Parker's daughte...
her husband's daughter in her arms

Honor felt an ache stab under her ribs. *Oh, Parker…how could you have been such a fool?*

But of course he wasn't a fool. He'd fallen in love and he'd been a good father to these children, she had no doubt. He'd just made a big mistake not divorcing her first.

"Did you know my mommy's in heaven? And my daddy, too?" the little girl asked, looking very seriously into Honor's face.

"Yes, darling, I did," Honor replied softly, gently rubbing the child's blond curls. "Now you've got your uncle Joe to look after you and your little brother."

"I *like* Uncle Joe!" the girl said, cheering up immediately. "Don't you?"

"I don't know if I do or not, Ellie. I just met him."

Dear Reader,

Christmas in a small town can warm your soul or break your heart.

My grandmother, born on a small, stony farm near Lake Ontario in 1893, begged her father to take her to town one snowy Christmas Eve. The dour farmer had some supplies to pick up in Medina, New York, perhaps something special for Christmas for his four children—a few oranges or a sack of nuts. Money was scarce north of the Ridge Road.

When they arrived, the whole place seemed lit up—to my grandmother's young eyes—by a huge Christmas tree in the center of town. Dangling from the lower branches were small gifts for the town's children. My grandmother watched as other children received their gifts. There was nothing for her; she was a farm girl.

My great-grandfather left her outside with the team to watch the festivities, snug under blankets on the sleigh. He returned a short while later with a doll my grandmother had seen earlier in a store window. She'd known better than to ask for it.

He handed the doll to her, unwrapped, with a rare smile. My grandmother was enraptured. It was just a doll, as they were at the turn of the century; she'd have to sew clothes for it when she got home.

My grandmother died at ninety-six, but she told me that story while she was in her late eighties. She'd never forgotten a child's unexpected joy at Christmas....

In my third MEN OF GLORY book, Joe Gallant and Honor Templeman seem to be at irreconcilable odds: in love but unable to grant each other's heart's desire. Somehow a way is found, as it so often is in small towns—and everywhere—at Christmastime.

I hope you enjoy Christmas in Glory, Alberta.

Judith Bowen

P.S. I'd love to hear from you! Write to me at P.O. Box 2333, Point Roberts, WA 98281-2333.

O LITTLE TOWN OF GLORY
Judith Bowen

HARLEQUIN®

TORONTO • NEW YORK • LONDON
AMSTERDAM • PARIS • SYDNEY • HAMBURG
STOCKHOLM • ATHENS • TOKYO • MILAN • MADRID
PRAGUE • WARSAW • BUDAPEST • AUCKLAND

ISBN 0-373-70814-9

O LITTLE TOWN OF GLORY

Copyright © 1998 by Judith Bowen.

This edition published by arrangement with Harlequin Books S.A.

® and TM are trademarks of the publisher. Trademarks indicated with ® are registered in the United States Patent and Trademark Office, the Canadian Trade Marks Office and in other countries.

Printed in U.S.A.

To my aunt, Edna Weeks

CHAPTER ONE

IT WAS FOUR WEEKS after the funeral before Honor Templeman could face clearing out her dead husband's apartment.

She and Parker had been separated, although not formally, for the past five years, and it had been at least three years since Honor had even been in his condo, two floors lower in the same building as hers. The arrangement was convenient. It meant they could attend the occasional company function together, show up at his father's for Christmas breakfast every year, keep up the ridiculous pretense that they were still married, happily or otherwise.

Despite all that, Honor was shocked to find how sparsely the place was furnished. A leather sofa and a large-screen television in the living room, a cheap department-store dinette set in the kitchen, a mattress with a duvet on the floor in the bedroom. Nothing in the bathroom beyond a few rolls of toilet paper and a tube of shaving cream in one drawer. Half-a-dozen towels.

She shivered. Honor knew Parker had spent most of his time on the road, traveling for Templeman Energy, scouting mineral properties. But even a longtime bachelor kept more of a home than this.

Dispiritedly she pulled back the closet doors. A

tweed jacket and two pairs of pants hung inside, along with four or five shirts. The thinnest scent of the man she'd once considered her best friend caught her nostrils. It didn't bring Parker back; Parker had been gone from her life for a very long time. Long before the terrible car accident that had killed him. It was all too apparent that clearing out the condo to put it on the market wouldn't be much of a job. She'd get at it this weekend.

Something wasn't right, though. Honor frowned, fingering the cheap cotton of the ready-made shirts. Parker had never lived like this when she'd known him. He'd enjoyed the good life, enjoyed what money could buy. This couldn't be the home base of the scion of perhaps Calgary's most prominent oil family.

She opened a drawer built into the closet and pulled out a handful of personal papers. There was an outdated credit card, a bankbook, a couple of letters and a yellowed newspaper clipping.

Honor held the newspaper clipping to the light, and the bottom fell out of her world. *Parker and Sylvie Templeman,* she read beneath the photo, *with Ellie, three, and the newest addition to the family, baby Alexander, at last weekend's Glory Fall Fair....*

Today was the last day of June. The newspaper was dated the previous September. There might be worse things, she realized in horror, than being widowed at thirty-one.

Such as finding out your husband had been living with another woman while he was still married to you—and that he had a family. Two children. And a life, obviously, somewhere else, in a place called Glory.

Two children. Trembling, she folded the clipping and stuffed it into her jacket pocket, along with the letters and the bankbook. She had a meeting in half an hour. She couldn't allow herself to think about this now.

At two o'clock, the meeting with some of her colleagues in the legal department over, Honor headed for the sanctuary of her office on the top floor of the Templeman Energy building. The glorious sunshine blazing down on the city of Calgary far beneath her had a glazed cold look.

She sank into the blessed comfort of Italian leather, but her fingertips, when she pressed them to her closed eyes, were numb. *Parker, Parker—how could you have done this? To me? To...to him?*

For Alec Templeman—her father-in-law and employer—would have to be told. And there was no one to bring him the news but her.

Honor took a deep breath, held it, then let it out slowly. *She would get through this. She would.* She dug the clipping out of her pocket with nerveless fingers and shakily smoothed out the crumpled paper on the polished surface of her desk. She weighted it down—using her fountain pen, a coffee mug, a thumb at each lower corner—so she could examine it more closely.

The photo was newspaper-grainy. A smiling woman, handsome and dark-haired, gazed at Parker. *Her husband. A man in love.* She hadn't seen him smile like that at anyone, not for a very long time. They were outdoors somewhere. Honor studied each background detail as though sifting through clues to a legal case she was building. A fall fair, the caption had said. And Parker had a young girl in his arms. *Ellie.* The woman held a baby wearing the kind of silly little sun hat babies often wore. *The latest addition to the family....*

Honor's fingers were clenched white on the edge of her desk. Who was this Sylvie? These should have been Honor's babies. These were the babies she couldn't have. The babies who'd died before they were born.

Tears dripped onto the shiny desktop, shocking her. She pushed the button on her phone to let Liz, her secretary, know that she was not to be disturbed under any circumstances.

Then she turned her chair around and stared south, way south. Past the river, past the hospital, gray and sprawling to the southwest, past the far-distant new subdivisions. Out there somewhere was Glory. The little town of Glory, south of High River. Where the newspaper had been published. Where Parker had lived a secret life with a woman he loved and their two children. Alec's grandchildren.

HONOR TOOK THE ELEVATOR to the fourth floor of the hospital. It was just past eight o'clock.

She'd taken the time to go home after work and change and even paw through her refrigerator for some leftover pasta salad and a cold breast of chicken. Staring at herself, drawn and hollow-eyed, in the mirror over the kitchen sink after she'd washed her plate and fork, she'd thought, *Don't put this off. It'll only get harder.*

So she'd slipped on a light cotton cardigan, pale pink to match the sleeveless shell she was wearing over tan chinos, and had gone down to the below-ground garage for her car. Ten minutes later she was at the Crowfoot Hospital parking lot. Alec R. Templeman, the man to whom she owed almost everything, was in a private suite here, recovering from the stroke he'd suffered the day after Parker's funeral. And from grief. The doctors had told her the stroke was not life-threatening.

They couldn't comment on the grief. Parker's death had toppled the old man like a five-hundred-year-old oak in a freak summer storm. With the death of his only son, all Alec's dreams had died.

Maybe that was where things had *really* gone wrong, Honor thought, stabbing viciously at the elevator button. Judging by the red light over the doors, the elevator appeared to have stopped on the second floor for an extended rest. Maybe fathers shouldn't put too much hope in their sons. Maybe fathers shouldn't dream of founding dynasties. Maybe fathers shouldn't snarl and prod and poke at their children's lives until the ones who wanted to please bled, and the ones with any spirit snapped in two or disappeared, leaving no forwarding address.

Which had it been for Parker? Both, Honor thought bitterly. He'd married her to please his father; he'd stayed married to her to please his father. *And she hadn't said no.*

The elevator doors opened grudgingly and Honor stepped inside. Would she find Alec staring at the ceiling in a darkened room as she had every time she'd visited in the past month?

Nothing had changed. There were fresh flowers on the nightstand, daisies this time, yellow and white. The lights were turned down, as Alec demanded, the curtains drawn. Honor had ordered that fresh flowers be brought in daily; she thought it might pique the old man's interest. The only passion Honor believed Alexander Royston Templeman had ever had, besides his son and making money, was his garden. Flowers didn't talk back. Neither had Parker.

"How is he today?" She recognized the nurse on duty, a young Filipina woman named Sue.

"Doctor says no change. You know," the nurse began with a tentative smile, "Doctor says he can leave if he wants—"

"He doesn't want to," Honor replied firmly. "Not just yet. Soon, though," she finished with a smile, lightly squeezing the nurse's hand as she prepared to leave Honor alone with her father-in-law. "Very soon."

She could only hope so. Alec was paying through the nose for this private suite. Honor knew the old man's pride demanded that he stay in the hospital, supposedly because of his illness. The stroke. He could not have borne the sympathy of his business cronies if he'd been immobilized by grief at home. But he wouldn't thank her for pointing that out.

Honor drew back the curtains covering the big window, letting in the long rays of the evening sun. She noticed the involuntary grimace, the fierce eyes narrowed against the unaccustomed brightness. She could get away with going against his wishes; only she could defy the old man.

Honor stooped to kiss the bristly cheek. Alec's

eyes followed her, but he made no effort to speak. She knew he was angry about the curtains. Good. He needed to feel again, to escape this miasma of self-imposed suffering. Anger, hate, love, revenge—anything was better than this.

"How've you been, Alec?" she asked, a tender note creeping into her voice. No matter how feared and, yes, even hated Alec Royston Templeman sometimes was in the fast-paced speculative world of the oil patch, no matter how much Honor privately despised the relationship he'd had with his son, no matter how difficult and peevish and arrogant the old man could be, he'd never been anything but good to her. He had brought her into his company, a struggling law student he'd met over the lunch counter at the Prince of Wales Hotel cafeteria, where she'd been working nights to help make ends meet. He'd put her on the fast track in his company's legal department. He'd married her to his only son. No one could have done more. Honor was not only grateful, she genuinely loved him.

As she'd expected the old man made no attempt to answer. His gaze returned to the ceiling tiles. Honor opened her briefcase and took out a sheaf of papers. Some were company documents, reports detailing land- and mineral-rights acquisitions she knew Alec took a special interest in; others were financial reports and newspapers.

"Look here," she said, holding up the *Financial Times*. "That Shute Bay deal looks like it's finally going through." She read aloud a lengthy account describing the ins and outs of a Newfoundland mining deal that had long been in the works. She moved to reading stock prices from the New York Exchange, from Nasdaq, from the London and Tokyo exchanges, then to a currency report, and ended by intoning the previous day's rates.

This was like reading "Goldilocks" or "Little Red Riding Hood" to a child. This was the stuff of the oil magnate's life, both inner and outer. This interested him more than what was on his plate for breakfast or the prospect of a holiday cruise or whether it rained or snowed. Still, Honor didn't see the slightest sign that he was even listening. He was shutting her out, just as he'd tried to shut out the knowledge of Parker's death. Of his part in it. His guilt.

Honor sighed and reached for his hand. There was a faint response then. Alec's gnarled fingers curled against hers for a few seconds. His hand was very warm and dry, the ropy old-man's veins standing out angrily against the paler freckled flesh. She nudged her chair closer and took his hand in both of her own.

"Alec," she whispered, "listen. It's time for you to come home. Do you hear me?"

His eyes never left the ceiling.

"I'll stay with you for a few days if you like, until you get settled. I'll bring you work until you feel like coming back to the office."

Honor thought he'd suddenly taken a deeper breath, but couldn't be sure. She tightened her fingers on his, hoping to encourage him to respond, then went on, still speaking very softly, "I'll hire someone who can take care of you at home. Someone to help Spinks." Spinks was his valet, driver and man-about-the-house. "The doctor says you need physical therapy, some help with learning to walk again. Maybe speech therapy, too. There are exercises you should be doing. Every day. Someone can help you with that.''

Help. That was not a word in the old man's lexicon. She paused and studied his profile—the bushy gray eyebrows that contributed to the habitually thunderous expression, the hawklike nose, the jutting stubborn chin. It was so unlike Alec to go unshaven, which meant he'd probably kicked up a fuss when the nurse's aide tried to shave him. Honor had to admit she was beginning to worry terribly about her father-in-law's recovery. Now, this news she had— would it help or hinder that recovery?

Honor sat quietly for a few more minutes, trying to gather her thoughts, trying to formulate a way to broach the subject. She'd gone over a thousand different angles in her mind since discovering the clipping that morning, and she still wasn't sure what to say. In the end, she knew, there was nothing to do but plunge in.

"Alec, dear—" she squeezed his fingers again, hers feeling clammy and damp "—I've got some news for you. It…it's very *good* news, Alec, but it's shocking, too. I don't want to upset you, but I have to tell you."

She bit her lip. The old man closed his eyes. Did that mean he was listening to her? Or still shutting her out?

"It's about Parker." Again, the deeper breath, held slightly, then released, which told her he was listening. "I found a newspaper clipping this morning in Parker's apartment. A newspaper from a small town south of here. Glory. Do you know the place?''

The old man squeezed her hand and nodded, ever so faintly. Honor returned the pressure, encouraged. ''You remember someone else died in that accident? There was a woman in the car when Parker was killed—a passenger, Sylvie Gallant. We didn't really know who she was, except maybe a friend or something, but it turns out she was living with Parker in Glory. She was his common-law wife, Alec.''

Honor broke off, her voice raw. Tears she couldn't stop—nor did she care to try—spilled down her cheeks. Alec looked faintly puzzled. His lips moved slowly, but no sound came from them. She clutched his hand, seeking comfort for herself now, as well as for him.

''There's more, Alec. Parker had been living with this woman for quite some time. They had two little children, a boy and a girl.'' She leaned over him and enunciated clearly. ''They're Parker's children, Alec. A boy and a girl. *They're your grandchildren.*''

Honor couldn't go on. The full import of the situation struck her. Sure, she and Parker had led separate lives for nearly five years, he with his apartment, she with hers. She hadn't thought the pretense mattered much to anyone but them. They'd thought they were doing it for the old man's sake, to save appearances. They'd talked of divorce occasionally, but neither had taken any action, both reluctant to face the old man's wrath and disappointment. Parker was no more guilty of wanting to spare his father's feelings than she was.

Perhaps if she'd been interested in someone else?

But that wasn't the case. She rarely went out. Some-times she even suspected she didn't have the same feelings other women had. Since children were to be denied her, it seemed she hadn't cared much about finding a mate, either.

She hadn't loved her husband for a long time, probably since those first early days when they'd been such great friends and then, for a while, lovers. They'd been married eight years, had lived apart nearly five. Her failed pregnancies had come one upon the other early in the marriage, and after the last one, which had required surgery, the doctors had advised against any more attempts.

Was that when Parker had stopped trying to make things work between them? Knowing how desper-ately his father wanted a grandson and heir, knowing Honor would never be able to give him one?

Honor couldn't believe Parker had been that cruel or coldhearted. She knew that deep down he hadn't given a damn what his father wanted, although he'd been willing to keep up appearances. No, the truth was he'd found someone to love, no doubt someone who'd truly loved him, and he'd hammered out his own life and happiness in secret. He'd never told her. Perhaps he'd had plans to ask for a divorce one day and then he'd present his new wife and children to his father.

What did they look like? Were they blond, blue-eyed? Did they look like Parker? Like their grand-father? It was hard to tell from a newspaper photo. Honor was seized with a burning desire to see them. Anger rose in her throat along with horror at Parker's deception and what amounted to his bigamy. These should have been *her* children. It wasn't fair. That might not be a rational reaction, but she'd wanted children so much. Under the law Parker was *her* husband, whether she'd wanted him or not. Whether she was able to have his children or not.

Suddenly Honor realized that Alec was trying to speak. His face contorted with the effort he was making. Spittle shone in the corners of his mouth and on his chin, and thick horrible sounds came from his throat. Inhuman sounds. Honor realized the sides of his face were wet, that tears ran from under the puffy reddened lids to disappear into the white linen of the pillow beneath his head. *He was weeping.*

His hand, which hadn't left hers, suddenly tightened and she winced. His illness hadn't diminished Alec's strength.

"What are you trying to say, Alec?" she cried. "I don't understand—what do you want me to do?" She mopped at her own damp cheeks with the cotton sleeve of her free arm.

Alec finally managed to get out a few gutteral sounds. He repeated them. They were the first words anyone had heard from the old man in many weeks.

"Get them." His hand still clutched hers. *"Get them."*

"Oh, Alec..." Honor leaned forward, ready to collapse, and rested her forehead on the old man's shoulder, drawing comfort from his so familiar oldman smell. Talc and spicy soap, special-ordered from England. Oranges and foot powder. She felt his hand in her hair, making a clumsy stroking motion. She took her time wiping her tears on the front of his paisley silk pajama top, then straightened.

His broken words summed up everything she felt. Every emotion that had ripped through her since she'd discovered the clipping. They all centred on the idea Alec had presented. Alec wanted to know these children, his grandchildren; so did she. Parker's babies. They were part of Parker, part of Alec…part of her life with them.

"I will. I'll bring them to you, Alec. *I promise.*"

CHAPTER TWO

JOSEPH T. GALLANT. The "T" stood for Thaddeus, she'd learned in her search of the provincial-poll records.

Joe Gallant was the man who had Parker's children. He was a farmer by trade and the twin brother of Sylvie Gallant. He was thirty-five years old. He'd be thirty-six in November.

Honor studied the land-registry page in the Glory municipal office, adding information to the file she'd already gathered on Gallant. His operation, Swallowbank Farm, consisted of more than 1400 deeded acres, with an additional 537 leased. He'd paid property taxes of over two thousand dollars last year. His farm was fifteen kilometers from Glory, on the Vulcan road. She had no idea what he'd paid in provincial or federal taxes—that was classified information. There was a fairly recent mortgage registered on the title of his land.

He was unmarried.

Honor pulled a notebook from her briefcase and jotted down the land description, including longitude, range and township. She made a note of the names of the owners on the adjoining properties.

"I'd like this photocopied. Would that be possible?" she asked the clerk behind the counter, passing over the big book open to a map that had Gallant's property boundaries on it, as well as secondary roads in the area.

"Certainly." The clerk slid the page out of its special binding and took it to the back of the office. She disappeared behind a glass-brick wall.

While she waited, Honor walked to the long window that overlooked a grassy square edged with wooden benches. A white-painted church with a bell tower stood on the other side of the square to the south. Storefronts faced the square on the street to the west. Some boys tossed a football in the middle of the green sward, and Honor watched as an elderly woman wearing gloves and a hat, with a small dog on a leash, stopped and sat on one of the benches to watch the boys play.

This was a quiet place. It was off the main highway that ran south from Calgary to the American border, and in all the years she'd lived in Calgary she'd only ventured off that highway once, during a brief trip to Lethbridge. That was before she'd married Parker.

She'd driven down here this morning and had planned to go back as soon as she had the information she needed. But now... Honor noticed a deli with a few sidewalk tables on the western side of the square. Maybe she'd stay and grab a sandwich and sit in the park here, have lunch. No reason to rush back to Calgary.

"Here you go, ma'am," the clerk said pleasantly, handing Honor the photocopy. She replaced the original in the big book and closed it. "Will that be all?"

Honor paid for the copy. "For now, anyway.

Thank you. You've been very helpful.'' She wanted to know more about Joe Gallant. ''Is the newspaper office near here? I think I'll drop in there next.''

''One block over. On River Street,'' the clerk said, then added, her curiosity clearly aroused, ''Is there anything in particular…?''

''Well…yes.'' Honor decided that small towns were small towns, no matter where they were. The clerk would probably have all kinds of helpful information about this grain farmer, and no doubt wouldn't hesitate to tell her. ''I'm gathering some information on one of the farmers around here on a…personal matter. Joe Gallant. Do you know him?''

''Joe?'' The clerk looked surprised, then frowned slightly. ''Of course I do. What would you be wanting with Joe?''

''It's more to do with his sister, really.''

''Nan?''

''No, Sylvie.''

''Oh, my, what a terrible shame that was! Those two dear little ones orphaned, my goodness, yes. Nan's helping Joe all she can, but—'' The clerk broke off cryptically and shook her head, lips pursed. ''It's a bad situation all round.''

''Bad?'' Alarm bells rang. What sort of person *was* Joe Gallant? And should he have the care of Parker's children?

''Oh, nothing like you'd think, ma'am. Not *that* kind of bad. Just that Joe's got his hands full running the farm, and Nan—that's his sister, Nan Longquist—has her own hands full looking after Harry and their five kids, not that their eldest, Ben, is around home much anymore. And they've been planning to take off this summer—the whole family, I mean—and go to California. How can they do that now, with Sylvie's kiddies to look out for? Poor little orphans.''

The clerk looked to Honor as though she might have some answers. Honor had none. ''Well, thanks again. I appreciate your help.''

The clerk waved as Honor went out the big beveled glass doors of the municipal hall. She smiled and waved back. Who knew where this would lead? She might need to speak to the clerk again before she had everything she wanted.

Honor stood at the top of the broad stone steps for a minute, trying to decide what to do next. The day was warm and sunny. She heard the shouts of the boys playing football on the green. School was out for the summer. Her heart suddenly ached—Parker had been dead for nearly six weeks. It was still so hard to believe.

At the deli she'd noticed earlier, Molly McClung's Delicatessen—an *Irish* deli?—Honor picked up a vegetarian special on kaiser roll and a container of fresh-squeezed orange juice. She settled herself on one of the park benches. There were a few more people in the park now, and the deli had been full. An unusual mix, Honor had thought, glancing around as she waited for her sandwich—some high-school kids joking at a window table, office workers perched on counter stools, two or three sober-looking farmers, ball caps pulled down firmly over lined and weathered faces, endlessly stirring their heavily creamed coffees.

Was that what Joe Gallant looked like? Well, no. For starters, he was only in his mid-thirties.

Honor took a bite of her sandwich. It was excellent. She noticed a pretty woman in a loose-flowing white cotton dress approaching. The woman had a book in one hand and a paper bag from the deli in the other.

She smiled pleasantly. "Mind if I sit here with you?"

"Not at all." Honor glanced toward the woman with the dog and saw that another elderly woman had joined her.

"Nice catch, Chris!" she heard the second woman call when one of the boys on the field had made a spectacular running catch.

The woman with the lunch bag sat down beside Honor, then turned with a smile. "I'm Donna. Donna Beaton. I run the gift shop on the corner. I haven't seen you around—you new in town?"

"Just passing through," Honor said. Her first shameless thought was that here was someone else she could grill about Joe Gallant. "My name's Honor—" She caught herself and stopped. The name Templeman was hardly unknown in the town of Glory. "I'm from Calgary," she finished a bit lamely.

The other woman didn't seem to notice. "Honor. That's an unusual name, but I suppose I'm not the first one to—"

"Donna!" one of the boys yelled, and waved. She waved back, then turned to Honor again. "Trevor Longquist," she said by way of explanation. "One of my son's friends."

Longquist. That was the name the clerk had mentioned. Honor considered her options. One was to come clean and just ask this nice woman about Joe Gallant and his role in Parker's children's lives. She'd know. It appeared the townspeople in Glory were singularly informed.

The other was to keep her mouth shut, pursue her own investigations, write a letter to Gallant requesting a meeting and generally conduct her business in an aboveboard straightforward manner. She was a lawyer, for Pete's sake, not a grubbing trench-coated PI.

She took a quick breath. "Longquist? That's a coincidence. The clerk at the town office mentioned that name when I asked her about someone else. Joe Gallant. Do you know him?"

So much for professional and upstanding. She *should* be a seedy private investigator—she had the tactics down pretty well.

Donna smiled and finished the bite of sandwich she'd just taken. "Joe Gallant." She stared off into the clear blue sky for a few seconds as though considering. "Sure, I know Joe." Then she turned back to Honor, still smiling dreamily. "Joe's a great ball player. One of the best first basemen the town's ever had."

Baseball?

Honor had the sudden desire to laugh. It was a good feeling. She wasn't sure she'd laughed since she'd heard the dreadful news about Parker. And maybe even for a while before that. Alec always told her she took life far too seriously.

"You like baseball?" Donna opened her drink.

She'd bought a small bottle of Evian water at the deli.

"I'm not much for any kind of sports," Honor admitted. "I do know the difference between a baseball and a basketball, though. And a soccer ball."

"Hmm." Donna smiled, her dark eyes alight with humor. She was a very attractive woman, Honor decided. "How about hockey? Joe's a terrific hockey player, too. He plays in the Glory Old Guy's League and— Say, do you know Joe?"

"No, I don't."

"Sorry, I thought you did. Why are you asking about him?"

You couldn't put it any plainer than that, Honor thought with respect. So much for her great PI technique. "I'm inquiring on behalf of a friend, that's all. A...a relative of the family's." Alec was mentor, father-in-law and employer. She supposed she could call him a friend, as well. Joe Gallant was the children's uncle and Alec was their grandfather. You could say the two men were distantly related...sort of. Still, it was almost a lie, which wasn't her style. It made her feel uncomfortable.

She finished the last of her orange juice and stood. "Well, it was nice chatting with you. I guess I'd better be on my way."

"Where you off to now?" Donna asked, shading her eyes against the sun.

"The *Plain Dealer* office," Honor said with a casual shrug. "Maybe I'll check out some of those old sports stories."

She bent to collect her lunch debris and pick up her battle-scarred leather briefcase. Donna touched her lightly on the arm. "Say, Joe isn't in any kind of trouble, is he?" she asked, eyes concerned.

"No," Honor said swiftly. "Not that I know of, anyway." She smiled and observed the flash of relief in Donna's dark eyes.

Honor had made a quick character assessment of Donna Beaton. She'd grown to trust her instincts about people in her many years of legal work. She liked Donna. She felt sure that if Donna liked and respected Joe Gallant, he must be an all right person.

Maybe more than all right, she reflected as she walked toward the newspaper office. Donna'd spoken of a son, so she was probably married. But she'd also had a certain soft smile on her face when she'd mentioned Joe's name, the kind of smile that could indicate a woman's feelings for a man went beyond affection and respect.

Hmm. Interesting.

Honor had to admit she was getting very curious about Joseph T. Gallant.

TEN DAYS LATER Honor had to face the fact that her dealings with the Glory farmer were not going to be as easy as she'd hoped.

It wasn't her fault; she'd done her homework and had a file on Gallant half an inch thick. And she'd been discreet, even with Alec. *Especially* with Alec. She'd kept her all plans to herself, sticking to the financial papers and general conversation—one-sided, so far—when she visited the hospital. Her father-in-law seemed to be starting to engage with life again. He wasn't speaking and he'd never referred by word or gesture to the news she'd brought him, but he didn't scowl quite so fiercely when she suggested taking him home.

If only she could bring his grandchildren to meet him.

But the first letter she sent the children's uncle came back in a hand-addressed manila envelope containing the opened envelope and the neatly refolded letter. Her letter. The letter she'd written asking for a meeting.

There was no note.

The next letter, the one she sent registered on company stationery, came back: delivery refused. Honor sent another. It, too, came back.

That one she received just after she'd returned from a trying business lunch with one of Alec's cronies, an irritating old man who should have been on the golf course, but who, like Alec, persisted in spending most of his waking hours meddling in the affairs of his own office. Not that Alec didn't still contribute plenty, despite his age.

Just looking at the returned letter made her angry. All the vague annoyance she'd felt toward her lunch companion centred squarely on Joe Gallant.

She'd had enough of this. She was being polite and professional. He was being an ass. She'd go to Glory and buttonhole him herself. She'd go this very afternoon. She was not going to take no for an answer.

Luckily the seventy-minute drive gave her a chance to cool off. The rolling hills, so close to the foothills, with the Rockies in the snowy distance, were green and lush with summer growth. The town of Glory, she'd learned during her research, edged ranch country to the west and farming country to the east. Vulcan was a small town just twenty miles to the east with the arguable distinction of loading the most grain in any one season on the Canadian Pacific Railway. Wheat, barley, mustard, soybeans, canola— which was the currently acceptable name for what had once been known as rapeseed.

When she got to the turnoff that led to the town of Glory itself, Honor pulled over to the side of the road. She dug a map from her briefcase and studied it, memorizing the route to Gallant's farm. Then she started the car again and put on her left-turn signal, although there was no one behind her.

"Joseph Thaddeus Gallant," she muttered aloud to herself, jaw firm, resolve steady, "prepare to meet your match...."

JOE HEARD THE CAR crunch to a stop on the driveway gravel, but in his position under the grain hauler he couldn't quite twist his wrist enough to check the time. He knew she was early, though. Damn. He'd hoped to finish the lube job and have a shower before any of the prospects Nan had lined up for him arrived at the farm for their interviews. And what about the kids? He hoped like hell his niece, Phoebe, could be trusted to have them spruced up and at least their faces washed.

Joe stopped, grease gun in his hands, arrested by the sight of first one shapely ankle, then a second, emerging from the car. The door slammed, and the ankles paused. Could she see him? He glanced down. Damn, his legs stuck out the front end of the hauler from the knees down. Mesmerized, he watched the ankles.

One step, a little hesitant. Another... Then a steady determined pace over the fresh gravel toward the grain hauler, with him under it. Damn again. What in hell was the name Nan had given him for the first interview? Betsy? Bonnie?

"Hello?"

She had a nice voice. Firm and quiet. Probably be good with kids. Those shoes, though, looked a little on the city side for a farm....

He cleared his throat and grunted, jamming the lube gun onto the last dirt-caked grease nipple. "Done here in a sec. Be right with you."

"Fine." There was a slight pause, and Joe saw the shoes turn and point toward the house, then back at him again. "As a matter of fact, I'm looking for Joe Gallant."

"Uh-huh. Be right there." Joe gave a last good squeeze on the trigger and was rewarded by a luminous lump of thick engine grease dropping onto his chin. He swallowed the epithet that had leaped to his lips, settling for another muttered "Damn."

Then he set the gun down and started to slither out from under the vehicle. He saw the shoes step back hastily and grinned. A grin that died when he saw her.

"I'm Joe Gallant," he said, looking up at her, squinting against the bright sunshine as his eyes adjusted. She was definitely too attractive for the job. He wanted someone quite a bit older, too, so there wouldn't be any talk in the district. And something else didn't add up—she wasn't dressed right. Short pale-gray skirt, jacket to match. Even the leather bag on her shoulder matched. The shoes, too. She was more a career-type city woman than a nanny prospect.

He scraped the clump of grease off his chin and wiped his hand on the grass beside him. He stood slowly, wishing there was an easier way to get to your feet in front of an attractive woman when you knew your hair was full of dirt and probably grass, your face was no doubt speckled with the black junk that had fallen off the underside of the hauler, and your jeans, shirt and hands were plain workingman filthy.

"I won't shake your hand," he said ruefully, wiping his hands on his jeans. He bent his head and brushed some of the debris from his hair. "Come on up to the house. I'll introduce you to the kids. Let me grab a quick shower and then we can talk—that is if you're still interested when you see the setup."

She hadn't said anything, but as he spoke her eyes narrowed. Blue eyes. Real nice blue eyes. "I wasn't expecting you this early, to tell you the truth," he added awkwardly.

"You were expecting me?" She seemed surprised.

"Yeah. Wasn't the appointment for four o'clock?" Suddenly he remembered. "Brenda Gibson, right?" He smiled, but got another narrowed glance for his trouble. Hey, who was doing the hiring here—her or him? They were at the bottom of the four wooden steps that led up to the veranda. "From the agency?"

"I don't know what you're talking about. I'm here

on behalf of Mr. Templeman,'' she said softly. ''Mr. A. R. Templeman.''

No. He had to be sure. ''Templeman Energy?''

''Yes. I sent some letters but…I guess you never got them.''

Well. That was putting it diplomatically. He'd sent every goddamn one back unread when he saw the return address. Except for the first one, which he'd scanned and returned the second he saw Alec Templeman's name. He wanted nothing to do with that old bastard, nothing at all.

''I got them. Just never read them,'' he said, pausing at the top of the steps. He glanced at his watch. Twenty-five minutes until this Brenda Gibson arrived. ''Look, I don't mean to be rude and I know you've got a job to do just like everybody else, but you might as well know right from the start that whatever's on Old Man Templeman's mind these days is nothing to me.''

He stared at her. She wasn't backing down, not an inch, although he could have sworn she'd flinched at what he'd had to say. ''Why's he sending you around, anyway? Why doesn't he do his own dirty work?''

''I'm inquiring on his behalf. I'm also his daughter-in-law. He's an old man. It would mean a lot to him to meet his grandchildren.''

''Grandchildren!'' Joe felt the bile rise in his throat. ''They never meant a thing to him when their father was alive, so why in hell would he care now?''

''He never knew about them,'' she said, her voice curiously shaky. Joe narrowed his eyes. Just who *was* this woman? And why did she seem to care so much?

"Never knew about them?" Joe walked to the side of the veranda, cleared his throat and spit into the peonies. Since Sylvie's death last month, his world had fallen apart. He had her kids to take care of, he had his own worries on the farm, so did Nan—and his heart had been torn apart with rage and grief. Sylvie, his baby sister by ten minutes, his truest childhood companion, his gift and his responsibility. He'd let her down. He'd looked the other way when she hooked up with Parker Templeman. She'd been in bad spots plenty of times in her life and he'd pulled her out. Why hadn't he pulled her out of this one? She'd be alive today if he had.

"Tell him to go to hell," he snapped. "I have nothing to say to him. He'll see my sister's kids over my dead body."

"Please!" She actually reached out and touched his arm. He stared at her hand. Soft pale delicate fingers, a hint of rosy polish at the short manicured tips.

He raised his head and looked at her. There were tears in those blue eyes. *What the…*

He frowned. "Who are you, anyway?" It struck him that she was taking more than average interest in this situation. Of course, she was a Templeman, too, the kids' aunt or whatever.

"My name is Honor. Honor Templeman. I work for Templeman Energy, too. I'm a company lawyer."

"Honor," he repeated. "That's quite a name for someone in your line of work."

She flushed, but made no motion to depart. Hell. He glanced at his watch again. Twenty minutes to get himself and the kids ready. If this Honor person only knew the truth about Alec Templeman, she wouldn't be standing here trying to change his mind.

"Well, you'd better come in. As I said, I've got an appointment at four, but maybe we can talk later. I've got some interviews lined up—I'm hiring someone to take care of the kids for a few weeks while my sister Nan's away. I might as well warn you, though, you're wasting your time."

He held the screen door for her. She looked scared. Why? He had the strangest feeling he was making a mistake, a big mistake, inviting her in.

"So, you married to Parker's brother?" he began in an attempt to get this conversation back on track. He'd come on pretty strong about Templeman; he hadn't meant to scare her. "I didn't know he had a brother—"

"He...he didn't. Parker was my husband."

"What did you say?" Joe froze, his hand on the inner doorknob.

"I was married to Parker Templeman."

CHAPTER THREE

As soon as she stepped inside, Honor knew she wouldn't forget the scene in that farmhouse kitchen if she lived to be a hundred.

"Hi!" A little girl stood on a chair at the counter wearing nothing but a pair of Minnie Mouse underpants and two enormous running shoes, clearly not her own. She was stirring mightily at something in a large bowl. There was flour and sugar and coffee and what appeared to be juice all over the counter. "I'm making a cake, Uncle Joe!"

In the center of the kitchen floor sat a baby in a diaper, happily stuffing grape jam into his mouth. His face was purple, as was his T-shirted tummy and the floor around him. He waved one chubby hand, greeting them as cheerfully as his sister.

Honor gasped and looked at Joe. He strode to a closed door that led from the kitchen, opened it and roared, "Phoebe, get in here!"

Two voices responded in unison, "But we're watching 'Days'!"

"One, two, three…" Joe began ominously. A girl of about fifteen materialized beside him.

"Oh, Uncle Joe, it's just about over. We'll clean up after that, honest." She glanced at Honor and smiled. "Sorry!" Then she turned back to her uncle. "I didn't know you had company."

"Look at Alexander." Joe pointed at the baby sitting in the middle of the floor. "Phoebe, this is not what I call looking after these kids. You and Jill promised me you'd keep an eye on them."

"But we are! Alexander kept climbing up on the table to get the jam, so I thought it'd be better if I put it on the floor for him. So he wouldn't hurt himself or anything." She nodded at the baby, clearly not seeing what the problem was.

"And Ellie?"

"Oh, she wanted to cook!" Phoebe laughed. "Jill set her up. It was Ellie's idea to take off all her clothes so she wouldn't get them dirty." Phoebe beamed, as though expecting her uncle to congratulate her on going along with such a good idea.

A voice called through from the room down the hall. "Pheeeeeb! Willie's going to the island now. He's getting in the boat with Sammy. He's got a knife."

Phoebe jumped up and down. "Oh, Uncle Joe, I've got to watch this—"

"Okay. Beat it." He shut the door behind his niece, who'd raced down the hall the instant he relented. He studied the two children for a few seconds, then turned to Honor. "I'm sorry about this," he said, lifting his hands helplessly.

Honor glanced around, then back at him. "Can I...can I help or something?"

He ran his hands through his hair in a desperate gesture, but at her tentative offer, spun to look at her again. "Okay. You take Ellie." His voice was hard.

He might not read her mail, but he'd accept her offer of help. *Good or bad,* she told herself gleefully, *you're in.*

"There's a bathroom down the hall," he continued. "Get that one in the tub. I'll take care of this little devil." He reached down and scooped up the jam-covered protesting baby and stalked off through the doorway.

Honor moved closer to the little girl. "Come on, sweetie. Your uncle says you have to take a bath."

"Good." She climbed down from the chair, careful not to lose her big shoes, and slid, one shoe at a time, toward Honor. "I'm tired of making this cake, anyway. These are Pheeb's," she said, pointing down at her feet. "She said I could wear them."

Honor wasn't sure what to do next. The little girl solved her dilemma by raising her arms and smiling sweetly at her. Honor stepped forward and picked her up, leaving the shoes behind. She didn't weigh much. *Parker's daughter. She was carrying Parker's daughter in her arms.*

"Which way to the bathroom?" Honor asked breathlessly, remembering only that Joe had said something about a hall.

"Down here." Ellie waved in the direction Joe and the baby had disappeared. "Don't you even know where our bathroom is?"

Honor shook her head. "Why would I? I've never been here before." The words came naturally, surprising her. She'd had very little to do with children in her thirty-one years.

Ellie giggled, then gazed at Honor soberly, eyes

wide. "Don't know where the bathroom is—that's funny!"

The bathroom was large with a big claw-footed cast-iron tub at one end. The floor was tiled in a black-and-white checkered pattern, giving the whole room an old-fashioned look. Honor set the girl down and turned on the taps. She noticed a bottle of children's bubble bath on a shelf and poured in a dollop. Ellie stripped off her panties, lifting her arms again for Honor to put her in the tub. Honor left her happily scooping up billows of white bubbles, sticking them to the sides of the tub, and went to search for some clean clothes for the child.

She felt vaguely guilty peeking into each room, looking for one that might belong to the children. She could hear the television blaring away somewhere nearby, but she didn't want to have to ask Phoebe for help. Or meet the still-mysterious Jill just yet. At one door she sprang back as though stung when she heard the unmistakable sound of a shower running and the joyous shrieks of the little boy. Obviously Joe had taken him into the shower with him.

She found a room, knee-deep in toys, that had a crib and a small bed in it. The room was sunny and bright, but had clearly filled another purpose not so long ago. The wallpaper was flowery and old-fashioned, and there were darker squares where pictures had once hung. On the dresser was a framed copy of the photo Honor had seen in the newspaper clipping—Parker and Sylvie and their two children.

Honor felt an ache stab under her ribs. *Oh, Parker...how could you have been such a fool?*

But of course he wasn't a fool. He'd fallen in love

and been a good father to these two children, she had no doubt. He'd just made a big mistake not divorcing her first. Or having the courage to face his father.

Honor yanked open a drawer. It was filled with baby undershirts and diaper covers and little stretchy socks with baseballs and animals on them.

The second drawer held clothes that might fit Ellie. She picked out a pair of clean underpants, some socks, shorts and a T-shirt that had "Glory Homecoming" on it. They might not have been what Joe Gallant had in mind for the children's meet-the-new-nanny experience, but they'd have to do.

Honor didn't know what she thought about that revelation; she hadn't really had time to think about anything. Not even how shocked Joe had sounded when she told him she'd been married to Parker. But the look on his face, the instant flash of pity that followed the shock—she'd never forget that.

She knew she was no beauty. She knew she wasn't the type men were drawn to—Parker had made that clear enough. Not that he'd been cruel. He'd just made it quite evident that he didn't find her sexually appealing. She didn't need Joe Gallant's pity, though, or the pity of any other man.

"I'm done!" Ellie stood up in the bath when Honor returned. Her hair was wet. Honor was sure she hadn't washed it—did a kid of three or four do that sort of thing for herself?

"Don't stand up, pumpkin. You might slip and fall," Honor said, turning to pull a large bath towel from the rack. When she turned back, the little girl's lower lip was trembling and her eyes were full of tears.

"My mommy called me that. She's in heaven. She called me 'punkin' all the time." The girl raised her arms to allow Honor to lift her out. Honor felt like weeping herself to have inadvertently aroused such memories.

She cleared her throat. "Here, let's get you all dried off and put some new clothes on."

"Did you know my mommy's in heaven? And my daddy, too?" Ellie asked, peering very seriously into Honor's face.

"Yes, darling, I did," Honor replied softly, gently rubbing the little girl's blond curls. "Now you've got your Uncle Joe to take care of you and your little brother."

"I *like* Uncle Joe!" the girl said, cheering up immediately. "Don't you?"

"I don't know if I do or not, Ellie. I just met him."

"What's your name, anyway?"

"It's Honor."

"Mine's El-oo-eese, but everybody calls me Ellie."

"That's a nice name."

Honor spread out the girl's clothes and was about to help her get into them when she heard a shout from down the hall. "What was that?" she asked the girl automatically, not really expecting an answer.

"Oh, that's Uncle Joe." Ellie sat down on the bathroom floor and began to pull on her socks. "He's just yelling for something, prob'ly."

Honor poked her head out into the hall. "Hello? Somebody call?" She felt absolutely ridiculous. Her new suit was probably ruined, although the stains on the dove gray fabric of her jacket and skirt were just water. Her white silk blouse stuck to her in several places, where more water had splashed.

"Hey! Can somebody give me a hand here?"

It *was* Joe. And he was bellowing from the bathroom off his own bedroom where he'd taken the baby. Honor could hear the rising strains of music from the soap opera as she dashed down the hall. It must be over. Maybe Phoebe and Jill would be available now to help....

"What do you want me to do?" she called from the bedroom side of the bathroom door.

"Come in here. Take this kid."

Omigod. Honor took a deep breath and opened the door to the bathroom. Steam billowed out. She was a grown woman, she reminded herself; she was *not* going to close her eyes and bang into things stumbling around in a bathroom where an attractive man was taking a shower. An attractive *naked* man.

"Honor?"

"I'm in here." But what am I *doing* in here? she thought wildly. That's the question. When I could be back in the office going over some nice fresh legal briefs. Or home making myself a cup of tea or—or shopping for paper products.

"Grab a towel and take this kid, will you?"

The shower curtain slid open about a foot and a half. Honor couldn't see anything of the naked Joe Gallant and she was trying very hard not to, but she could see the slippery, flailing, wailing baby he thrust toward her. "Got him?"

Honor bundled the child securely in the big white towel she'd grabbed. "Got him."

The curtain snapped back into position. "Okay.

Put a diaper on him or something. I'll be out in a sec.''

Honor speedily retreated. She held the howling baby firmly on one hip and closed the bathroom door behind her. She heard the shower stop. She was out of here! When Joe Gallant said ''a sec,'' he probably meant it, and all she needed right now was for him to stride out, either magnificently naked or magnificently clad in nothing but a towel. It had been a long, long time, but Honor was no more immune to six feet plus of very attractive male than the next woman.

Events were moving far too quickly. She glanced at her watch as she hurried along the hallway with the baby. It was four o'clock. Any second now the doorbell would ring and the first of several applicants for the job of taking care of these two darling children would come across the threshold.

This whole business of a hired nanny was a surprise to her. She didn't like the idea of strangers looking after Parker's children. They were Alec's grandchildren. If Alec had custody...well, they'd have a paid nanny, too, wouldn't they? But it would be the best, most qualified nanny around. Alec R. Templeman would spare no expense for his grandchildren. Still, all the money in the world couldn't bring back their mother and father.

At least, according to Ellie, they liked their uncle Joe. They didn't even know they *had* a grandfather.

There was no time to ponder that.

''Hi!'' Phoebe emerged from the kitchen at the end of the hall, accompanied by a red-haired coltish girl of about twelve. ''This is Jill, my sister. Here,

I'll look after that little guy now.'' Phoebe plucked the still-wailing Alexander from her arms, and her sister grabbed for the baby's hand.

"Here? See? Your thumb, Alexander!'' Jill popped the boy's thumb into his mouth and he immediately brightened, even managing a teary smile now that he was safe in his cousin's arms.

The two girls disappeared into the children's bedroom with the baby, and Honor stood alone in a very damp designer suit in the hallway of a stranger's house.

Ellie.

Honor returned to the bathroom in time to see the little girl pulling on her T-shirt. It was backward, but suddenly Honor didn't have the strength to care. She didn't think anyone else in this household would, either. She took a deep breath and smiled. "Ready?'' She held out one hand and the girl clasped it.

They walked hand in hand back to the kitchen. She'd forgotten the mess in there, but luckily Phoebe had kept her word and cleaned up, after a fashion. The mixing bowl and spoon were in the sink, the counter had been wiped off, the chair was back at the table and the jam—or most of it—had been washed off the floor. Ellie spotted her cousin's shoes again and, with a sigh of bliss, stepped into them. Honor grabbed a broom and began to sweep up the coffee grounds and sugar the girls had missed.

Joe walked in, barefoot and looking much different in a clean chambray shirt, unbuttoned, and tan pants. He ran one hand through his damp hair as he entered the kitchen, eyes alert. "Anyone here yet?''

"Just me.''

He grinned and Honor felt her knees give way. "Well, that's a lucky break," he said, still grinning. "Here, let me have that broom."

She sank gratefully into a chair, not sure her legs would carry her much farther. "I'll finish up here," he said, rapidly moving the neat pile of coffee and sugar she'd swept up toward the porch door. He unlatched the screen door, jammed it open, and with one large manly swipe managed to send most of the pile outside. Presumably the wind would carry it away.

"There!" He turned and raised an eyebrow. "Nothing to it."

Honor couldn't help herself. She smiled back and something started to hum deep inside her. She wanted to laugh. She recognized the sign as incipient hysteria and managed to beat back the impulse. This was the craziest half hour she'd ever spent in her life, bar none!

Joe slowly buttoned up his shirt, his eyes not leaving hers. He continued to smile. Honor thought she saw admiration in his gaze, too. "Thanks. I sure needed your help with the kids. Good thing you happened by. How do you feel about interviewing a couple of nanny prospects now?"

He had to be joking. All she wanted to do was get in her car. Drive back to Calgary. *To her empty apartment.* Maybe send him another registered letter.

"I think I could handle that," she heard herself reply. "After the last ten minutes, I think I could handle just about anything!"

But in the bathroom, where she tried to repair the

damage to her hair and makeup and suit, she changed her mind.

"Don't do it," she mentally told herself in the mirror over the sink as she dragged a brush through her hair in an attempt to tame it. "You're not in this *with* him, you're in this *against* him. For some reason he doesn't want anything to do with Alec. Your goal is to unite the children with their grandfather. Maybe more."

A contrary little voice inside argued, *But why not try to get on the good side of him? Help him out now, and who knows...?*

No way, she decided, smoothing the wrinkles in her skirt. There was a lot more at stake here than getting on the good side of Joe Gallant. There had to be some serious reason behind his point-blank refusal. *Over my dead body,* he'd said. What could it be? She'd ask Alec. She needed to think. And something told her she wouldn't get a whole lot of rational thinking done in the same room as Joe Gallant.

"Actually, I have some appointments—I've got to get back to the city," she said coolly when she returned to the kitchen.

"Oh?" Joe's dark gaze searched hers. Did he see though her quick little story about having to leave? Just then the doorbell rang.

"Hi!" A cheerful teenager with a perky blond ponytail and jeans came in. "I'm Brenda Gibson. Sorry I'm late. I'm here about the nanny job?"

Joe waved her to a chair in the kitchen and followed Honor out onto the porch.

"You'll be back."

It wasn't a question.

"Yes," she said. "I need to discuss this situation of the children with you. My father-in-law is determined to have some contact with them. What I told you is the case—he had no idea my...uh, Parker had any children. He had no idea he was living out here with your sister." She paused and bit her lip until it hurt, trying to contain her emotion. "None of us did," she added quietly, pleased that her voice was so firm.

Joe shook his head. "I find that hard to believe."

"It's true!"

"Okay, okay." He glanced toward the kitchen. If ever a man looked like he had a lot on his mind, it was Joe Gallant. "How about Saturday? Can you come back then?"

She nodded. "Saturday's fine."

"We can get this over with. I'm warning you, though, there's nothing to discuss. I'm not changing my mind."

She thought about Alec—old, broken, bitter, lying on that hospital bed staring at the ceiling. "Nor am I," she said, and left him frowning after her as she walked down the porch steps and across the gravel to her car.

She regretted her decision to leave the minute she turned out of the farmhouse driveway. She wanted to be there. She wanted to see the person he hired to look after Parker's children. She wanted to have some input. Damn it, she had a right to be part of their lives, have some say in the decisions that affected them. She was what? Their aunt? She felt a sob rise and lodge under her breastbone and ache and ache. She was their *stepmother*....

She managed to return the stiff nod of the woman driving an older-model compact slowly and carefully along the farm lane, a severe-looking woman in heavy plastic-rimmed glasses.

Another nanny prospect. Looked like it was either ponytail or perm for Parker's babies, Honor thought glumly.

Poor little orphans.

WHEN SHE WENT to the hospital the next afternoon, Alec was sitting in a recliner chair, the first time she'd seen him out of bed. His eyes actually brightened when she entered the room, and he turned his face toward her expectantly.

"How are you today?" She bent and gave him her customary kiss on the brow and took a chair beside him.

She smiled, not hiding her pleasure at seeing such a change in the old man. "You've had a haircut," she said.

He made a disgusted sound. It was an attempt at communication, at least.

"Dr. Peterson is coming in later," she added. "We're going to talk about you going home."

Another disgusted sound and a deep frown.

Honor leaned forward and patted his knee. "The Cumberland deal went through. I thought you'd like to hear that. We got everything we wanted."

His eyes caught and held hers. Honor was happy to be able to bring him good news on a mineral-rights-acquisition case she'd been working on for the past six months, a deal that had gone through only that morning. It had been Alec's pet project for almost a year. Within a week she'd have the paperwork completed and Templeman Energy petroleum engineers could finalize plans to drill on the land.

"How much?"

Honor was delighted to hear the growled inquiry. He'd not only been following what she'd been saying—she'd kept him up-to-date at every visit on the progress of the deal, hoping to engage his interest—but he was wondering what it had cost the company. For a man to whom money was everything, or nearly everything, it was a very good sign indeed.

She laughed and patted his knee again. "Plenty— don't even ask. But it's a good deal for Templeman Energy. You'll see. The reports are all very positive on the initial drilling."

The old man seemed to relax and leaned back in his recliner. Honor noticed the nervous movements of his fingers on the arm of the chair, alternately drumming and clenching.

It was time to tell him. "I went to visit the children, Alec. I saw Parker's children yesterday—"

The old man made a noise, what sounded to Honor like a strangled curse, and turned to her, his eyes oddly bright. It came as almost a physical pain to see just how much he wanted to hear her news. She'd come to believe she'd never see that light of hope in his eyes again.

"They're beautiful, Alec," she went on softly. "Just lovely. Ellie, the girl, is about three or four and she has blond hair and blue eyes, just like Parker. The little boy is blond, too, but he hasn't got a whole lot of hair—" Shocked, Honor caught herself. She'd forgotten momentarily that the little boy was named for his grandfather. How would *that* news affect the old man?

Alec gave her a quizzical look and held up his right hand, with first one, then two fingers displayed.

"Oh, he's just a baby. Maybe one, one and a half—I really can't tell."

"'s name?"

She reached forward and grasped his hand in hers. "His name is Alexander. They must have named him for you. Isn't that wonderful?" Honor blinked back tears. "Parker must have planned to tell you about them. He must have looked forward to bringing them to see you sometime."

And her. What about her? When had her husband planned to ask her for the divorce she'd have been ready to give him so he could marry the mother of his children?

"Gallant." Alec frowned.

"Yes. That was the name of the children's mother," Honor said, frowning slightly. "Sylvie Gallant, although I think she went by Parker's name, too. I'm not sure. Her brother has the children now. He's their guardian."

"Gallant," he repeated, his voice thick and hoarse.

What was he going on about? Then she noticed moisture at the corners of the old man's eyes. This was affecting him deeply. Maybe he'd had enough for one day.

"Mrs. Templeman?"

Honor stood as the door opened and a white-coated doctor came in. She shook the hand he proffered. He smiled at her, but his steady gaze was for his patient.

"And how are you this afternoon, sir? Just about ready to go home, Sue tells me," he said, mentioning Alec's regular day nurse.

Honor knew Alec despised the doctor's bluff heartiness. But she couldn't blame the doctor; he must be thoroughly fed up with this difficult old man.

"Your father-in-law can go home anytime," he said, turning to her. "I've told him there's nothing more we can do for him here."

"I've told him that, too," she said, "more than once."

"What about it, Mr. Templeman? I'll sign your release forms today, and you can be out of here after breakfast tomorrow."

Alec scowled mightily and muttered a phrase Honor was pretty sure could not be repeated in polite company.

"I like that idea," she broke in quickly, determined to put the plan into action. "I'll talk to Mr. Templeman's valet and we'll get everything ready for him. We'll be able to set up home therapy right away?"

The doctor nodded. "I'll give you the name of a private outfit. Mr. Templeman won't need much. He's got nearly full movement of his upper body, a little compromise with his left leg that I think will show progress over time. He'll need some sessions with a speech therapist. They'll do their own assessment. We'll monitor him on a regular basis for the first few months. Physically, aside from the stroke he suffered, he's in great shape for a man his age."

"Alec?" Honor wanted to nail down the old man's agreement in front of the doctor.

He glared at her, then nodded and slapped his right hand down hard on the arm of his chair, a gesture of frustration and resignation. Still, at least he was allowing them to get him home, where Spinks could take over—

"Great!" The doctor shook her hand again and reached over and grasped his patient's hand briefly. "You'll do just fine at home, sir. I know you will."

With a parting wave and nod, he left.

Honor turned to her father-in-law. She laughed out loud when she saw his look of disgust. Then he made a grotesque effort to smile. One side of his mouth lagged behind the other.

"Kids," he said, raising one arm and waving it at her. "Kids. Home."

He wanted her to bring his grandchildren to him. He'd figured out that the chances of that happening would be much better if he was home than if he remained here in the hospital. That was why he'd agreed—it had nothing to do with the doctor's wishes or hers.

She'd promised him. How in the world was she going to deliver?

CHAPTER FOUR

SATURDAY WAS BRIGHT and hot. Joe was glad he'd sent the children down to Nan's after breakfast with Phoebe. The woman he'd hired to look after them wasn't going to start until the day before Nan and Harry and their kids left for California, next Thursday. With that lawyer woman coming out to the farm again today...well, he was just as glad Alexander and Ellie were out of the way.

Every time he thought of Parker Templeman his blood boiled. He'd known, of course, that Parker had never married his sister. That hadn't bothered Sylvie any. They'd passed as husband and wife for more than four years—a common-law arrangement, which wasn't something his sister and Templeman had invented. But he'd always assumed they just hadn't gotten around to getting married yet. Or that Parker was still too gutless to go against his father's wishes. He knew Sylvie didn't care much about appearances, to the dismay of many of the townsfolk.

But he'd never dreamed the real reason was that Parker Templeman was already married to someone else.

Honor Templeman. The woman as he'd seen her last Tuesday drifted into his consciousness. He hadn't been wrong about the city shoes or the fancy suit. She was a city woman through and through. A lawyer, she'd said. Just about as slick, probably, and as slippery as all the rest of the Templeman clan. Nice hair, nice figure…a nice smile, although he didn't get the feeling she smiled much. No wonder. That bum Templeman had wrecked her life, too. Walked out on her, took up with another woman… Well, there likely were reasons all around for the way things had turned out, good and bad, and she sure wasn't coming out to the farm today to cry on his shoulder.

And his sister hadn't just had her life wrecked— she was dead.

The lawyer lady was coming here on business for Templeman. No doubt she had Joe Gallant figured for some hick she and the old man could work over. Well, he'd warned her she was wasting her time—

Speak of the devil.

Joe shaded his eyes as he stepped off the porch. Yes, that had to be her, all right. The same upscale sedan. If he could afford to drive a BMW, it'd be bright cherry red, not dark blue like hers. Said more about the lady than she probably knew.

But she didn't look anything like she had last week. She was wearing white jeans, which fit her as if they'd been custom-made, sandals and a sleeveless shirt, pale pink. Big sunglasses and a hat. Probably slathered on the sunscreen this morning, too, after the weather report. She was the careful type. She carried a matching pale pink sweater in one hand and over her shoulder was slung a video camera. Joe frowned at this reminder of why she was here.

"Hello!" She actually sounded cheerful. He came

forward. "This too early for you?" she went on. "Sorry, I should have called first."

"Not at all." He glanced toward the sun, an automatic movement, although he knew without checking that it was dead on half-past ten. Early to go visiting. Just right, though, if you had unpleasant business you wanted to get out of the way.

"Maybe we could sit in the backyard?" He looked around, glad he'd managed to get the grass cut yesterday "There's plenty of shade."

"Sure." She fell in easily beside him as he held open the gate of the white picket fence. They followed the gravel path that led to the lawn at the side and back of the farmhouse. He noted the pale pink ribbon on her broad-brimmed straw hat. Nice touch.

"I'll get us some drinks," he said, gesturing her toward a motley collection of outdoor furniture, some plastic, a cast-iron bench, a picnic table, two aged wooden Adirondack chairs, a hammock slung between two trees at the side of the yard. "Iced tea okay?"

"Fine." She began to dust off one of the Adirondack chairs with her sweater as he went in the back door.

Joe poured two tall glasses of iced tea, then reached for a metal tray that hung on the wall. He wiped his shirttail over the surface, which featured a rather ghastly historic photo of some prize team of plow horses from Glory's yesteryear. He realized he couldn't remember when the tray had last been used.

He picked it up, then set it down again. Didn't look right, somehow. He studied the two glasses. Ice! He swung open the refrigerator door and rummaged in the freezer portion for ice. Luckily there were two full trays, so he tipped one tray into the sink and fished out the four best-looking ice cubes, two for each glass.

On the way out, he grabbed the radiophone from its cradle. Maybe Nan would need him for something.

His guest had settled right in. Her hat and sweater rested on the second Adirondack chair—which left the obvious uncomfortable choice of the cast-iron bench for him—and she'd pushed her sunglasses up onto her hair. The video camera lay in its case at her feet.

"Thanks." She lifted a glass from the tray he proffered and took a small sip before depositing it on the weathered pine table beside her. Joe sat gingerly on the iron bench. She *would* have to use both his favorite chairs.

"Well." She gave him a tentative smile, which did something to Joe's insides. Something very pleasant.

He raised his glass, damning himself at the same time, because the two of them had nothing to toast. "Cheers," he said, and drained half his drink.

She smiled again, but didn't lift her glass to meet his. She glanced around. "Where are the children?"

All the good feelings Joe had toward this delicate-looking woman slammed to a halt. He answered carefully, "They're over at my sister's. Phoebe and Jill's mom." He gestured with one thumb. "They have a house just down the lane a ways. Nan's husband, Harry, works for me."

"I see." She studied him for a few more seconds, then added evenly, "I expected to see them."

Joe grunted noncommittally and finished his tea. Why hadn't he thought to bring out a pitcher?

"I rented the camcorder so I could take videos of them today to show their grandfather."

Joe set down his glass. "I'm afraid that wouldn't be a good idea."

"Why not?"

"Maybe I haven't made myself clear, Mrs. Templeman," he began slowly.

"Please. Call me Honor. I think, after last week, we're on a first-name basis, don't you?" She smiled, still the friendly smile, although Joe thought he saw steel gleam in those soft blue eyes. She was probably one helluva lawyer.

He nodded, acknowledging their hectic first meeting. "Honor. Look, we should get a few things straight. I warned you that you'd be wasting your time coming out here, and I'm afraid that's exactly what's happened—"

"Is it wasting my time to try and bring a grandfather and his grandchildren together?" she asked sweetly, reasonably.

He stared at her for a full moment. "In this case, I'd have to say yes, it is. You're wasting your time and mine. Old Man Templeman is never going to have anything to do with these kids. Period. He's never going to *see* these kids. As far as they're concerned, they don't *have* a grandfather, not on their father's side."

"So you say. But, in fact, they do. And he's a very wealthy man who could do many things for them. He has the right to see them. He *wants* to see them. They're his flesh and blood. And they have the right to get to know their own grandfather—''

''The *right!*'' Joe laughed, but he knew the sound held no humor. He turned to her. He didn't like this one bit, but it was time he spelled the situation out. *Past* time. ''Look. My sister is dead. My twin sister. I loved her more than I have ever loved anybody in this world.'' He felt the familiar wash of grief at Sylvie's death and choked it back. He went on evenly. ''She had two children, Alexander and Ellie. Her will clearly names me guardian of those children in the event of her death.''

''But their father has rights, too,'' Honor said hotly. ''He was killed, too!'' Were those tears she blinked back so quickly? He hoped not. He couldn't stand a woman's tears.

''The legal beagles see it this way. My sister and her common-law husband were killed in a car accident. When it isn't clear which party died first, the law assumes the husband did. Which means the spouse inherits. Then the spouse dies a split second later and her heirs inherit. Like I said, my sister's will was clear. I am the legal guardian of my niece and nephew, and that's the end of it. Did your husband name a guardian for his children in his will? No, he did not, at least not according to what my lawyer tells me. The children's father was not married to their mother. His relatives have no legal claim whatsoever. Considering the accident that killed them, even if my sister *had* been married to the father of her children—which she wasn't—her wishes and legal will would have prevailed. Is that putting it plainly enough?'' She was a goddamn lawyer. This should make perfect sense to her.

''Is that what we're talking about here? The *law?*''

''Yes, damn it. We're talking about the law.''

She stared at him for a few seconds, then turned to gaze into the trees, the windbreak some long-ago pioneer had planted to shade the house and keep the prairie wind from driving everyone mad. He studied her straight nose, well-shaped lips, a small firm chin. She had a classic regal profile.

''Have you made arrangements for care of the children?''

''Arrangements?''

''One of those nannies who came out last week...''

''Oh, that. Yeah, I hired one. An older woman who lives with her sister in town.'' He shrugged. Her unexpected change of subject had thrown him. ''She'll do.''

''The one with the perm?''

''Perm?''

''I passed her driving in. She looked very determined—glasses, gray hair.'' She smiled, but it was a sad little smile that broke Joe's heart. Damn, how could he do this to her? She was only trying to help in her own way. Was it *his* fault that bastard Templeman had gone out and hooked up with another woman while he was still married to this one? Joe caught himself wondering how a man could leave such a woman, then quickly focused on what they'd been discussing.

He stood. To prolong the discussion was pointless.

At least now she knew the facts. "Sorry, I can't be of any help to you on this. That's just the way it is."

"Why do you hate him?" She squinted up at him in the brightness. "What has he ever done to you? Why can't you help him? He's a lonely old man."

Her voice wobbled dangerously and Joe sat back down. *Damn.* "And what about me?" she asked. "Don't you think I want to get to know my husband's children? Don't you see how important that is?"

Stick to your point, Gallant. Take your time. Stay calm. "You're right, Honor. I do hate him. There's a reason behind my decision, but I'm not going into it with you. Let's just say your father-in-law did something a long time ago that hurt my sister. I've never forgiven him for it. I'm not going to forgive him now." He looked away, toward the trees she'd studied earlier, aware that she was watching him. He couldn't bear that appeal.

"What did he do that was so terrible you still want to punish him all these years later?" she demanded in a low voice.

"Never mind," he shot back. "It's history. But it happened. You're going to have to trust me on that. Believe me, I owe him."

"Tell me what it was."

"Ask your father-in-law if you want to know so badly," he returned. "Maybe he'll tell you."

"I'll do that."

For a moment their eyes held, neither backing away.

"And as for you," Joe continued softly, "why do you care so much? I'd have thought you'd want to stay well out of this whole sorry mess. Start over. After all, this guy was married to you, right? And for the last four or five years he was living out here most of the time with my sister and their two kids, passing himself off in town as pretty much married to *her*."

"I know," she said simply. She dug a tissue out of her handbag and blew her nose. "I don't think you could understand the situation between us. I only found out about his…his other life two weeks ago. I had no idea. But it's true—we hadn't been living as husband and wife for quite a while. Years. There's some history with me, too. I…I never had any children, you see."

She looked up at him and he felt the full raw force of her pain. "I couldn't have children. It just wasn't in the stars for me. Seeing Alexander and Ellie last week was—I don't know…" She made a sound that was half laughter, half tears, then went on in a whisper, "It was just like they were my babies, somehow. The babies I never had. Can you understand that?"

How in thundering hell had he gotten himself into this situation?

Joe asked abruptly, "You want some more iced tea?"

He didn't wait for her answer, just picked up the tray and left. He filled a pitcher with tea and ice cubes, then sat down to wait. He had to leave her alone for a few minutes; she had to get hold of herself. If she didn't… Joe had a horrifying image of taking her in his arms and soothing her, holding her close, maybe even tasting those soft pink lips, promising her... what? He couldn't stand to see a woman in a state like that.

And she'd told him all that stuff about not having kids. Told *him,* a perfect stranger! Why had she done that? He wished she hadn't.

He peeked through the slats of the blind on the back kitchen window. She looked okay. She was standing there, admiring the bed of old-fashioned roses that Nan somehow managed to keep alive year after year. He glanced at his watch. He'd give her two more minutes.

When the time was up, Joe took a deep breath, balanced the tray on one hand and pushed open the door. Just get through this, Gallant. Get through the next ten or fifteen minutes without doing something really dumb, and you'll be home free. You'll never see her again.

Luckily he'd just reached the sitting area when the radiophone beeped. It was Tim Abbott, the agriculture student he'd hired for the summer. Tim was in Calgary looking at combine equipment and wanted to discuss some details with him. He asked for Honor's permission with a raised eyebrow, which she responded to with a dismissive wave and a weak smile. He turned and walked to the trees and back several times as he talked, giving her a few more minutes to herself.

He kept glancing her way and, by the time Tim had finished, noted with satisfaction that she'd restored the broad-brimmed straw hat to her head and picked up the video camera. She was leaving. The relief he felt was mixed with something else. Regret? That he had to disappoint her? That she was departing in such a vulnerable state? His mind was made up on the issue of the old man, but that didn't mean he didn't feel any sympathy for the role she'd been forced to play in this miserable business.

"More tea?" he asked as he came up to the sitting area, knowing she'd refuse.

"Oh, thank you, but I think I...I'd better be on my way," she said. Her cheeks were flushed and her eyes bright. Joe cursed himself. He felt like he'd just kicked a lame dog.

He felt helpless as he watched her prepare to leave. She set the camcorder down on the pine table and began to put on her sweater, despite the heat of the day. Worried about sunburn, he thought. No, she wouldn't want to burn that pale ivory skin, such a contrast to the gleaming dark richness of her hair—

The phone rang again and he was damn glad it did.

"Joe? Is this Joe Gallant?"

He didn't recognize the screechy tone. "Speaking." He held up one finger to indicate to Honor that he'd be right with her. The least he could do was walk her to her car, wish her a safe trip, a happy life....

"This is Elsie Groundwater. You don't know me. I'm Bea's sister—Bea Hoople's sister?"

Joe frowned. *Trouble, he could smell it.* "Yes? Anything wrong? Bea's coming out to work for me next week—"

"That's just it, she won't be. Bea's broke her wrist. Can't work for you, after all." The woman sounded triumphant.

Joe ran one hand over his face. "What happened?"

"Well, she was standing on a chair trying to peer out the window at the house across the street last night. They have a lot of parties over there, y'know, and we've had plenty of trouble over it, believe you me. Anyways, she took a step and fell off. Broke her arm in two places."

"I'm sorry to hear that. Thanks for letting me know."

Joe punched the off button on the phone and stared glumly at it for a couple of seconds. Now what?

"Problems?"

"Yeah. The sitter I hired was standing on a chair so she could spy on her neighbors and she fell off and broke her wrist."

"The Perm? Spying on her neighbors?" Honor was actually smiling, and he didn't think the reason was his misfortune or the nanny's, more that she had the same image in her head he did of the older woman perched on a chair trying to see what was going on across the street.

"Uh-huh."

"So what will you do now?"

"I'll try and get hold of that other kid, the first one who came out here—"

"The ponytail?"

Joe met her smiling blue gaze, hesitated, then grinned. "That's the one."

"Is there anything I can do?"

"No. Thanks for asking. I should be able to round somebody up, although this is getting to be pretty short notice."

"Short notice for what?" Then she hurriedly added, "If you don't mind me asking."

"My sister Nan is leaving next week. She's been keeping an eye on Alexander and Ellie for me, but the whole family's going to California for the summer. They'll be back around Labor Day." Joe ran both hands through his hair and closed his eyes for a moment. *Damn the luck he had.*

"Nan offered to cancel the trip, but I wouldn't let her. They deserve a holiday, all of them. They've had this planned for a long time. I just need someone temporarily, until Nan and Harry get back..."

"Is Nan going to look after the children long-term?" she asked. "When she gets back, I mean?"

Joe stared at her. Was she questioning his fitness as guardian? No, she couldn't be. He was so damn up and down about this, he kept jumping to the wrong conclusion. "No. Nan's got her hands full. I've got to find a more permanent arrangement. I haven't had time yet." He grinned suddenly. "Maybe I should just get married. That's what Nan says." He shook his head, as though to say, *Women!* when he noticed she wasn't smiling.

"I'll give that kid a call, Brenda Gibson. I wasn't too keen on her. She struck me as too young for the job." He didn't add that she'd struck him as flaky, too. "Shall I walk you out to your car?"

"No," she said quickly. She was still frowning. Why? Maybe he shouldn't have told her so much about his child-care circumstances. "I'll wait until you speak to this Brenda person. I...I'd just like to know things are settled for the children."

That was fair enough. Joe took the porch steps two

at a time. Now, if he still had the kid's phone number...

He did. He punched in the last number as he reached the porch again. Brenda's mother answered on the second ring. No, Brenda was not there. No, Brenda would not be back today. Yes, Brenda had taken a job for the summer in Lethbridge and she'd left three days ago.

He punched the phone off and set it down on the windowsill next to a pot of straggly geraniums.

"She can't make it," Honor said. It wasn't a question.

Joe shook his head. "Nope. Already got a summer job." He squared his shoulders and managed a smile. "Don't worry, I'll get somebody," he said.

She turned with him and walked slowly in the direction of her car. Joe racked his brain for any other prospects he could come up with on short notice. Sure, he could round up a sitter for a day here, a couple days there, but what he needed was a commitment until Labor Day. And it couldn't be just anyone, either, not for Alexander and Ellie.

Honor paused as she reached her car. Amazed, he watched as she fished in her pocket for a key to unlock it. She'd locked her car? Here? He didn't think he'd ever locked his car on his own place. Big-city habit, that was all. And an indication of a careful methodical mind.

"Well, have a safe trip back," he said gruffly, waiting for her to get in. What else was there to say? *Goodbye, nice lady. Try not to marry any more jerks.*

"Thanks." She made no move to get behind the

wheel. Suddenly she turned to him and looked him straight in the eye. Joe's stomach did a flip.

"I have an idea," she said. She seemed nervous; she licked her lips, which didn't do anything to quiet the emotions that raced through him, seemingly with a red-blooded life of their own. Damn, why didn't she just *leave?* "I'll take care of the kids," she said quietly.

"What?" He couldn't have heard right. He took a step back, as though she'd thwacked him in the chest with a garden spade.

"I mean it. I can look after the children. I'd like to."

"What about..." His mind failed him. Never in a million years had he thought of anything like this. "What about your job?"

"That's not a problem. I'm long overdue for a vacation, plus I've just finished a big project. I've got some time on my hands right now."

"Hell, I don't think this would work, Honor."

"Think about it!" She seemed suddenly lit from within. She had a glow he'd never seen before; it scared him, plain and simple. "I'll take care of them. That'll give me a chance to know them a little. I won't do anything you don't want me to, I promise." He knew she was thinking of the old man. "A-and you could keep looking for someone who could be with them right up until Labor Day. Although," she added, "I could do that, too. But you might not want me that long."

Her eyes searched his. He still felt like he'd been poleaxed.

She put her hand on his forearm, as she'd done

that first day she'd come to the farm—so soft and pale and feminine against the tan of his skin. He felt dizzy. "Think about it, Joe. Please. Call me." She fumbled in her bag and brought out a card, which she gave him. "Here. I'm serious. Call me."

She got into her car then, and he took another step back. She reversed carefully, turned the car around and drove away. He stared after the vehicle.

On the one hand, it was the craziest thing he'd ever heard of—his sister's lover's widow looking after his niece and nephew, while he hunted for a replacement...or a wife?

On the other hand, he had to agree with her. It made a lot of sense.

CHAPTER FIVE

A. R. TEMPLEMAN LIVED in an area of palatial residences situated along the Elbow River, which meandered through south Calgary, just below the old-money residential area of Mount Royal.

The three-acre property had been purchased in the 1950s from a business partner who'd gone broke, and beyond extensive new landscaping, the estate hadn't changed much in forty years. A cast-iron gate and electronic security system were among the few modern additions, and they'd only been installed a year ago when Spinks discovered a vagabond living in an old car parked in some trees at the back of the property. The two Templeman Labrador retrievers, rather than doing their duty as guard dogs, had been joyously bounding down for extra rations from the vagabond's table every evening, it turned out.

By now, the house, built in the 1930s, looked much like an aging dowager, still in carmine lipstick, South Sea pearls and a twin set, but determined to make the best of things on finding herself suddenly thrown in with a gang of young, moneyed, virile newcomers in Armani suits and Rolexes. The large modern houses on each side of the Templeman estate and across the road were all testament to Calgary's boom of the past two decades.

Alec despised excess. No one in town made money in a more raw or brash way, but he preferred the status symbols of his youth. The silk pajamas and smoking jacket, the finest Cuban cigars in his study, the worn English-leather club chairs. The Egyptian cotton bed linens, the Chinese carpets on the hardwood floor, the *good* Bavarian china, the fine rosewood baby grand—unplayed, untuned. These necessities spelled luxury to that generation born between the wars. Only in the area of transport was the oil magnate unabashedly North American. In a sea of BMWs, Mercedes and Jaguars, he kept a Cadillac. It, too, was a mark of the highest success of his age.

Spinks tended 33 Elbow Lane. Everyone called him Spinks. Honor hadn't even known his first name—Cecil—until she'd been married for several years. No one, Parker had told her, knew exactly where his father had found him.

Tended, Honor thought with a smile as she turned into the drive, was exactly what Spinks did. The house at 33 Elbow Lane was his; Alec R. Templeman simply paid the bills.

Her father-in-law had been home nearly a week now. She'd visited him every day and had begun to feel cautiously optimistic. He'd complained about the arrangements Spinks had made and the physical therapist the doctor had recommended and every single suggestion of hers, but Honor considered that a good sign. The father-in-law she knew and loved was an ornery man. If he was starting to complain, he was starting to heal. Anything was better than the terrible deadly quiet of the hospital room.

If only she could bring him and his grandchildren together...

Perhaps going to Swallowbank Farm was the chance she needed. She'd have the time to convince Joe Gallant to cooperate, no matter what had happened between him and Alec in the distant past. The early-morning phone call she'd received agreeing to the proposal she'd put to him on Saturday still sent shivers running down her spine. She'd known instantly who he was the moment she'd heard his voice. All day she'd been thinking about it, feeling tremors of anticipation at this opportunity to get to know Parker's children. She could hardly wait to tell Alec.

Was it too much to expect things would work out? Maybe. Honor parked at the side of the big house and got out of the car. There was no single easy way of bringing Alec and his grandchildren together. She'd realized that ever since meeting Joe Gallant. He was a stubborn proud man. So was Alec Templeman.

Alec's single-minded obsession with seeing his grandchildren worried her a little. There'd been no love lost between Parker and his father. How would he relate to grandchildren? Alec wasn't a man who understood family feeling. He wasn't a man who particularly liked children. He'd never had time for anything that didn't relate to business.

Unless it was his flag irises.

On impulse Honor bent to pick one in the raised bed along the drive. She held the shaggy purple bloom up, enjoying its wise and oddly dignified appearance.

Her heels tap-tapped and echoed in the long hallway, dim and cool and smelling of lemon oil and lavender. She popped the single iris blossom in with a bowl of daisies and ivy on the hall table. Spinks had outdone himself. Every surface in the old house was polished and shining, as though the grizzled majordomo had attempted to work out his own grief over his employer's illness and Parker's death by aspiring to an even higher standard of housekeeping than usual.

Spinks was in the library with Alec. He rose when she entered and immediately set off to make tea. Honor knew he'd bring a plate of his famous shortbread, too. Spinks didn't attempt much in the way of cooking, but what he did was always exquisite. Her father-in-law's valet and companion was a very unusual man.

Alec smiled as she walked toward him. He reached out a hand, which she took and squeezed warmly in both of hers.

"You look marvelous, Alec," she said. The change from the hospital gloom was impressive. He had color in his cheeks, and he was freshly shaved and wearing a shirt and tie and sitting in his favorite chair. She'd known the calm reliable Spinks would be the medicine he needed.

"Ha!" Alec waved at her, then gestured toward the nearby sofa.

"You do. You look great. How's the new physical therapist working out?"

He grimaced, then mischievously winked. She laughed out loud. "You old scoundrel!"

"Nice young girl. Very nice," Alec grudgingly

admitted with another wink. "Knows her stuff." The "young girl" had to be in her late twenties, but Honor had to admit she was a very attractive woman. And the type who knew just how to jolly a cantankerous old man along.

Honor felt confident she was leaving him in good hands. Spinks could handle anything that came up while she was gone. Alec had talked more the last few days than he ever had at the Crowfoot Hospital, but that could be because he was making more of an effort.

He had something to live for now.

It was a chilling thought. What if this didn't work out? How could she bear to face his disappointment?

"I've got some news, Alec," she said, still holding his hand in hers.

His eyes, clear and sharp as a hawk's, sought and questioned hers.

She cleared her throat. "I'm going out to Glory for a little while to look after Parker's children—"

"What's that?"

"Parker's children. Little Alexander and Ellie. Their uncle needs someone to fill in for a few days while he finds a nanny for them." Sometimes she wondered if his memory was as good as it had been.

"Aargh!" Alec released her hand, grabbed the cane that leaned against his chair and smashed it onto the hardwood floor in front of him.

His eyes flashed defiance and anger as he met her gaze. She held her tongue. She wouldn't give him the satisfaction of demanding an explanation.

"Bring 'em here. *Bring 'em to me.*"

"It's not that easy, Alec. Their uncle doesn't want

to…to upset them just now." It was a white lie, but how could she tell the old man that she didn't dare even mention his name to Joe Gallant? Let alone insist that she bring the children to Calgary.

Alec smashed the heavy cane on the floor again. He tried to speak, but was so angry the words wouldn't come. With a hoarse garbled sound he shut his jaw grimly and refused to make a second attempt.

Honor reached out and grasped his hand again. Poor old man. Lonely, sick…angry. Nothing was going the way he wanted it to, and he wasn't used to that. Alec had his virtues, she knew that very well; she also knew that patience was not among them.

"I'll try to talk their uncle into letting me bring the children to see you soon. I'm sure it will all work out," she said soothingly, patting his hand. "Everybody just needs a little time. This is all so…so new to everyone." Including herself. She could only imagine what her sudden appearance had meant to Joe.

"Uncle?" Alec was frowning.

She'd told him, back in the hospital. He'd obviously forgotten.

"He's the mother's brother. The children's guardian. Joe Gallant is his name. He's a farmer—"

The cane smashed on the floor again. Spinks came in, hurriedly set down the tea tray, then wrested the heavy cane from his employer's grasp. "Here, sir. I'll take that," he said quietly, laying the stick aside, well out of Alec's reach.

Honor jumped at the opportunity. "Alec, what in the world is wrong between you and Joe Gallant? Was it to do with Parker?"

"Gallant," growled the old man, and shook his fist. "Joe Gallant." And he followed the farmer's name with a few coarse oilfield expletives that had Honor shuddering and Spinks looking properly shocked, although Honor was pretty sure he'd heard worse in his time.

She got up and poured the tea, hoping her bent head hid her expression. There was more here than either Alec or Joe had let on; apparently Alec had no more regard for Joe Gallant than Joe did for him. Something was terribly wrong—if only she knew what. It was clear that Alec couldn't—or wouldn't—tell her.

She set a cup of tea beside Alec's chair, then opened the briefcase she'd brought. "Here," she said, and handed him a sheaf of papers. He took them eagerly, mood shifting instantly, as she'd known it would. "The Cumberland acquisition. Don Wetherall will make sure these contracts are signed tomorrow. I'm leaving for Glory first thing in the morning."

"Ah." She watched as the old man settled back in his chair, fury forgotten, and began to read the company documents avidly, as she'd known he would.

THERE WAS AN ENORMOUS amount of activity at the Gallant farm when Honor arrived. Dogs barked and ran frantically around the yard. What seemed like a hundred teenagers milled about, the younger ones, mostly boys, kicking balls and tossing sticks for the dogs to chase.

Honor recognized Phoebe and waved. The girl waved back briefly and called hello before returning to her friends, all of whom, it seemed, were deeply involved in tearful farewells.

You'd think they were moving to Sudbury, Honor thought, not going on a family trip to Disneyland. She got out of the car, smiling to herself. Joe had told her when he called that the Longquists planned to leave at noon on Thursday. It was just eleven o'clock now.

She was looking forward to this. She had two packed suitcases in the trunk, enough for a week's stay, and a satchel of gifts for the children, including something for Phoebe and Jill and their two younger siblings. As she recalled, the clerk at the town office had said there were five Longquist children, with the oldest not living at home.

Where was Joe in all this confusion? Honor looked around casually. Ah, there he was, about thirty yards away. She didn't know if her heart seemed to stop because their gazes connected so directly, or if it was the realization that the man he was walking beside was in a motorized wheelchair.

The small boy, Alexander, was sitting on the lap of the occupant of the wheelchair. Ellie skipped along beside the men, a black-and-tan puppy yipping excitedly at her heels. The instant the girl saw Honor, she ran toward her, yelling her name.

Honor was stunned. She held out her arms, an automatic reaction, and Ellie threw herself into them, and flung her own arms around Honor's neck. She whispered something Honor couldn't make out, then, as quickly, wanted down. Head spinning, Honor set the child on the grass. Ellie grabbed her hand and hung on to it.

"Look—there's Auntie Nan! There's Auntie Nan!" the little girl yelled, pointing as a large blue-and-cream motor home nosed from behind the trees that screened the lane and continued at a snail's pace toward the Gallant farmhouse.

Joe and the other man reached Honor.

"Hello." The man in the wheelchair extended his hand and she stepped forward to grip it. "You must be Honor. What a piece of luck you were able to step in and take care of the kiddies like that."

Honor's eyes sought Joe's—what had he told everyone? Joe nodded, his smile strained.

"Honor, I'd like you to meet Harry Longquist, my brother-in-law. Nan's husband. Harry, this is Honor Templeman, Parker's sister."

Sister? Honor's gaze clung to Joe's. She read the entreaty in his, the appeal to say nothing about her real relationship with the man these people regarded as part of their extended family. But it hurt. It sliced through her like a knife to have her position reduced to a lie, well-meaning though it was. Yet at the same time, did she want to draw the Longquists into her tangled life? Why spoil their holiday with the knowledge that their sister's common-law husband had been married to another woman?

"I'm very pleased to meet you," she managed, dredging up a smile. Joe's relief was palpable. Again Honor felt the sense of hurt, although she knew that was sheer foolishness....

Nan joined them, a handsome woman with threads of silver streaking her thick dark hair. "My goodness, I'm going to have to get used to driving that thing! What a beast."

Joe quickly performed the introductions, again referring to Honor as Parker's sister. She shook Nan's hand and smiled at Alexander, who continued to regard her with suspicion and clung to his Uncle Harry's shirtfront.

The adults looked at each other. Honor sensed tension in the air. Finally Joe spoke. "Well? Let's all go inside—"

"Yay!" Ellie cried, still clinging to Honor's hand and pulling her toward the house. "I'll show you all my stuff and where everything is!"

Honor followed the child. At least Ellie seemed happy she was here.

Joe and Harry and the baby disappeared down the hall. Nan poured cold drinks for everyone, then sent Phoebe out to the veranda with a tray of glasses and a big jug of Kool-Aid. She handed Jill two bags of store-bought cookies from Joe's cupboard and sent her out after her sister. Finally she turned to Honor, who was standing uncertainly near the kitchen table.

"Sit down, dear," the older woman said. "I want to go over this list with you. What the kids like to eat, bedtimes, that kind of thing. I can't tell you how relieved Harry and I were when we heard you'd be here. Not that Joe can't manage just fine," she quickly added. "It's just that he's so busy this time of year."

Honor was grateful for her help. She didn't have a clue what to do with children in the way of routines. She'd told Joe she could look after the kids— but could she? She had no experience to draw on, as Nan did.

The next hour or so flew by. Then all of a sudden

the activity seemed to intensify as the Longquists piled into the motor home. Nan looked harried and constantly asked her children did they have this? Did they have that? At the last moment their oldest son, Ben, showed up to say goodbye. Nan burst into tears and hugged him and made him promise not to get into any trouble while they were gone and to be sure to water her African violets in the kitchen window. Ben was returning from his job at a ranch on the other side of Glory to sleep at the Longquist house several times a week and to look after everything there; his mother had given him a list, too. The Longquist dogs were under Joe's care. Just as the motor home was pulling out, Honor remembered the gifts she'd brought and distributed them.

Then they were gone, in a last flurry of waves and honking of horns. The teenagers who'd come to see their friends off left, too, most in their own cars, others on bicycles.

Suddenly it was almost quiet and Honor became very aware of the tableau they presented: her standing on the veranda beside Joe, the little girl in front of her waving a small hand energetically and calling goodbye as her cousins and aunt and uncle drove away. Joe had the baby in his arms. She sent him a quick sideways glance. They looked like a small intact family—a mom, a dad and two adorable children standing on the steps of their home in the country, waving goodbye to their visitors.

Joe was staring after the motor home as though wondering, as she was, what came next.

WHAT CAME NEXT turned out to be lunch, which was a messy affair with Alexander in his high chair and

Ellie at the table. Joe went into his office to make a few phone calls, and when he came back out, she had the children started on a macaroni-and-cheese boxed dinner she'd found in the cupboard. She was spooning some into Alexander's mouth while he regarded her skeptically with solemn blue eyes. He beamed when his uncle returned to the room and blew macaroni all over his chair tray.

"Ugh!" Honor involuntarily jumped back. "I think he's had enough."

"You get used to it," Joe said dismissively. He went to the counter for a couple of paper towels, which he used to wipe off the baby's face. "His naptime now." He looked at her intently. "You want to take care of it? Or should I?"

"Do you mind? I mean…well, I think it might be better if I watched today, just until he gets used to me being here. He's not all that sure yet that he wants me around," she confessed with a shrug.

"Oh, he'll get over it," Joe said softly, lifting the baby from his chair and holding him high. "Won'tcha, tiger?" He grinned at the boy, who giggled back and swiped at his uncle's face with a hand that still had a few pieces of macaroni stuck to it. Joe laughed out loud, and Honor had the strangest feeling that this man was already so completely and totally bonded to his niece and nephew that he'd become, in effect, their father. Which was a good thing, she thought, considering that Joe Gallant was their legal guardian and would be responsible for them until they were grown.

It was a sobering thought.

Dead. Parker and Joe's sister, Sylvie—dead. No one today had even mentioned them, except that Joe had introduced her as Parker's sister.

Honor followed them down the hall. So far, she hadn't been shown to her own room, although she was assuming the vacant one across from the children's room would be assigned to her. Joe's bedroom was at the end of the hall.

Honor kept her attention focused on the center of Joe's back. It was all too easy to see him as a very handsome sexy man, an *interesting* man. It was all too easy to allow herself to admire the way his jeans fit, or the breadth of his shoulders under the plaid cotton shirt he wore, or the way his dark hair curled at the back of his neck.

But she was only here on his sufferance and at his extremely reluctant agreement to her proposal. And it was only for a week or so, until he lined up someone else. She couldn't afford to see him as anything other than he was—the obstacle between Alec and his grandchildren. An obstacle that somehow she was determined to get around. Joe Gallant wasn't a man to her—he couldn't be—he was a problem. She had to remember that.

In the children's room, she was amazed at how quickly and expertly he settled the little boy in his crib. He changed his diaper, maneuvered him into clean sleepers, then placed him on a small lambskin, the washable type she'd seen in baby departments. Alexander sighed heavily and stuck his thumb in his mouth. Joe lowered the blinds and turned the knob on a music box that sat on the dresser. As the tinny carousel sounds of "Ring around the rosy" burbled out, Joe beckoned to her and they left.

In the hall he paused to close the door quietly behind him. "He's usually asleep before that thing runs down. I jimmied it so it runs three times as long."

Joe made no move to leave, and Honor glanced up at him. "I guess you want to see where you'll be sleeping," he murmured.

"That might be a good idea," she said dryly. "Why don't I go out to the car and get my stuff?"

"That's okay. I'll bring it in." As she'd expected, he walked across the hall and pushed open the door, which stood ajar. He looked around quickly. It was a plain room, with a bed, a chair, a dresser, a closet, a few framed pictures on the wall. Nothing personal. "This do?"

"Of course." She hadn't considered how closely they'd be living, she and the children and their uncle. In the same house, naturally. But somehow the logistics of that kind of living hadn't entered her brain yet. She'd lived on her own for so long.... She turned to leave.

"Hold on." He touched her shoulder gently and she froze.

"Something else?" She regarded him coolly.

"Yes. I'm heading for Glory right away. I'll take Ellie with me. That'll give you a chance to settle in a little on your own. I'm meeting someone in town who might be able to take over from you."

"Already?"

He frowned. "It's something I need to take care of. Permanently. You know that."

"Yes, I understand." She did, but she couldn't

help feeling a little disappointed that he was angling to get rid of her before she'd even unpacked. Still, she had her chance to be with the children, didn't she? Even if it was only for a few days.

She had to be grateful for that.

CHAPTER SIX

HE MUST BE NUTS, Joe thought as he made a left turn onto Macleod Avenue, not snapping up Jane Oldham's offer right on the spot. She was free to look after the kids as soon as she finished her summer-school course. She'd be able to take care of them until school started in September.

Jane Oldham was a teacher. He'd dated her a few times three or four years before, but it had never amounted to anything on either side. Or so he'd thought. He didn't like the way she'd smiled at him today.

Damn. That was a problem, certainly not the biggest one, but still a problem—with these good-looking single women who were willing to take care of the kids and live in his house. People talked. Not that he really gave a damn. He might be in the marriage market these days, but he didn't want to get his arm twisted into tying the knot with Jane before he was good and ready.

Still, he had to think about what kind of example he was setting, especially for Nan and Harry's kids. There'd been enough talk in the community about his sister, Sylvie, over the years, not much of it good and none of which had stopped when she'd teamed up with Templeman. The best solution all round would be if he simply got married. Unfortunately he didn't have a likely candidate in mind.

Joe pulled into the dusty parking lot at the side of the post office. He got most of his business mail in town. He glanced at his niece. Ellie was sound asleep, leaning against the armrest on the locked passenger door. Poor kid. She'd had a big day. Maybe he should've left her at the farm with Honor to have an afternoon nap like her little brother.

Honor. Joe dared to examine his thoughts on the subject. Ever since he'd called her early the day before, he'd been having second thoughts. She was bad news. Sure, she'd be okay with Alexander and Ellie, no question. But she wasn't Parker Templeman's sister—she was his widow. And it wasn't only that she wanted to get to *know* the kids—she had some kind of agenda concerning Old Man Templeman. He didn't trust her. And she wasn't too old or too young or too fat or too thin—she was just right. Just *how* right she was he didn't want to think about yet.

He'd put Jane off, and it wasn't because Ellie had whispered to him that she didn't want Miss Oldham, she wanted her new auntie to take care of her. And it wasn't because Jane couldn't start for another ten days that he'd said he'd keep looking, if it was all the same to her.

It was because he didn't want Honor Templeman to go back to Calgary. Not yet.

"Afternoon, Myrna," he said, nodding to the postmistress as he entered the box area of the post office. Myrna Schultz had her cage open at the counter and was attending to a customer with a postage meter.

"Nan and Harry get off all right, Joe?" she called.

"Just fine. They left around noon."

"Woulda been a darn shame if they'd had to cancel—"

"Sure would," he interrupted amiably. The postmistress gave him a sharp look, which he ignored. He leafed through some of the mail he'd pulled from his box, tossing a handful of junk mail into the recycling box that stood near the door. He nodded as the other customer left with his postage machine.

"So, who's looking after Sylvie's little ones now that Nan's gone?"

Joe glanced up and met the postmistress's curious gaze. "I'm still checking into that, Myrna. I'll be sure and let you know the minute I've got things settled."

With a casual wave and a grin, he left. *Old busybody.* But her interest underlined his situation with Honor: in a town like Glory, Honor Templeman's arrival was big news.

Joe didn't have a chance to speak to Honor, adult to adult, until after the children were in bed. They'd shared a quiet supper—if it was possible to call a meal with children quiet in any sense of the word. He and Honor hadn't spoken much, and after the meal he went through the children's usual evening routine of baths and stories and bedtime. He had it down to about forty-five minutes on a good night. Both children were sound asleep by eight o'clock.

Joe took a cup of coffee outside to the veranda to watch the sun set. He had a lot to get organized between now and the middle of August. There wasn't just the arrangement for Ellie and Alexander; there was his business to consider. Oats and barley had to be taken off two sections of land and hay off a third. Then, if the season permitted, he did custom combining for some of his neighbors. The farm supported two families, his and his sister's, and provided the salaries for two or three seasonal workers. There were seed and fertilizer and equipment loans to meet, and a mortgage again, since Harry's accident two years ago.

The screen door slammed, and Joe jerked his thoughts back to the present. Honor Templeman.

She carried a steaming cup in one hand and with a simple "Mind if I join you?"—not waiting for his invitation—sat down in the old swing love seat on the veranda.

"Sure. Nice night," he said lamely. The woman had a knack for catching him off stride.

"Very nice."

He heard the squeak-squeak of the love seat hinges as it gently rocked. Another Sunday-afternoon job, oiling the mechanism.

"So," he began again in what he hoped sounded like a straightforward friendly tone, "how did your first day go?"

She hesitated. "Quite well, I think," she said, and Joe had the sense that she was giving him the scrupulous truth. "I believe Ellie will adjust quickly." She took a sip of whatever she'd brought out in her cup. "I don't think the little boy likes me at all."

"Oh? Why do you say that?" Joe turned so he could see her expression. In the slight shade of the veranda roof, she looked serious, but that didn't surprise him. He had the definite impression that she was a very cautious sober woman. Probably a good trait in a lawyer. She wore a flowered skirt of some kind, a pale pink T-shirt and sandals. She appeared to have a preference for pink.

"He cried most of the afternoon when he woke up from his nap. I did everything I could think of to comfort him, but—" she drew a shaky breath and Joe realized it was bothering her a lot "—he just wouldn't settle down for me."

"He'll get used to you," Joe said. "He was like that with me when…" He frowned. He still couldn't bear to speak of Sylvie's death. "After the accident. It was a big shock to both of them." After a pause he corrected himself. "To all of us." If she could be honest, so could he.

"I'm sure it was," she said softly. "Were you and your sister very close?"

"I told you we were twins," he said, as though that explained everything. "We did everything together when we were kids."

"What was she like?" came the soft query. "If you don't mind talking about it."

Oh, he did, he did. But he couldn't tell her that.

"We were the same age of course, but I always felt like I was her big brother. It was strange. I felt I had to look out for her. Be the responsible one." Joe stopped, suspended for a moment in memories of his dancing, laughing, devil-may-care sister. "Sylvie loved life, I guess you could say. And she never let anything get in her way. I hauled her out of more than one scrape when we were growing up. And later."

"Do you…" He heard the pain in her voice and steeled himself for what she was about to say. "Do you…is it your opinion that Parker and she were happy together?''

She was asking him. She wanted to know the truth.

''She was crazy about him. He…well, it always seemed he was crazy about her, too. I believe he was.'' Joe glanced at Honor. She was clutching her cup in both hands. No way was he going to go into all the history between Parker and Sylvie, not now, not with this woman who was practically a stranger, who had drifted into his life on the most unlikely of connections.

''Look, I'm sorry if that hurts, but it's the truth. I have no idea what went on between you and Parker, but he made my sister very happy. That's the only thing I can forgive him for, to be honest. He cared for Sylvie and he loved those two kids.''

''I'm glad,'' he heard her say, so quietly he could barely make out her reply until she repeated it. ''I'm glad of that.''

An awkward silence fell. Joe felt a desperate need to change the subject or at least redirect it. ''What about you? Tell me a little about yourself.''

She leaned forward slightly, still holding her cup in both hands. She didn't hesitate. The words spilled over him, low and soft, until he wished he'd never asked. There was too much *to* this woman. He didn't want to know.

''I grew up in Edmonton. My father died when I was a little older than Ellie. I was five. I barely remember him except that he had a sad smile and large hands and he loved to read me stories. After he died my mother and I moved a lot.''

She paused and took a sip from her cup, then

laughed briefly. "I think it had to do with my mother's luck. When she was lucky and was working, we lived in a nice neighborhood. When she lost her job and we had to go on welfare, we moved to a smaller place. I made up my mind that I wanted to escape that life. I worked hard in school. I got scholarships. And...and eventually it happened." She shrugged.

"What about your mother? Is she still in Edmonton?"

"She'd always been in poor health, that's why she lost so many jobs. She died when I was in my second year of university, when I was eighteen."

"I'm sorry to hear that."

"Yes," she said simply. "I miss her. She was very proud of me. I often wonder if I would've done the crazy things I've done if I'd been able to talk things over with her."

"Crazy? Like what?"

"Like marrying Parker."

Joe set his empty cup down on the step beside him and moved so he could lean against the top balustrade and observe her. *Why had she married Parker?* He wanted to know.

"I'm sure you're wondering why I'd say something like that." She paused, then went on with a burst of passion in her low voice that surprised him. "I liked Parker. Maybe I could even say that I'd fooled myself into thinking I loved him. For a short while, anyway, when we were first married. We got married because of his father—the man you hate so much."

She stopped and Joe held his breath. So Alec was

behind this, too. He wasn't going to ask her to go on, but he wanted to hear the whole story.

"Who was Parker's father to me? That's what you want to know. Well, he rescued me. I met Alec when I was in my final year of law school. I was waitressing in a hotel to make ends meet, wondering what I'd do if I didn't get a decent position articling, and he offered me the world. He gave me a job and put me on a fast track in his company's legal department. I did more in three years there than I would have been able to do in ten at another place. That's where I met Parker. Alec thought we were a perfect couple. He pushed Parker to marry me. He wanted Parker to have children. Heirs. That was very important to him. Parker didn't object. Neither did I. I'm not a very romantic creature, I guess."

That bastard, Joe swore silently.

She shook her head sadly. "I'm only telling you this because I think you have a right to know. At least, your sister had a right to know and now she's dead. I mean, he was living right here in this town most of the time for the past four or five years, with a family and everything, and we knew nothing about it up in Calgary. I didn't. His father didn't. It was a complete shock when I found out."

"How did you find out?"

She shook her head again and sighed. "I was clearing out Parker's apartment and I came across a newspaper clipping. I guess I should've suspected something when his lawyer told me after the funeral that Parker had nothing except his apartment and furnishings. I realize now that he was providing for another family and had made sure they were taken care of. I'm glad he did that. Legal wife or not, I certainly don't need the money.''

Joe swore again to himself.

But Honor hadn't finished. ''Don't get me wrong. Parker and I were happy enough at first. I wanted children and he wanted to please his father. I h-had three pregnancies in three years. Two were stillbirths and one was a tubal pregnancy. I had to have surgery. The doctors told me there was little chance I'd ever conceive again and if I did, I'd likely never carry the baby to term.''

Goddamn, Joe groaned, *why didn't she shut up? He didn't want to hear this!*

''I wanted you to know the whole story, Joe. I'm not saying that's why Parker and I separated. I don't blame him. I'm glad, actually, that he was happy with your sister. He deserved a life of his own. He'd had a rotten time of it, always under his father's thumb. His mother died when he was a boy. As I said, we weren't in love. After all that, the babies I lost and everything…well, we just kind of drifted apart.''

She looked directly at him and he heard her shaky laugh. God forgive him, he wanted to go over and take her in his arms. Dead or alive, he wanted to tear that coward Templeman and his goddamned interfering father limb from limb.

''We were both to blame. Neither one of us had the courage to face up to his father. Or our situation. Why didn't we just go ahead and get a divorce the way other people do? I don't know. We should have.'' She shrugged and dug into the pocket of her skirt, produced a tissue and blew her nose heartily.

It was a very human gesture, and Joe felt some of his outrage on her behalf fade. *He still wanted to take her in his arms.*

"And this is the man you want to introduce to Alexander and Ellie as their grandfather?" Joe growled. "This domineering, interfering, heartless old fool?"

She looked at him, startled. "Oh, no, Joe. It's not like that. He's not a monster. He's just a sick lonely old man. He has no one now except me and I'm not even really related. If you could meet him, you'd—"

"Never!" Joe picked up his mug and stood. "I had a low opinion of the man before, as you know, and for good reason. After what you've told me..." He shook his head. "I don't know how you can sit there and make excuses for him."

"He's just a man, Joe. He's made mistakes in his life. We all have. Nothing would make him happier than to meet Parker's children—"

Joe couldn't stand it anymore. With a terse good-night he turned and walked into the house. How could he tell her? Alec Templeman had more to answer for than wrecking his own son's life, and hers. He couldn't tell her how Alec had interfered with Parker and Sylvie—not this time, but when they'd first met, years ago. No, he had plenty against Alec Templeman, and nothing this woman said now was going to change that.

HONOR HAD A HARD TIME getting to sleep. It was so dark in the farmhouse and so eerily silent. Besides Nan and Harry, she had no idea how close or how far the nearest neighbor was, nor had she realized how accustomed she'd grown to the comforting noise and lights of the city.

She lay there and stared at the ceiling, thinking of where she was and how she'd gotten there. Every once in a while, her mind would drift and she'd hear Joe's voice again when he spoke of his sister. Rough, raw. He was obviously terribly broken up over her death. Had he had the chance to grieve properly?

Probably not. He'd had the children to look after immediately after the accident, and then she'd come calling with her terrific ideas about getting his niece and nephew together with a grandfather they'd never known existed. A man he clearly despised.

She hadn't meant to spill everything out there on the veranda tonight. Sure, she owed him some sort of explanation about Parker, if only because of his sister. But to go on and on like that about her own father, her lost babies, her hopelessly incompetent mother....

Something about Joe Gallant unsettled her. She'd felt it from the first day she met him, slithering out from under that big farm machine, all covered with dirt and grease and with the clearest most direct gaze she'd ever seen on a man. It was as though he saw straight through her, so what was the point of keeping secrets, anyway? She shuddered. She'd hate to face him across a negotiating table.

Honor recognized part of the feeling, and was mortified. *Sexual attraction.* She was sexually attracted to him, pure and simple. He was a very attractive man. Fit, handsome, healthy. Somehow she'd reached the grand old age of thirty-one with very limited experience when it came to men. She'd been married for eight years, but five of those years had been in name only. Before that? One could hardly qualify a few gropes in the backseat of a car after a high-school dance as useful experience.

Mostly she hadn't cared. She was used to being ignored by men. Sure, times had changed, but the fact was, most men were put off by brainy women, and she'd always been a studious serious person. She'd preferred to immerse herself in her career and Templeman Energy. Even since she and Parker had separated, she'd rarely dated, let alone had an affair or a real relationship.

Yet something raw and primitive and exciting about Joe Gallant seemed to cut through her, straight to the woman she was beneath the lawyer's exterior. The woman she'd almost forgotten existed.

This man of all men—Joe Gallant.

She had to be careful; she was only here for a short time and couldn't afford any more complications in this already delicate situation. Whatever feelings Joe aroused in her had to be suppressed. Imagine if he supposed, even for a moment, that the lonely cast-off widow had her eye on him! He'd figure she was trying to throw herself at him to get him to change his mind about Alec and the children. What could be more pathetic or humiliating?

She fell asleep, finally, to be awakened hours later by Ellie's muffled sobs from the children's room across the hall and her whispered pleas for "Mama." Honor didn't know what to do, so she did nothing, just lay there in her own bed and ached for the little girl.

Ellie would not remember Parker. No one would

keep him alive in the girl's heart, certainly not Joe
Gallant. That was tragic, yet Honor knew it was true.
She had only to examine her own thoughts and mem-
ories to know how easily a father could be forgotten.

IN THE MORNING she felt quite different, calm and
confident again. She didn't know if Alexander was
getting used to her already, but when she went into
the children's room, he was sitting up in his crib and
raising his arms to her to be lifted out. He didn't
smile, but yesterday he would have balked.

That's progress, she thought, quickly fastening on
a clean diaper and then picking up the little boy. He
sighed and popped his thumb into his mouth. There
was no sign of Ellie. She could hear a radio playing
from the kitchen, though, and smell the aroma of
good coffee.

Honor carried Alexander toward the kitchen, glad
she'd taken the few extra minutes to wash, brush her
hair, put in her contacts and pull on jeans and a T-
shirt before going to the children's room. She hadn't
slept well, but considering everything that had happened since yesterday, she felt amazingly good.

"Morning, Sleeping Beauty," Joe said, one eyebrow raised in query and a smile on his face.

Honor glanced at the kitchen clock on the wall. It
was just half-past seven, which hardly qualified as
oversleeping. "Good morning," she returned evenly.

Joe waved the spatula in his hand and growled,
and Alexander giggled and held out both arms to his
uncle. Joe, also in jeans and a T-shirt, stood over a
griddle of pancakes at the stove. He held up one
hand. "Not now, tiger. I got pancakes to finish up

here and Miss Muffet over there is just about done with her curds and whey and ready for a pancake.''

He winked at Honor, a sexy slow wink that completely rattled her. She hid a smile and carried Alexander over to his high chair and settled him in.

"Hi!" Ellie waved her spoon. "I'm having curds and whey just like Miss Muffet.'' Honor glanced at the bowl in front of the girl. It looked like yogurt and fruit to her. She smiled and fastened Alexander's bib around his neck, with a warm feeling under her ribs. Joe liked playing these little games with the children. And why not? It made life more pleasant for everyone, including her.

Joe brought over a plate of pancakes with a flourish and another grin. Well, you could say one thing about the man, she thought, he certainly was a morning person. "Dig in, everybody. Syrup and butter on the table. Coffee on the counter. I'll get some juice for the kid." He walked to the refrigerator and pulled out a jug of orange juice which he brought to the table. Honor couldn't help noticing he was barefoot.

As he walked behind her chair, he paused, and she felt him snag the scarf she'd used to loosely tie back her hair. With one quick tug he'd whisked it off and draped it over her chair back.

"Hey!" She whirled around.

He had an odd look on his face, as though he'd surprised himself with his action. "Sorry. Couldn't resist."

That was all the explanation he offered. Honor shook her head slightly to settle her hair around her shoulders and felt her cheeks grow warm. She wasn't going to make a big deal of it in front of the children, but she decided she'd have to get a few things straight with Joe Gallant in private. If she didn't know better, she'd think he was flirting with her.

"Look, Ono—" Ellie was having trouble with Honor's first name "—I got a bunny." She pointed to her plate and Honor saw that Joe had made the child a special pancake; he'd added two long ears and a tiny blob of batter for a tail. No wonder Ellie said she liked her uncle Joe.

"What's Alexander got?" Honor asked, taking the small plate Joe handed her and positioning it in front of the little boy.

Ellie studied the pancake for a few seconds, then shouted, "A bear!"

Honor swung her gaze to meet Joe's. "A bunny with an ear challenge," he said with another wink.

She smiled. It was hard not to. She speared a couple of pancakes to put onto her own plate. Suddenly she was hungry. The pancakes looked excellent. Joe Gallant was full of surprises; obviously he could cook, too. Which was good to know, as they hadn't discussed that aspect of her caring for the children.

"Ono?" Ellie said, frowning as she leaned both elbows on the table. "Can I just call you Auntie 'cause it's so hard to say your name?"

Honor glanced, stricken, at Joe. She didn't want to perpetuate his white lie about her relationship to Parker. On the other hand, what did it matter?

"Why don't you call me Honey, Ellie. That'd be easier for you," she said hastily. "That's what my mother always called me."

"She called you Honey?" asked the little girl,

beaming. "That's nice. Honey. Honey. Honey," she repeated, practicing in a singsong voice.

"Can I call you Honey, too?" Joe asked quietly.

She stared, shocked at his intimate tone, and felt herself flush. "Certainly not," she snapped, attempting an acid response she didn't really feel. "*You* may call me Mary Poppins. *Miss* Poppins, *ma'am.*"

Joe laughed. The sound—big and bold and so very male—echoed in the farmhouse kitchen.

"And *you,*" he said, leaning toward her confidentially, eyes gleaming, "can call me the Big Bad Wolf."

Despite herself, she felt an answering grin tug at her own mouth.

This week, the week she was committed to spending with these children, was going to be *interesting,* to say the least.

CHAPTER SEVEN

RIGHT AFTER BREAKFAST, Joe excused himself, saying he had business in Glory that morning and would be going to Calgary in the afternoon. He wouldn't be back until late. Tim and another seasonal employee were working around the place somewhere, but they'd both brought their lunches, he told her.

Honor watched him whistle as he took a shirt, sports jacket and dress pants on a hanger out to his pickup. Not back until late, he'd said. Now, why would she have the idea that he was meeting a woman? He waved cheerfully to her as he left the yard and she waved back, Alexander in her arms. She was relieved, frankly. She looked forward to getting to know the children on her own.

Joe's behavior at breakfast had thoroughly unsettled her. Still, judging by her observations of the way he acted with the children and with his sister, Nan, and her family, Joe seemed to be one of those naturally physical guys. Maybe he wasn't flirting. Maybe it was nothing at all. Maybe he dealt with everyone in a way that might be considered intimate in other circles. She was probably reading too much into the whole thing.

The house seemed very empty after she put the children to bed that evening. She read for a while, then watched a television program that never quite engaged her attention—all the while listening for Joe's return. At about half-past nine she went to bed.

She didn't sleep. She lay awake until she saw the lights on her bedroom wall and heard the crunch of tires on gravel. It was just before midnight. She heard him come in and do a few things in the kitchen, then turn off all the lights and go quietly down the hall. She heard him pause at her door—he was probably looking in on the children. A few seconds later he continued on to his bedroom and she heard the door shut.

The next few days went by quickly. Honor studied Joe's routine with the children and tried to duplicate it. She'd bought several books on raising children, ranging from Dr. Spock to Penelope Leach, which she studied secretly in her room before she went to sleep. Something must have worked, because gradually the little boy seemed to accept her. He stopped gazing intently over her shoulder when she approached, as though hoping to see his uncle, or perhaps his mother or father. Who knew what went through the head of a fourteen-month-old child?

Ellie, bless her heart, fell all over herself to help, for which Honor was grateful.

Honor called Calgary several times and talked to Spinks. Once she spoke to Alec, but the old man didn't seem to understand her very well and his responses were hard to make out over the phone. One message came across loud and clear—he wanted to see her and the children. She finally promised she'd come to Calgary for a short visit that week, although she knew Joe would never consent to her taking the children.

Sunday morning she broached the subject.

Joe came out to the backyard where she was sitting in the shade watching the children splash in the small inflatable pool she'd found the day before in the Longquists' garage. Most mornings she took Ellie and Alexander with her to feed Jill's fish, a daily task she'd told Joe she'd be happy to take on while she was at the farm. He continued to feed the Longquist dogs, a collie mix and a terrier of some kind, who appeared content to show up on Joe's back porch to join his dogs for their meals.

Honor hastily put down her book when she heard the click of the picket gate. Then, feeling silly, she deliberately left the turned-over book in clear view on the pine table beside her. Why shouldn't she be reading child-rearing literature? How else was a person supposed to learn?

"How's it going?" he asked easily, sliding into the Adirondack chair next to her. He glanced at her book but said nothing.

"Fine." Honor thought that was an honest answer. She and the children were getting along much better. She could actually say she was getting used to the long day, with only a break while they napped, so different from her normal working day at the office. "Did you have something you wanted to see me about?"

"Not really." He studied her for a few seconds. "There are quite a few things we haven't discussed, though. Maybe we should."

"Oh?"

"For instance, how long you'll be staying." Joe ran one hand over his face in a weary gesture and blinked a few times. He'd been out late the night before, the third time that week. The man seemed to have a very active social life—none of her business, of course.

"Well, that depends, I guess," she answered warily, glancing toward the children. Ellie was happily pouring water over Alexander's head, and he was giggling. "Have you found a replacement yet?"

"Nope." Joe grimaced. "Not yet. I'm meeting with someone on Monday who might work out. Won't know until I see her." He paused, then added, "I've got a couple of different plans in mind. What's your time frame?"

"I told you, I'll stay until Nan gets back if necessary. I realize you'd prefer to find someone more permanent, but the children seem relatively content with me."

Joe nodded. "They like you."

Honor felt herself color slightly, but she welcomed his comment. "Do you really think so?"

Joe nodded again, his eyes on the children. "Ellie talks about you all the time when she's with me. Alexander is definitely adjusting. But tell me—" he turned to her and she met his gaze "—how can you just up and leave your job for so long? I don't get it."

He could certainly be persistent. "I'm between projects," she answered. "I'm on holiday, so my time is my own. My employer, who is also my father-in-law, is home convalescing, and he's entirely supportive of my coming out here like this."

"Convalescing?" Joe frowned. "What's wrong with him?"

"He's been sick. I've told you that." Although Joe had never questioned her about it. "He had a stroke shortly after Parker was killed." Surely he could understand how important it was to Alec Templeman that he meet his grandchildren. "It was a terrible shock. His only child…"

"Doesn't sound like they got along all that great," Joe said with a snort.

"Well, no. Maybe they didn't. But now he's lost any chance he ever had to make things up with his son, hasn't he?" Honor returned heatedly, then caught herself. She shouldn't prattle on like this, pleading Alec's case. She had to go carefully. After all, Joe had lost his sister, too.

She might as well let him know she'd be going to see Alec. "Joe?"

He swung to look at her again. Honor felt that same rush of recognition she always felt when their eyes met fully. Almost a sense of déjà vu, and she'd never believed herself to be an intuitive person. "Yes?"

"I need to go visit Alec soon." She didn't like the way he frowned. "That's the one drawback to my looking after Alexander and Ellie. He counts on my visits. He…he's very lonely."

Joe was silent for a long moment, as though considering what she'd said. "I have no problem with that. When?"

"Maybe tomorrow?"

He nodded. "I'll take the kids with me to interview this nanny prospect in Glory tomorrow. They may as well meet her, too. You go ahead.''

She'd wondered about that—what they'd do with the children. She'd hoped, in a way, that he'd have some pressing obligation, something that couldn't accommodate the children and then she'd just slip in with, *Oh, why don't I just take them with me?* And he'd say, *Okay, why don't you?*

Sure, Honor Templeman. And the moon's made of green cheese.

"All right. I'll do that.'' She gazed back at the children. Ellie was topping up the pool with the garden hose and Alexander was shrieking with delight. "I'll only be gone a couple of hours.''

They sat side by side for a few more moments, neither speaking. Honor never felt completely relaxed and comfortable in Joe's presence. Would she ever, during the short time she was here?

Madly she cast about for a safe topic of conversation. "You, uh, mentioned some other ideas you had.'' She looked at him. "To do with the kids?''

"Yes,'' he said, and ran his hands through his hair, then leaned back, arms on the wooden armrests. "Well, as you know, I'm looking for a nanny. One, two, maybe six months' employment at the outside. I've also decided I should get married. That's a more long-term plan, I'll admit, but it's something I need to get started on. The middle of summer's one of my slower times, so until harvest starts— Why are you looking at me like that?''

Honor was taken aback by his question. Had her shock been so visible?

"It just...seems a very odd way to go about the

question of marriage," she said quietly. Odd? Compared to what she and Parker had done?

His eyes searched hers. She knew he was thinking exactly the same thing, but was too polite to mention it.

"Maybe so," he said finally, "but I think it'll work out. How hard can it be? I've always figured on getting married one day. I've made up my mind to put some real serious effort into it now, that's all, which is something I can't say I've ever done before. On Friday I went out with a woman I used to date in Calgary." He frowned and stretched his legs out and examined the toes of his dusty boots. "It didn't work out quite as well as I'd hoped—" he grinned at her boyishly, and she couldn't help smiling back "—but I haven't written her off yet."

He cleared his throat. "And then, Saturday, I took out somebody I used to date right here in Glory. It might be better to stick closer to home, anyway. You know, a farm girl?" He gave Honor a sideways look. "Somebody who's already used to the life, so to speak. Might be easier all round."

"Uh-huh." Honor kept her eyes on the children. She wanted to laugh out loud. Joe sounded so darn serious, as though he actually wanted her advice.

"I definitely have some options, no question. I've just got to sift through some of the likelier candidates, that's all. It'll take a little time." He flashed her a grin, which she quickly turned away from to study the children again.

"Mmm," she murmured agreeably.

"What do you think?"

"Me?" She turned back to look at him. "You

sound like you know what you're doing, Joe. At this rate, hey, you should be married by the end of the month. Then I can go home to Calgary and you can get on with your life.''

"You think I'm crazy."

"No, I don't. You need someone to take care of the children, right? You're thinking of getting married, anyway, right? Why not now? Makes a lot of sense to me.'' But it wasn't true; she *did* think he was crazy. And there was something else, something she couldn't put her finger on. Something that made her simmering hot and angry inside and very aware that she had to make an effort to remain calm during the rest of this conversation.

It was the thought of another woman coming into these children's lives and taking the place of their mother. These were *her* children, damn it. She couldn't get the thought out of her mind, no matter how foolish it was.

"Day care's no option out here in the country,'' he continued, frowning. "Besides, I'd never do that to Alexander and Ellie after what they've been through. They deserve a solid stable family life, and I'm in a position to make sure they get it.''

"I can understand that.'' No, she couldn't see Joe Gallant putting the children into day care. And it wasn't fair to expect Nan to raise them when she was still raising her own family.

"Besides,'' Joe went on, "even if day care was available, it wouldn't be convenient. My hours are too crazy. When the harvest is on, I'm out in the fields all day and all night.''

He seemed to be working things out in his own

mind, so Honor didn't answer. He seemed to feel some need to put forward all the factors he'd considered in arriving at his decision—to justify himself to her somehow.

For a few moments they were silent. Honor started to relax a bit. At least he was straightforward. You couldn't get any more straightforward than that—blurting out your marriage plans and then asking for someone's opinion.

"Say, Honor…" His voice was low and tentative. Intimate. *Sexy.*

She swallowed. Now what did he have in mind? "Yes?"

"How'd you like to go to a ball game?" He broke into his trademark grin, a warm devilish look that zipped clear to her toes and back.

She laughed, a silly nervous sound. "A *ball* game?"

"Yeah." His eyes were full of laughter, and she had the strangest notion that it didn't matter what he asked, she'd do it. "Baseball. Over at Black Diamond. I've got an exhibition game there this afternoon. It's about twenty miles away. We could take the kids and buy 'em hot dogs and lemonade. What do you think?"

"Okay." She was surprised at how quickly she'd agreed. "You won't believe this, but I've never been to a ball game—"

"You're kidding!"

"Not kidding!" she said, mimicking him. "Just watched the World Series on television and—"

He reached over and grasped her hand, shocking

her into silence. He leaned forward, eyes shining. "You're going to love it. That's a promise."

She swallowed again, wishing he'd release her hand. He seemed to have forgotten he'd grabbed it.

"How will you introduce me?" she asked suddenly. "We haven't talked about that. I...I don't want to lie about who I am," she finished, her voice barely audible.

"You mean what I told Nan and Harry?"

She nodded.

"I just wanted to spare your feelings," he said gently. "I thought you'd rather I told them you were Parker's sister. I figured you'd be, you know, embarrassed or something if I'd told them he'd been married to you, left you high and dry, took up with Sylvie..."

"Oh, Joe, I appreciate that," she said, fighting back emotion. "I really do. I can't lie about it, though. Someone's bound to know. And besides, it's just not how I do things." A new thought struck her. "Maybe you'd rather people not know for Sylvie's sake."

"Hell, no! Sylvie's dead. There's nothing I can do about that. But you're not—" Joe stopped and Honor could swear the look that came into his eyes was a tender one. "Don't you care what people might think? Really?"

He felt sorry for her! The abandoned wife.

She pulled her hand away and sat straighter. "Joe, don't worry about me. I can handle it. I'm tough."

"You don't *look* tough."

"Looks can be deceiving."

"Maybe." Joe said. He sounded doubtful. "Black

Diamond's a fair distance from here," he said slowly. "We're probably not going to run into too many Glory folk, anyway, except for the players. What's your maiden name?"

"Sanders."

"Sanders," he repeated with a wicked smile. "For today, Honey Sanders, it is."

SHE'D NEVER BEEN to a baseball game and she'd never ridden in a pickup truck. She'd suggested they take her car, but had demurred to Joe's preference for his own truck with the rumble seat in the back fitted with the children's car seats.

And now here she was, sitting on the lowest bench of the splintery wooden bleachers at a prairie baseball diamond, sucking on a cherry Popsicle so cold it made the roof of her mouth ache. The afternoon was hot and quiet with a big blue sky above. She listened to a magpie's chatter from a nearby willow tree, interspersed pleasantly with the catcalls and encouragement from the small group of spectators.

Ellie had found two other children to play with and was swinging on the swing set that was part of the playground, along with a sandbox and a seesaw, to one side of the bleachers. Alexander sat at Honor's feet, drooling and making *vroom-vroom* noises with a plastic truck, one of the toys she'd brought.

And she was watching her man play first base.

Well, not right now, since the Glory Magpies were at bat. And not *her* man—but that was obviously what some of the players and their wives and girlfriends had assumed when she and Joe had shown up, kids in tow. Joe had introduced her as "a good friend of mine, Honey Sanders.'' Friends, it appeared, came in only one variety when they were attached to an attractive single man like Joe Gallant. Joe hadn't bothered to correct that impression.

She didn't mind; even the attention was a novelty. And it meant nothing. She'd likely never see these people again. Certainly the two principals—she and Joe—were in no danger of mistaking their relationship. And Ellie persisted in calling her ''auntie'' most of the time. Now it was Auntie Honey.

''Right on!'' She heard a cheer break out at the same time as a bat cracked against a ball, and she craned her neck to see what had happened. Obviously someone from the Glory team had made a base hit. It wasn't Joe. She'd recognize him even in his baseball uniform, looking a lot like all the other players.

The game was nearly over and it was close, with the score tied at the bottom of the eighth and no runs scored so far in the ninth. Despite herself, Honor realized she'd gradually become caught up in the excitement of the game, and she watched the pitcher and batters avidly.

''Hi!'' A pleasant-looking young woman Honor had smiled at earlier came over and stood beside her. She reached down and tousled Alexander's blond curls. ''Yours?''

''No, just baby-sitting,'' Honor replied. She reached into Alexander's carryall and retrieved a soda cracker, which she held out to him. He grasped it in his chubby hand and directed it to his mouth, beaming.

''He's a sweetie.'' The woman took a sip of the

drink she carried. "I guess your husband's playing, huh? First base?"

"No, he's not my husband and, yes, he plays first base," Honor answered easily. "Joe Gallant. A friend, that's all." This wasn't nearly as difficult as she'd thought it would be. People were friendly but accepting. She hadn't had too many questions yet that she'd qualify as plain nosy.

"Hey, I've heard of Joe. My husband—that's him out there in left field—" told me they had a great guy playing first. We don't play Glory enough to get to know the team."

Honor nodded. "Uh-huh." She kept her eyes on the diamond. The crowd on the other side of the bleachers started to cheer and Honor watched as a fly ball hit by someone on the Glory team was caught by the woman's husband.

"*Yesss!*" she shouted with a big grin and a clenched fist to the sky. "*Way-ta-go, Bobby-o!*"

Honor smiled back, perfectly content. Of course it would be nice if Joe's team won, but she didn't really care. She was just enjoying the outing.

"Hey, see you around," the woman said suddenly, turning to her. "Take good care of that friend of yours." She winked and patted Honor lightly on the arm. "He won't be single for long."

She was gone before Honor could decide what to say. But then, nothing was probably best. Let people think what they wanted to; they would, anyway.

"Auntie Honey!"

Honor turned to see Ellie waving madly at her. She picked up Alexander and walked toward the girl.

"I want Alexander to teeter-totter with me," Ellie

begged. She ran to one end of the seesaw and climbed on. "Put him on the end. Please?"

"I'll hold him and you'll have to go very slow," Honor warned. "Okay?" She looked over her shoulder. The game had gone into a tenth inning.

Alexander giggled and clung to the painted iron bar in front of him. Honor kept both hands on him, careful to hold him upright. "Okay, you push now, Ellie."

"Whee!" Ellie pushed herself up and the seesaw gently went down at Alexander's end. The little boy crowed with delight. Honor grinned. "Now, up we go!" she said, and took off some of the weight she'd put on the plank. Ellie's end gently drifted down again. Alexander screamed with laughter.

After a few more times the little boy wanted off, and Honor diverted Ellie's attention back to the swing. An older girl, possibly twelve or thirteen, offered to push Ellie, so Honor left her there and wandered back to the ball diamond.

She kept Alexander on her hip and stood close to the chain-link fence behind home plate. The Magpies had a runner on second and Joe was at bat. The other team, the Black Diamond Oilers, yelled catcalls and insults, all in fun. Honor could almost feel Joe's intensity as he swung the bat a few times, then stepped up to the plate and narrowed his eyes to watch the pitch.

Honor looked at the scoreboard. Bottom of the tenth and still tied at six runs each. She looked back at Joe. He swung at the first pitch and missed. The second was fouled to the right.

"Ball one!" called the umpire.

Joe let the next pitch go by.

"Ball two! Two and two."

The pitcher eyed the runner on second, who had made a halfhearted attempt to take third but then abandoned the idea. The pitcher turned back to Joe.

Honor watched him wind up, then let fly a vicious-looking ball. They were all vicious-looking, in Honor's opinion, but she was admittedly no judge. There was a mighty crack and a huge cheer went up from the Glory bench. Joe had hit the ball well into the hole in left field. He was running…running…

Honor was screaming with excitement. *"Run, Joe, run!"* He dived for second base a split second after the ball arrived, making him the third out. But it didn't matter—the runner on second had come in. Glory had won the game.

Half the spectators were cheering, the other half were grinning. Everybody, it seemed, liked a ball game, regardless of who won.

Honor hugged Alexander, who'd been wriggling up and down in her arms, kicking his legs rhythmically as she yelled. She reached over and kissed the little boy.

"Hi!" Suddenly Joe was there. Grinning, filthy dirty from sliding into second, sweaty, his ball cap on backward. Honor didn't know when she'd ever seen a happier, handsomer man. "We won."

"I know."

He put his arm around them both and hugged Alexander between them. "We won! How'd you like that?"

He bent to give the boy a kiss on the cheek, just as Honor had. Then he grinned and put his other arm around her and leaned down, and Honor just knew he was about to kiss her cheek, too. But he didn't.

Honor didn't trust her voice. She smiled, wondering if she looked as dopey and dazzled as she felt.

"I said you'd love it, didn't I? Huh?" He hugged them both again.

"You did. It was great. I loved it. Every minute." She blinked.

"Me, too, Uncle Joe. Pick me up, too." They both looked down. Ellie was tugging on Joe's jersey.

With a growl he scooped her into his arms and kissed her. Then, with a detour to the bleachers to pick up the rest of Honor's gear, including Alexander's carryall, the four of them made their way toward the parking lot.

And home.

CHAPTER EIGHT

THE NEXT MORNING Honor left Joe with the children and drove to Calgary. His interview with the nanny prospect was for midafternoon.

Now she sat with Alec over yet another pot of tea. When she produced the photograph of Parker and Sylvie and their two children, which she'd guiltily taken from the children's room—telling herself she wasn't *taking* the photograph against Joe's orders, merely borrowing it—Alec eagerly reached for it.

Her rationalization was, strictly speaking, true, but definitely against the spirit of Joe's request. She could argue that his wishes were unreasonable, and no doubt she would soon. She hadn't tried to change his mind on the subject of the children in the week she'd been at the farm. It was time to start working on that when she got back. Surely whatever had happened in the past between the Gallants and the Templemans could be overcome if there was reason and goodwill on both sides. She'd certainly try to bring that about.

Alec stared at the picture so long Honor began to worry. When he looked up, his eyes were bright. Honor was glad she'd risked Joe's wrath by bringing it with her.

"Keep it?" Alec's voice was hoarse. "Mine?"

"Oh, no." Honor kneeled beside his chair, next to Major, the big Labrador retriever. His mate, Sadie, was stretched out near the window, careful eyes watching them both. "It belongs to the children. To Joe, I guess. It's in the children's room to remind them of their mother and father," she said softly.

Alec frowned. "Want this," he said firmly, and waved it at her. His eyes were wild.

"I'll get you one." Honor took the picture and rubbed at the fingermarks on the glass with the tail of her shirt. She'd get a copy made before she left town, a quickie color copy at a corner printer, and pop it in a drugstore frame. She tucked the picture back in her bag.

Alec was smiling when she looked at him again, the fierceness gone as quickly as it had arisen. "Nice," he said simply. "Very nice."

Honor sat down on a nearby chair. "They're darling children, Alec. Lovely and sweet-tempered and polite, especially considering everything that's happened. They seem happy with their uncle. He's good with them."

Alec growled several curses adroitly linked with Joe's name.

"Alec!" She laid her hand over his. Impatiently he shook it off and regarded her with angry eyes.

"Listen here," she said, trying to make her voice very firm. "This attitude isn't going to help. Joe Gallant is the children's guardian, whether you like it or not, and the only thing that's going to have the slightest chance of working with him is persuasion. Let me handle it."

"Ha!"

"I'm serious. You can keep your threats to yourself." Major sighed and thumped his black tail against the polished oak floor. Honor smiled. "Right, Major?" The dog thumped his tail more enthusiastically and cocked an eyebrow in her direction, not bothering to lift his massive head.

"Conrad." Alec had a steely glint in his eyes. "Conrad can help. We'll see." He shook his finger, a warning gesture. Conrad Atkinson was Alec's personal lawyer.

"Keep him out of this, Alec," Honor said as her father-in-law's meaning dawned. He and his lawyer could be bullies, both of them. "I'm serious. There's nothing Conrad can do for you. What are you thinking? Custody? Challenging the mother's will?"

She could tell by Alec's quick sideways glance that she'd struck a nerve. "Forget it. You'd be crazy to get Joe's back up any more than it already is. He's a stubborn man. You're both stubborn men." Honor glanced at her watch and stood. She needed to start on some of the other errands she hoped to get done before she returned to Glory.

"That's most of the trouble, I'm afraid," she muttered. She reached for her jacket and shrugged it on. "Two stubborn men."

She bent to kiss Alec. "Bye for now. I'll stop by on my way out of town in about an hour or so."

It was more like two hours before she dropped off the framed photocopy of the children with their parents. Spinks thanked her in his usual grave, polite manner and said Mr. Templeman was napping. He gazed at the picture he held carefully in his hands, and Honor could imagine what was going through his mind. Parker had been special to him. More than once, Spinks had intervened between her husband and his father.

Honor was relieved to hear that Alec was asleep, then felt badly for feeling that way. She just didn't want any more run-ins with Alec. Not today. The old man's mind was stuck on a single track. Maybe by the next time she saw him, he'd be showing an interest in his company again. That would be the best possible medicine; nothing like a gloves-off oil-patch dustup to get the old man feeling alive and useful. She wasn't even sure this was a good time to bring Ellie and Alexander for a visit. Right now their grandfather was too obsessed with seeing them to do anyone much good.

And she was anxious to head out of town. She'd been thinking of Joe's interview that afternoon in Glory. Had he hired someone to take her place? How many more days did she have with the children? Work was fine; she'd checked with Liz and there was nothing on her desk that required her presence. She wanted to be back at the farm with the children.

And Joe. She frowned as she got into her car. *Don't be a fool,* she told herself.

But it was true. She *was* a fool. In less than a week she'd developed what amounted to a ridiculous crush on the man. Something she hadn't experienced since junior high. Her common garden-variety attraction to him—which she'd noticed and admitted to herself shortly after her arrival—had grown. Living in the same house hadn't helped. Neither had that hug after the baseball game.

Sure, it had been a pretty innocent thing. But it

had brought her into close physical contact with a healthy virile man. She'd wanted more. She'd felt the strength of his arms around her and Alexander; she'd been enveloped in a powerful sweaty male embrace that hadn't felt the slightest bit innocent. At least not to her.

Honor was worried. She was overwhelmed with the thought that she might do something stupid and give herself away. Like blush. Or get caught staring at him. Or...or generally behave like some moonstruck adolescent.

It was embarrassing. Yet, in a way she welcomed the feeling. It was proof that her life as a woman wasn't over. That she wasn't turning into some dried-up prune of a career woman headed for a lonely old age. If she felt this way about Joe, she could feel this way about other men. Perhaps when she returned to Calgary, she should start dating seriously. And sex. Sex was part of life. Maybe she should give it another try. See if things could be different.

She wouldn't be starting completely from scratch—she'd had one or two fairly persistent suitors in the past year, both from within the company. Not that either particularly appealed. But there was that nice Nigel Harrison, a journalist, who'd taken her to the opera twice. She'd never allowed herself to give any relationship a chance because, in some old-fashioned way, she couldn't forget that she was still married, even if she hadn't seen much of her husband in recent years. They weren't living together, but they weren't divorced, either. She was a widow now, free to pursue her own life again, on her own terms.

Honor smiled as she turned onto the secondary highway that led to Glory. *Men. Dating. Sex.* A new phase in her life.

It was a pleasant notion to contemplate.

AGAIN, JOE FOUND that he was in the position of second-guessing himself. He didn't like that. It wasn't something he was all that familiar with. He liked to make a decision, stick to it and forget about it. Put it behind him. Move on.

That just wasn't happening with this nanny business. There'd been nothing wrong with the woman the agency had sent out for the interview—and she'd been ready to start, too. At the last moment, though, he'd gotten cold feet and said he'd give it some thought. *Don't call me, I'll call you.*

But he wasn't going to call her. He knew that for a fact. He slammed his right hand against the steering wheel and swore under his breath. What was he waiting for—Mary Poppins? Hell, he already had Mary Poppins. Right out there at the farm.

"What'd you say, Uncle Joe?" Ellie looked as innocent as an angel. An angel with a glint in her eye. Alexander was asleep in his car seat.

"Nothing," Joe said, glancing in the rearview mirror.

"Oh-yes-you-did," Ellie sang out. "I heard you say something."

"Okay." Joe grinned. "What did I say, Ellie? Huh? What'd I say? Tell me." If Honor could hear this interchange, she'd be trying to break the guardianship provisions. She and Alec Templeman.

"Good ham. You said *good ham,* Uncle Joe."

Joe kept smiling. *Out of the mouths of babes...*

"Is that what we're having for supper, Uncle Joe? Ham? You said we could have chicken from the scary drive-in place."

"You bet. It's Grizzly chicken for us." Joe wheeled into the town landmark, the Grizzly Drive-in, home of Grizzly burgers, Grizzly ribs and Grizzly chicken. The drive-in was built in the shape of a huge snarling bear's head. You placed your order at the ferocious-looking mouth, with some bored teenage girl behind the window, nicely framed between the top and bottom teeth. Or else it'd be that unflappable Mrs. Perkins who'd run the Grizzly ever since Joe could remember. If you had to go inside for some reason, there were doors in the ears. Sun-bleached picnic tables outside were used summer and winter. Either that or you ate in your truck, parked off to one side of the pot-holed parking lot. There were signs posted everywhere warning you to put your trash in the barrels or risk no service next visit. Ma Perkins never forgot a face.

"Whoopee!" Ellie scowled at the bear, as all kids did. Joe remembered every one of Nan's kids doing it when he'd brought them here over the years. *"Grrrrrr!"*

"Grrrr!" returned Mrs. Perkins pleasantly as she always did, snapping back her order window. "What'll ya have, Joe?"

"Barrel of chicken with all the trimmings and extra salad. Gallon of root beer." Honor looked like the salad type. He was hoping he'd get home before her and surprise her with the meal already prepared. So far, they'd taken turns cooking on a casual basis.

He glanced at the clock on the wall behind the cash register. Nearly five.

Would Honor be back yet? Joe found himself hoping so. Amazing how quickly he'd gotten used to having another adult in the house, someone who'd be around in the evenings. Someone to say good-morning to at the breakfast table.

Not that he'd been there much in the evenings lately. Joe sighed and wiped one hand over his jaw. *Damn.* The courting wasn't going as well as he'd hoped, either. He hadn't realized how reluctant some women might be to step into a ready-made family, now that he'd made his mind up to take the plunge. When he thought about it, who could blame them? And the kids weren't even his—they were his sister's.

"Ketchup? Vinegar? Extra napkins?"

Joe shook his head. "Don't bother. We're taking it home." He set the cardboard bucket of chicken on the floor of the passenger side, then reached for the frosted jug of root beer. He paid, nodding in farewell, and raised his hand in the side mirror to the truck that had driven in behind him. Jeremiah Blake. From the Diamond 8 ranch west of town. Joe made a mental note to give him a call and ask if he'd be playing on the Glory Old Guys' Hockey League this fall. It was just pickup hockey, for fun.

He ought to stop in at the Chesley place on his way home, he thought, pulling up at the stop sign before turning onto the Vulcan road. He had a mortgage payment due soon, and now that he was considering buying another combine, maybe Ira'd give him a week's slack on it. Even used farm equipment was worth a king's ransom. Joe had borrowed a whack of money from Ira Chesley two years ago when Harry had his accident. He'd been laid up for nearly a year, Harry had. Accidents happened now and again on a farm or ranch, even to the most careful of workers. Unfortunately it had happened to his brother-in-law, and the accident was a bad one. The Longquists had little savings, and Joe had found himself in the position of partially supporting his sister and her family. As it turned out, Harry was stuck in a wheelchair. His sister Nan had had a lot to bear in her life; there was no way he was saddling her with raising Sylvie's kids on top of everything else.

But he'd driven right past the Chesley farm before he'd even realized what he was doing. And then he wondered why…and didn't like the answer. He wanted to get home. He wanted to see if Honor was there waiting for them.

He hoped she was.

JOE TRIED TO IGNORE the disappointment, like a waft of arctic air that exited his lungs for no reason, when he drove into the yard and didn't see her car. He took the food in and set it on the kitchen table, then went back out to unbuckle Alexander's car seat.

Ellie skipped beside him as he walked to the house, Alexander in his arms. She rubbed her tummy. "I'm starving, Uncle Joe. Can I have a french fry out of the bag?"

"You unpack everything and put it on the table, Ellie. I'll change Alexander's diaper and then we can eat." He grinned at the little girl, who regarded him with beseeching eyes. "Sure, go ahead. Have a french fry or two. Don't forget to wash your hands first, though.'' It was tough remembering all these little things he was responsible for teaching the kid now, like washing before meals. And putting shoes on the right feet and brushing her hair in the morning and not picking her nose in public.

"I won't, Uncle Joe,'' she yelled, and raced down the hall to the bathroom.

Joe smiled as he followed her, carrying Alexander into the children's room. He stretched the boy out on his crib mattress. Alexander was growing fast. Another few months and he'd be talking a blue streak. Then it'd be all that manners stuff to teach again.

Joe expertly whipped off the boy's wet diaper and pulled a clean one from the pile stacked on the dresser. He saw right away that the photo of his sister and Parker and the two kids was missing.

Shock bounced down his spine. Leaving the boy happily kicking bare legs on the cot, he strode across the hall and wrenched open the door to the room Honor was sleeping in.

His relief was almost unbearable. Joe glanced back at the children's room, stunned. *His first thought had been that she had packed up and left.* But she hadn't.

He returned to finish buttoning up Alexander's overalls, his brain spinning. The boy squirmed, reaching for a plastic car on his bed, trying to turn over. "Hold on there, tiger," Joe murmured. "Almost done here."

He must be nuts. Just plain nuts. If she'd left without telling anyone, he'd be better off without her. Wouldn't he? She was trouble, anyway, he knew that. Then he could call the woman he'd talked to that afternoon, Penelope George, and tell her the job was hers for as long as she wanted it. No danger there of neighbors getting the wrong idea; the woman was professional starch through and through and had to be fifty if she was a day.

Alexander grinned suddenly and held his arms up to be lifted out of the crib. Joe felt his heart soften at the sight of the little boy's happy face. He'd never thought he was cut out for kids and fatherhood and all that stuff, but these past few weeks with his niece and nephew had shown him he was wrong. Sometimes he felt like they really were his kids. Like life was playing catch-up with him. Like maybe he should have started on this part of living ten years ago. Ellie and Alexander were even more special than if they'd been his—they were part of his sister, his twin. They'd keep Sylvie with him always.

Then Joe realized that Alexander's grin was directed over his shoulder. He turned.

"Hi."

Honor stood at the open door, a plastic bag in one hand, the missing photograph in the other. Again he felt the relief that had hit him when he knew she hadn't left.

"Hi yourself," he said, hoping his smile looked a hundred percent natural. "Good trip?"

She nodded, then glanced down. "I brought back the children's picture," she said, coming into the room and repositioning it carefully on the dresser. Then she glanced up and met his gaze. "I took this to show Alec," she said softly. Her cheeks were pink. *Caught in the act.*

"I figured you must have."

"Yes. Well." She dug into the plastic bag and pulled out a red rubber airplane that Alexander eagerly reached for, eyes alight.

"You're spoiling them," Joe said, watching her closely. He might as well not have been there. She was studying Alexander as he inspected the airplane and made small burbling noises that Joe was pretty sure expressed appreciation and pleasure.

A frown flashed across her face as she looked up at him. "Maybe." Then she smiled at the little boy and he smiled back and buried his face shyly on Joe's shoulder. She held out her arms. "May I?"

He handed her the child, who went willingly from hiding his face on Joe's shoulder to hiding his face on Honor's. "What's spoiling, anyway? I don't see that it matters much, do you?" she asked calmly.

Joe didn't have an answer.

"You had supper yet?" Joe hoped his face didn't reveal what had just blazed, red-hot, through his mind. *They belonged together, those two. They looked good together, mother and son. They fit together, just the way a family should.* Nobody he could possibly hire would care for them the way she already did. They were her husband's children. She'd married the guy; she'd had some feelings for him once. He cleared his throat, waiting for her response.

"No," she said, glancing at him quickly, then returning her attention to the child in her arms. "I'm looking forward to it. I see Ellie's got everything ready. We'd better not disappoint her."

"No."

Joe held the door while Honor went out before him, carrying his nephew. He followed her down the hall, strictly disciplining his thoughts and his gaze, which had a disconcerting tendency to wander. By the time he reached the kitchen, he knew he'd made up his mind. As soon as he realized that, he felt a whole lot better about everything.

"So," Honor said, when they were settled at the table, "did you hire somebody to take my place?"

Was her smile strained or was that his imagination?

"No," he answered. "As a matter of fact, I've changed my mind about it."

"Again?"

"Yeah. Does your offer to stay until Nan and Harry get back from California still stand?"

She set down the chicken wing she'd taken from the bucket and carefully wiped her fingers on her napkin, eyes locked on his the whole time. "Yes. It does."

"Good. Until Labor Day?" he asked, picking up his glass of mostly flat root beer and trying to hold back his grin.

She lifted her own glass. He had a notion that she was having a hard time holding back a grin, too. Maybe as hard a time as he was. "Until Labor Day."

They clinked glasses. Ellie squealed with pleasure and raised her glass.

Honor smiled then. She smiled at him across the bucket of chicken, a large carton of too-green coleslaw, a tub of rapidly congealing gravy and a plateful of limp french fries—and it was a smile to snag any man's heart.

Lucky man, Joe thought, whoever he might be one day.

CHAPTER NINE

JOE DROVE to Ira Chesley's farm right after breakfast on Monday.

Ira was a dark, stooped, worried-looking man of about sixty, a bachelor. He'd been a neighbor since Joe'd bought up the old Suggett place north of his ten years before. Joe had always dreamed of putting down roots somewhere, all during the boyhood years he and his family had drifted from one town to another, his mother and sisters and brothers trailing his itinerant horse-race gambler of a father, Sam Gallant. Sam and the oldest brother, Nicholas, lived out in British Columbia somewhere, about as far as they could get from where the Gallants had started out in a small Acadian town on New Brunswick's Chaleur Bay. Nick had done all right for himself out on the West Coast. As for Sam, Joe had no doubt that his father was still hanging around the racetracks, buying up nags and living on dreams. He'd never change. Joe and his siblings just tried to make sure old Sam had a warm place to spend the winters and enough money to keep him in tobacco.

The Suggett place, east of Glory, had been abandoned for several years and was going cheap when Joe heard about it. Some of the fields were overgrown in scrub alder and willow, but Joe figured he could make a go of it with hay and maybe some feed grain. There were ready local markets for such crops. Ira had been a good neighbor right from the start. He'd gone to bat for Joe with the banks to arrange a mortgage. Joe had saved a down payment by working for three years in the oil patch after ag college, but of course he'd had little practical experience. Ira had also helped him out with practical farming advice; he still did. This last time he'd needed money, Joe hadn't wanted to go back to the banks. Ira had offered to lend him enough to tide Nan and the kids over until Harry could work full-time.

Now Joe needed money again. A farmer's life always seemed to be one hop ahead of the moneylender's, Joe had discovered over the years. If you wanted to do a good job farming, you needed the equipment. Equipment wasn't cheap. Fertilizer wasn't cheap. Everything depended on the weather. A good year could have you paying down your debt, a bad year could wipe you out.

Then you needed decent help to run the farm. Harry had been great, and having Nan and their kids on the place had been a bonus. But since the accident, Harry hadn't been able to work much. He helped out in the office and drove a grain truck and a combine that Joe had converted to hand controls. This year Joe had hired Tim Abbott, who was turning out to be well worth his salary, but the kid went back to school right about the middle of harvest. His nephew Ben—Harry and Nan's oldest—was off to college this fall, too. Joe knew he'd need to hire someone else. And one of the ways he planned to stay solvent enough to pay another man's wages was to acquire a second combine. He and Harry and maybe the new fellow could do extra custom combining as well as taking off their own crops.

It was a delicate balancing act—robbing Peter to pay Paul. So far he'd been lucky enough to manage. Finding himself suddenly responsible for his twin sister's kids had hit him hard, that and having to deal with Sylvie's death. He hadn't even known she'd named him their guardian. Still, he was managing that all right, too—and the kids' existence was the reason Honor Templeman had turned up in his life. He wasn't complaining—yet.

"Joe." Ira tweaked his greasy ball cap in greeting. He motioned his visitor onto the porch where he sat in a shabby upholstered rocking chair, enjoying the morning sun. Five or six hounds lunged to their feet and set up a roiling multilayered ruckus. Ira took a tennis ball from a pail he kept on the porch and tossed it out into the junk-strewn farmyard. Predictably the hounds streaked after it and set up a noisy dispute among themselves as to which was the rightful owner of that ball.

"Come on up, young fella, and get yourself a cup of coffee while it's warm." Ira heaved himself to his feet. Joe knew his neighbor's rheumatism was bothering him. One day soon, he reckoned, he'd hear that Ira had put the farm on the market, that it had gotten to be too much for him. Joe followed him into the dark cluttered kitchen to pour a cup of coffee. One cup was all a man could take of Ira's poisonous brew.

They returned to the porch. "So what's new,

Joe?'' Ira said with the semblance of a smile, settling into his rocker.

Joe backed into the reason for his visit, as was the habit among his rural neighbors. He reported how the kids were doing, mentioned Honor's showing up to look after them and said they'd already received a postcard from their cousin Phoebe. Ira's grizzled brows waggled with interest as Joe explained just what Honor's relationship to Alexander and Ellie was.

"This Honor—she a looker?"

"She's all right," Joe said noncommittally, with a sharp glance at his old neighbor. Why would Ira care?

"Good cook? Young?"

"Young enough. We've been sharing the cooking. She seems all right."

"Grab her, Joe. Time you got married, eh? No sense ending up a miserable old fool like me, eatin' outa cans and talkin' to yourself. Nothing but hounds for company and not a decent brain between the whole pack. Eh? You gotta think of the future, boy. 'Specially with you takin' over them kiddies now."

Joe knew Ira thought the world of his dogs, even took a kind of perverse pride in their ineptness at every normal canine pursuit except hot-trailing a rabbit or a raccoon. His hounds would chase a coyote clear into the next province and not even stop for a drink of water, Ira often boasted. As he was fond of saying, "Them ain't dogs—them's *hounds!*"

"I've been giving the idea some thought lately, Ira," Joe said carefully. "Marriage, that is. Not every woman wants to take over a ready-made family, you know.''

"No," his neighbor muttered gloomily. "No, I don't suppose most would." He paused and rocked for a while as though considering, then sighed. "So, what can I do for you today, Joe?''

"That payment I owe on the mortgage Saturday. I don't suppose you could see your way to giving me an extra week or two on it," Joe said.

Ira was silent for a few moments. "I guess I could. I ain't short. Truth is, I've been meaning to speak to you about that business. My sister's boy over in Swift Current got himself into a heap o' trouble and I could use that money to help her out."

"You mean, could I pay off the principal earlier than we figured?''

"I was wondering, uh-huh. Maybe about October or so? After harvest comes in."

Joe had to be honest. "It'd be tight, Ira. I'd have to raise it somewhere else now that I've put an offer on that combine." He stood and replaced his hat on his head. There was the children's money, money from their father's insurance, but that was in trust for them. No way he'd touch it. "Unless I put the combine on hold until next year. I suppose I could do that. I'll check into a few things and see what I can work out."

He clapped the old man on the shoulder and said, "I'll stop by next week."

"I wish I could do more for you, but my sister's in a terrible state over that boy of hers, and she's got nobody to turn to but me. Law trouble, y'know.''

Joe patted the old man's shoulder again. "I understand, Ira. I appreciate everything you've done for me so far. Anything I can do to help out, just call me.''

Ira nodded gravely and raised a hand in farewell. As Joe approached his pickup, the seething mass of hounds surged his way and leaped and stumbled and howled, first at his feet, then at the door of his pickup as he jumped in and slammed it shut. He grinned out the open window as he put the pickup in reverse. ''Got a couple of coyotes over at my place you can set these fellas onto. Give 'em something to do.''

Ira smiled—or mustered the expression closest to a smile in his repertoire—and waved again as Joe left.

WITHIN ANOTHER WEEK Honor felt as though she'd always lived in the country. Her legal work, which she checked on from time to time with her secretary, Liz, seemed to belong to a different life in a different world. Which was crazy, as Glory was just over an hour's drive from Calgary.

But drawing up contracts to acquire mineral rights and property leases and rights-of-way seemed a distant dry business compared to actually experiencing the land. Evidence of southern Alberta's oil-rich Devonian rock was all around: you couldn't go more than a couple of miles without seeing the diligent grasshopperlike structures that labored night and day to pump black gold from the depths of the earth. Until now she'd never thought about the kind of impact that might have on landowners' rights—what she'd trained herself to think of as surface rights, not homes and farms and ranches. She'd never consid-

ered how an oil rig in the middle of a herd of dairy
cattle might cause problems, or how a gas flare near
a farmer's family home might pose a health hazard
to his wife and children. She'd always concentrated
on the money side, her experience proving that every
problem in the oil industry could be solved with a
sufficient infusion of cash. That was A. R. Templeman's philosophy, and it had always worked for him.
Honor had enjoyed the negotiating part of her job
and was good at it. In the end Templeman Energy
always got what it wanted. But then, so did the other
party—even if their satisfaction was measured only
in dollars.

Driving to Glory with Ellie and Alexander to do
the week's grocery shopping was an activity guar-
anteed to require an entire morning's effort, she
thought, unfastening them from their car seats in
front of Henderson's IGA in Glory.

She'd tried the co-op food store the week before
but was intimidated by the knots of palavering neighbors—mostly men clustered at the ends of aisles
while their determined-looking lipsticked and home-
permed wives pushed huge carts up and down the
aisles. She'd decided to try one of the smaller stores
in the center of town this trip.

Even the business of provisioning for the five of
them was daunting. You couldn't just run to the corner store for a carton of milk if you ran out. In Calgary she was used to dashing across the street to the
deli for a prepared salad or pickles at the last minute,
or going out to eat several times a week in restau-
rants, either alone or with friends. Looking after children was different. They needed regular meals,

plenty of nutritious snacks, a fridge stocked with milk and eggs and fruit juices.

Then there was Alexander's nap to plan the day around, as well as excursions here and there to keep the children—and herself—occupied. Honor had made a list of activities to do with the children and was methodically working her way through it—trips to the library, swimming, a picnic, the occasional afternoon movie. At the bottom of her list was a trip to Calgary to visit their grandfather, which she was beginning to think was one item she wouldn't be able to cross off anytime soon.

She hadn't had much of a chance yet to discuss the topic with Joe. Sometimes she wondered if she was avoiding the issue. She'd read more fiction since she'd arrived at the farm than she had in the entire year. Her habit, after she'd put the children to bed, was to retire to her room with a book. She knew she was avoiding spending time alone with their uncle. Of course Joe was often out in the evenings—pursuing his marriage agenda—which suited her just fine.

It was an odd situation to be in. She wasn't his employee, nor could she exactly claim to be his friend.

"Why, hello! What a surprise." Honor looked up. It was the woman she'd met in the park on her first trip to Glory. She had a plastic shopping basket in one hand. "Honor, wasn't it? Remember me? Donna Beaton." She held out her other hand and Honor shook it.

"Of course I remember you. Honor Templeman."

Honor felt genuine delight, as though she'd met a long-lost friend.

Donna gave Alexander a curious look. "I see you must have tracked Joe down, after all," she said with a smile and a wink. "Baby-sitting today?" She glanced at Ellie, who was pushing a child-size grocery cart up and down the aisle, oblivious to the two women.

"Actually I'm taking care of these two for Joe while the Longquists are away," Honor said. "A couple more weeks. Labor Day."

"Oh?" Donna raised one eyebrow and gave Honor a friendly smile, then frowned. "Did you say your last name was Templeman? I guess you're related to the kids."

Honor took a deep breath. No time like the present. She'd made up her mind that she wasn't going to play the Honey Sanders name game she and Joe had played in Black Diamond. She ignored the elderly couple who had rounded the aisle and were perusing the shelves on the opposite side. "Yes. Actually I was married to the children's father once." That made it sound as though she'd been divorced. Was that fudging? She tried a laugh, which came out rather shakily. "I'm sort of their stepmother, I suppose you could say. I'm glad to have the chance to take care of them...."

Donna was nodding, still smiling, looking from her to the baby, firmly belted into the kiddie seat in the shopping cart, to Ellie, who was muttering as she deposited the occasional low-shelf item in her small cart. "Well, that's lovely. Isn't it great you turned up when you did? What a coincidence. I know Joe needed someone to look after the little ones.''

Just then Honor saw that the elderly gentleman had said something to his wife and held up a jar for her inspection, receiving the distinct response, ''Hssst!''

Oddly Honor felt relieved that the truth was out. With this old gossip across the aisle hanging on her every word, she had no doubt the news would be all over town by the end of the day. She was relieved to put the fiction of being Parker's sister to rest, just in case that particular notion had spread.

''Yes, I was married to Parker Templeman. We'd been separated for a long time. Five years. Of course, Joe's looking for a more permanent nanny for the long term, but I was pleased that he agreed to let me step in and take care of the children while Nan's away....''

Donna, too, seemed to realize that they were being overheard, and that Honor was glad of the chance to air her situation. She winked and gave her a conspiratorial smile. ''I'll be out to the farm to visit you soon. So pleased everything's worked out.''

''It has. I'll look forward to your visit.'' With smiles and waves, the two women continued on their separate ways. As Honor passed the elderly couple, she noted that the woman's eyes were wide and round; she could practically hear the ''tsk, tsk.'' She smiled to herself. Let them wonder. Let them all wonder.

Honor was still feeling good about the morning's interchange when she arrived back at the farm. Ellie helped her carry some of the smaller purchases into the house. Before they'd finished unloading the car,

Joe appeared, walking toward them from one of the toolsheds, and offered to bring in the rest of the bags.

She started lunch while he made the last few trips to the car. When he'd deposited all the bags on the counter, he began to methodically put the groceries away. So far he hadn't said much. She liked that about Joe. He was used to living by himself, doing things for himself—which extended to his own cooking and laundry, she'd noticed—and didn't expect other people to take up any slack for him.

"You can forget the Honey Sanders business," she announced with a small smile as she fastened a bib around Alexander's neck, readying him for his bowl of yogurt to be followed by chicken noodle soup. The hungry baby reached eagerly for the crackers she held out to placate him until his soup cooled.

"What's that?" Joe smiled, but his eyes were curious. "What are you talking about?"

"I ran into Donna Beaton in the IGA this morning."

"Oh? I didn't realize you knew her."

"I met her during the first trip I made to Glory." She paused, then, "Back when I was checking you out."

Joe shot her a surprised look but didn't say anything. He crossed his arms and leaned against the counter to listen.

"I told her that I was here taking care of the children for the rest of the summer and that I'd been married to their father at one time."

"You told her that?"

"Why not? I appreciate you wanting to spare Nan's feelings by telling her I was Parker's sister, but I've never been comfortable with it, Joe.'' She ladled out some soup and carried it across the kitchen to set in front of Ellie. "I'm not a bit ashamed of my situation. I'm not the first wife whose husband preferred another woman. And I won't be the last."

Joe regarded her speculatively. Honor wasn't sure she liked the gleam in his eye. "That's true," he admitted.

"So." She placed a bowl of yogurt and a loop-handled baby spoon on Alexander's tray. "So I thought you should know that our conversation was overheard by at least two people—"

"That was Ryan and Barnaby's grandma and grandpa, Uncle Joe! They were shopping, too," Ellie chimed in. Honor hadn't even realized the child, who was happily spooning up her noodle soup, had been following the conversation.

"—and I expect the facts to be all over town very soon."

"The facts," Joe said, still with that strange light in his eye. She had the distinct feeling he was teasing her. "Which facts would those be?"

"That you've invited the widow of the man your sister lived with to move out here for the summer to look after your niece and nephew. Those facts." She didn't think Ellie would be able to follow the various relationships she'd rapidly described.

Joe laughed. Again it was the big bold male sound of it that startled her and warmed her from the inside out. He reached into the refrigerator and pulled out a can of beer.

"Uncle Joe?"

"Yes, angel?"

"When are you gonna dig that hole you promised me you'd dig?"

Hole? Honor frowned at the girl. Joe was going to dig her a hole?

"This afternoon, Ellie. I promise. Right after your rest."

"Awww!"

Joe ignored Ellie and popped the tab on his beer. He grinned at Honor. "Townfolks talking, huh? Know what, Honor Templeman? I always had you figured for trouble." He raised his can in a salute and winked. "Right from the start." Then, still smiling, he left the kitchen.

The afternoon was a scorcher. Honor put Alexander down for his nap right after lunch, and the little boy fell asleep almost immediately. His cheeks were flushed and he seemed a little more subdued than usual. She hoped he wasn't coming down with something. Before she tiptoed out of his room, she turned the fan in the window on low so the sleeping baby could get the benefit of the moving air. Ellie had insisted she wasn't tired enough to have a rest, and Honor hadn't wanted to push the issue, fearing that she'd disturb her brother. At least if Ellie didn't lie down now, she'd probably go to bed earlier.

Ellie changed into her bathing suit and disappeared into the backyard for a splash in the inflatable pool while Honor cleared the table and washed the dishes. She made a mental note to check the temperature of the water when she went outdoors later. With this hot August sun, the water was probably warmer than a bathtub.

By the time Honor went out, armed with a book,

a large sun hat and a tube of sunscreen that she intended to smear all over Ellie at regular intervals, the girl had abandoned the pool for something far more interesting.

She was watching her uncle dig a hole.

CHAPTER TEN

"WHAT IN THE WORLD are you doing?" Honor asked as she stepped closer. Ellie had her hands on her bare knees, very grubby hands, Honor noticed, and was watching every movement of Joe's spade.

"What does it look like I'm doing?" he asked, shading his eyes with one forearm. He'd taken off his shirt and his tanned muscled chest glistened with sweat.

"Digging a hole."

"Yep. That's what we're doing—right, Ellie?"

"Right, Uncle Joe!"

Joe grinned at Honor but offered no further explanation.

"So, what I'm wondering is, why are you digging a hole?" Honor said, deciding she had no choice but to play along.

"We're digging a hole for fun, right, Ellie?"

"Right, Uncle Joe!" Ellie yelped, jumping up and down in excitement. "I'm gonna play in it. Dig and make mud!"

"Play?" Honor directed her query to Joe.

He took another stab at the turf that rimmed the hole he'd already dug, which was about three feet across and a foot deep. He tossed the chunk of sod onto a pile already heaped in a wheelbarrow positioned near the hole. Honor allowed her gaze to linger on his bare torso, feeling guilty about it, but knowing her dark glasses screened her eyes. *How pathetic can you get, Honor Templeman?* she asked herself.

Pretty pathetic, she answered silently, continuing to admire Joe's attractive physique.

"You must have enjoyed getting dirty when you were a kid," he said, straightening and leaning on the spade handle. His amused glance bored directly into her eyes, dark glasses or no dark glasses. She had the distinct impression he was quite aware that she'd been secretly admiring him.

"I can't remember." It was true; had she ever felt free to play in the dirt? And with whom? They'd moved so often she'd always had to make new friends. Books had been her distractions more than shovels and spades and skipping ropes had.

"Well, Ellie likes holes. And so do I," he stated, picking up the spade again and removing more dirt. "When it's done, I'm going to turn it over to this little girl." He grinned at his niece. "She knows what to do with it, right, Ellie?"

"Right, Uncle Joe!"

Honor grabbed a plastic lawn chair and hauled it into the shade. Then she settled down on it, first calling Ellie to her and pulling a T-shirt over the girl's head. "Remember we talked about how important it is not to get sunburn, sweetie?"

"Uncle Joe doesn't got a shirt on," Ellie pointed out.

"No," Honor agreed, glancing Joe's way again. "He doesn't, does he? But he's a grown-up and he has to take responsibility for his own sunburn. You can remind him if you like.''

Ha, thought Honor, watching the girl's determined march across the lawn. *Serves you right.*

Joe laughed when Ellie told him to put his shirt back on. Then she saw him whisper something to Ellie. The girl covered her mouth and giggled. Now what had he said to her? Honor felt annoyed—but she noticed that Joe reached for his shirt and pulled it on, although he didn't do up the buttons.

"Small mercies," she muttered to herself, finally opening her book. She'd brought out the Dr. Spock baby-care manual, wondering if Alexander's flushed cheeks and drooling and feeling out of sorts were symptoms of something to do with his age. She supposed he could be getting new teeth. That would be preferable to a summer cold—

"I'm off for the afternoon," Joe said, suddenly looming over her. She shaded her eyes and looked up at him.

"Off?"

"I'm helping Tim finish up the cut on the last field of hay. I should be back around suppertime. Don't wait for me. I, uh, I'll be going into town right away."

"Big date?"

"Yeah." He grinned, but Honor thought he looked a little sheepish. She saw that he'd buttoned up his shirt.

"So what's the deal with the hole?" Honor glanced at the hole Joe had dug, where Ellie was raptly stamping around and around on the fresh dirt.

"It's just something to amuse her. Kind of like a

sandbox, only a little more interesting. She knows the drill. I've filled up a washtub of water by the back door—'' Joe pointed at an old-fashioned washtub near the door ''—and when she's ready to come in, she rinses off in that.''

''I see.'' It was certainly a novel approach—dig a hole and let a kid play in it. Cheap entertainment. Time would tell just how much amusement Ellie got out of it.

''I, uh…''

Honor raised her eyebrows, curious about his hesitation. Was there something more on his mind, maybe about his big date?

''I'll see you later, okay?''

''Okay.''

''If you need anything, call me on my cell phone.''

''Sure.''

He left and Honor watched him go. He always seemed reluctant to leave her with the children, and she wondered if he worried about her ability to take care of them on her own. Surely she'd proved that she was capable. Or was he afraid she'd spirit them off to Calgary?

She had to have it out with Joe one more time about bringing the children and their grandfather together. Much as she hated to disrupt the ease and evenness of their day-to-day life, it had to be done. Her conscience was bothering her. Even if she'd felt some of the urgency dissipate once she'd settled in at the farm, what about Alec? It was selfish of her to ignore *his* needs just because her own desire to meet the children had been more than satisfied.

She had to come to some agreement with Joe

while she was here, and if she couldn't, well, she'd just keep working at it when she got back to Calgary. It wasn't as though the facts were going to change or disappear. Alec was their grandfather and he had a right to know his grandchildren. That was all there was to it, no matter what Joe thought. No matter what had happened between them in the ancient past.

Once Alexander was awake, Ellie had had enough of the mud hole and grumpily washed herself off in the washtub Joe had provided. Honor could see she'd have to supervise the girl until they had the routine down, or the house would be full of mud in no time. Typical of a man not to think of that. She quickly corrected herself; he *had* thought of that. He'd provided the washtub. Of course, he'd just assumed Ellie would use it.

Alexander's cheeks were still flushed, and he, too, was grumpy. Honor gave the children a snack and then rocked them in the hammock for a while, catching the occasional breeze that swept through the trees nearby. It was too hot. That was part of the problem. Alexander obviously wasn't feeling well, and Ellie should have had a nap today. Honor felt some of the frustration she'd always imagined to be the occasional lot of motherhood. You were constantly meeting the needs of others, mainly your children. Your own needs had to be put on hold. It was a situation not every woman could handle.

Could she? She'd mourned her lost babies terribly, but she'd managed, every time, to immerse herself in her career again. She'd always been able to focus. It was a quality that had not only helped her through her lonely childhood, but allowed her to secure the high marks and scholarships necessary to climb out of the world she'd grown up in and never have to go back.

Along the way, though, she'd lost something. Even cranky and whiny as these children were right now, there was a primitive and very human satisfaction about being tumbled in a tactile sweaty heap with them, feeling the warmth and solidity of their small bodies against hers, the child-scent of their hair and skin. Somehow she knew that this physical contact was what the children wanted, too, what they'd missed sorely since the death of their parents. Joe's sister, Sylvie, would have cuddled them; Parker would have hugged them and told them stories.

Honor's eyes filled briefly. How pleased she was, deep down, that Parker had known this special family happiness, however briefly. She regretted that she hadn't been able to turn him free to marry Sylvie, hadn't helped him face up to his father. If only he'd confided in her.

But then Joe Gallant would have had nothing to say about it. Alec would have known his grandchildren—and she'd never have met Joe.

Not that it mattered a whole lot.

Honor gave the children an early supper and they were in bed asleep by seven o'clock. Her research had shown her that Alexander was probably getting some molars, causing his discomfort. If he didn't improve soon, she'd have to consult Joe and perhaps take the toddler to the doctor. Just to be sure. She'd hate to be responsible for ignoring something important, some disease she was sure a real mother would have known by instinct.... She gave herself a shake. That was foolish thinking. Every mother had to learn as she went, just as every child did.

Honor flipped on the radio in the kitchen and cleared away the dishes from the children's meal. She found an easy-listening music station and hummed along as she worked. There wasn't much to do, just wash a few bowls and plates and glasses and wipe off the table. She gathered up a load of the children's dirty clothes and threw it into the washing machine in the laundry room off the kitchen entry.

Then she thought about preparing something for herself to eat. Joe would no doubt be eating in town, taking his date somewhere fancy. Well, as fancy as Glory had to offer. She glanced at the clock. Nearly half-past seven and he wasn't back from the fields yet.

She tried hard not to think about Joe's matrimonial pursuit, but she couldn't help it. She wondered how the wife search was going. The very thought annoyed her. Sure, she'd botched up her own choice of a mate, but setting out on a methodical hunt the way Joe was doing didn't strike her as any improvement. She didn't think for a moment that Joe wouldn't make some woman a good reliable husband, just that his methods seemed…not right somehow.

She didn't feel this way because she wanted him for herself. Well, okay—be honest, Templeman— maybe briefly, for a quick fun romp to see if she could attract a man like that.

More and more, her time away from the office had convinced her that continuing on a nice, even, up- ward path as a single, successful career woman wasn't all she wanted out of life. She wanted companionship, too. She wanted a companion.

An image of Joe's sweaty hard-muscled body flashed into her mind. Yes, *that* kind of companion....

She decided to take advantage of whatever breeze there was. She hauled a card table onto the veranda and set it up. The sun had moved behind the farmhouse, so the table was in the shade. She pawed through several drawers before giving up on finding any kind of tablecloth. Joe's house was reasonably well furnished, but there was a lot missing. A couple of frying pans, four saucepans, three large plastic bowls, a microwave and two cookie sheets did not a well-equipped kitchen make, in her view. He had plenty of dishes and tea towels, but obviously no tablecloths. Well, she thought, shaking out a couple of clean tea towels to use as a cover for her small table, it was a man's establishment, after all.

She laid her place, feeling positively cheerful. The children were sleeping soundly, she'd put on a saucepan of rice, and as soon as she'd had a quick wash and brushed her hair, she was going to make a simple veggie stir-fry. Then she'd settle down at the table with her novel and a glass of wine.

Ten minutes later she'd tied on an apron and was getting ingredients out of the refrigerator when she heard Joe's truck drive up. The screen door slammed and then Joe stood in the kitchen, regarding her. His hair was dusty and his shirt had bits of grass and hay stuck to it. He'd already taken off his hat and hung it on the entranceway hat rack. Honor could hear the sound of the washing machine's spin cycle in the background.

"Looks like I'm just in time." He smiled and gestured to the table set up on the veranda, visible through the open kitchen window. Honor turned down the radio volume slightly.

"Didn't you say something about a big date tonight?"

"Yeah." He paused and sighed. He didn't look all that thrilled about it, which for some reason pleased her. "I'd better grab a quick shower and be on my way. I'm running late." He glanced at the kitchen clock as he passed through to the hallway.

Honor washed some broccoli and red peppers and set them on the chopping board. She'd have to do her stir-fry in the frying pan. Not that she'd expect he'd have a wok. She noted the sudden drop in water pressure, which meant Joe was in the shower. She forced her mind away from the images that had tumbled through her brain the first day she'd driven out to the farm, when he'd yelled at her to come into the bathroom and take the dripping Alexander from him.

Only three weeks ago. So much seemed to have happened since then. Not least the fact that she was relatively comfortable living in the same house with this man, a stranger, and her husband's two children. If only her secretary or Nigel Harrison—the man who'd taken her to the opera—could see her now. Or Alec.

Honor got out the wine and poured herself a glass. She jammed the cork back in and replaced the bottle in the refrigerator. The aroma of sautéeing onions, peppers and garlic filled the air, the wine was delicious, and her book awaited.

The phone rang. Honor walked to the wall near the table, picked up the receiver and said hello.

"Is this Joe Gallant's place?" It was a woman's voice, soft, feminine, a little puzzled.

"Yes, it is. Would you like to speak to him?" Joe appeared in the hall doorway, hair tousled, wearing a clean shirt and pants. She handed him the receiver and tried very hard not to overhear his end of the conversation.

It was brief. Joe hung up and turned to her with a grin that shouldn't have been there.

"The date?" She couldn't help the query, nosy or not.

"Yeah. It's off. She had a panic call from her cousin and she has to drive over to her place tonight. Down at Stavely."

"Too bad." She gave him a sidelong glance.

"Yeah. Too bad." He walked over to the counter and reached for a wineglass.

"You don't sound all that broken up about it," Honor continued, unable to resist.

Joe opened the refrigerator and pulled out the wine bottle. He uncorked it and poured some into his glass before answering. When he did he raised his glass to her. "Know something? I'm not." He took a sip of wine and smiled. "Is there enough for two of whatever you're making?"

"I guess so," she said, knowing her cheeks had

gone a bright pink. "Veggie stir-fry and rice. Getting a little weary of the wife chase, are you?"

"Veggie, huh?" Joe reached into the freezer section of the fridge and took out a package. "I can thaw these steaks in the microwave in no time." He threw her a quick look. "So that's what you think—I'm out hunting for a wife? I guess I am. To tell you the truth, it *can* get a little tiring."

"Oh?" She glanced at him again as she turned down the heat under the frying pan.

He waved the brown paper package in front of her. "You want one?"

"Sure. If you're willing to cook it."

"Absolutely." He grinned at her as he set them in the microwave. "I'll fire up the barbecue and you bring out another plate. And some more wine."

"I guess I can do that," she said, feigning reluctance. "If you're positive you can afford to waste a whole evening like this when you *could* be out doing some serious courting."

Joe laughed. "I can use a break."

Suddenly Honor felt even more terrific than she already had. She'd looked forward to an adult meal alone on the veranda.

But she was looking forward to his company even more.

THE STEAKS WERE perfectly cooked. The wine—even the second bottle—was perfectly chilled. The music, low as it was, lent a romantic ambience to the hastily-put-together al fresco meal. A tiny breeze even sprang up before they'd finished, relieving the heaviness of the August heat.

Joe was an amusing and interesting conversationalist. That surprised her. But then, she reminded herself, she'd spent very little time alone with him. Either he'd been out—on his courtship forays—or they'd been with the children.

He knew a lot about the history of the area, and about the various neighbors, some of them pretty eccentric, who lived nearby. He told her about his childhood and the town he'd been born in back in New Brunswick. He even sang a few lines of an old Acadian song in such an odd French that she couldn't make out a word. He had a lovely baritone voice. She was delighted. He made more than one reference to this evening—their meal together—as a date. At first she thought he was joking; later she wasn't so sure.

At the end of the meal, feeling a bit dizzy from both the wine and the conversation, Honor leaned back and looked out over the landscape, to the grain in the fields stirred by the slight wind.

Now what? It wasn't quite nine o'clock. Not for a moment had she forgotten that a very sexy virile man sat opposite her at the rickety card table. A single man. Or that they were all alone.

Well, not exactly alone.

Honor pushed back her chair. "I think I'd better check on the children," she said.

"Everything okay?" Joe's swift look of concern went straight to her heart. There was no question in her mind—Joe Gallant loved his niece and nephew dearly. If her father-in-law entertained anything more than a passing fancy of trying to get custody of those children, he'd have a fight on his hands.

"Alexander's been a little under the weather," she said. "I think he might be getting a new tooth."

Joe frowned. "I could take him in to see Kate Pleasance tomorrow. She was Sylvie's doctor." Pain creased his face briefly. That was something else she ought to remember. Joe never, ever forgot that his sister had died so recently and so tragically. "She delivered them both."

His eyes, when they met hers, shimmered with feeling. Honor walked into the house, thinking hard. Now what? *Now what?* The whole evening alone with him loomed before her. And after they'd had such an enjoyable meal together, she surely couldn't escape to her room with her book—could she? Or sit with him in some room and ignore him?

The children were both sound asleep. Ellie had thrown off her sheet, and Honor gently covered her up again. She adjusted the fan she'd placed in the window, turning it to its lowest setting. Alexander was asleep, too, frowning slightly, his little face flushed and warm to the touch. Maybe Joe was right; maybe she should take him to the doctor tomorrow.

She left the room, closing the door softly behind her. Then she took a deep breath and walked back toward the kitchen. She noticed as she entered that the dishwasher was humming. Joe must have brought in the dishes and stacked them in the machine.

He had. When she stepped onto the veranda, she noticed that their wineglasses were still outside, as well as the half bottle of wine they hadn't finished. In the center of the table was a bunch of marigolds he'd obviously plucked hastily from the border that lined the front walk and thrust into a drinking glass. It was a touch of brilliant gold, an intense contrast to the deepening blue of the sky. Soon the sun would set, night would fall...

As she stood on the veranda, Joe came forward and reached for her hand. He bowed slightly. "I'd like to dance with you, Honor."

"Dance?" she croaked.

His eyebrows lifted. "Yes. Why not?"

"I..." She didn't know what to say. She felt her heart hammer like a schoolgirl's. This was so silly! She was a grown woman, for heaven's sake. What was she worried about? He was only asking her to dance, not take her clothes off and lie down with him in the grass.

"Sure," she said, forcing a smile. "Then you can pretend you're on a real date." She swallowed. "You could probably use the practice, right?" she joked, trying to keep things light.

He grinned. "Right." He took her hand and pulled her toward him. He put one arm around her, then swore softly. "Forgot the music." He released her and walked toward the open window, reaching through to turn up the radio that sat on the kitchen table. Some sappy waltz was playing. Elevator music, she thought.

But it didn't feel like elevator music when he took her in his arms again. His eyes held hers and his arm secured her to him, close but not too close. Her hand felt sweaty and small in his. She hoped he didn't notice. She felt hot all over, and it wasn't simply because of the August evening.

"Joe," she began, "do you think this is such a good idea?"

He smiled, a devastating smile that tickled her heart and fluttered her stomach. "It's an excellent idea. The best idea I've had all day."

He spun her into a turn and pulled her closer and murmured into her hair, "Maybe even the best idea I've had all summer."

Honor was struck dumb. Her whole body hummed from the proximity to Joe's. Her senses were overwhelmed with his scent, the warm, male, musky embrace, the brush of his thighs against hers, his belly... She felt faint, as though she'd swoon right there in his arms, on the porch of some forgettable frame farmhouse out in the middle of the prairie with no one else around except two sleeping children, a few snoozing dogs and a magpie that darted from fence to roof to tree, belting out its raucous song.

Honor felt like weeping. She'd rarely been so overwhelmed in her life. She felt so tender and vulnerable and fragile in Joe's arms, and cherished. As though the tinny music would go on forever, as though Joe would never let her go, as though...as though...

Luckily the song faded to a close. Unluckily it

segued directly into another schmaltzy tune, and Joe didn't relax his embrace, not in the slightest. It seemed that he intended to dance with her all night, up and down the veranda, around the card table, adroitly missing the boot-scraper at the top of the stairs, to the other end of the veranda, where the creaky love seat swung stiffly on its hinges.

Finally that song was over, too. The quiet monotone of the disc jockey broke in. Honor was suspended, mesmerized, helpless, in Joe's arms. His gaze never left hers.

He froze, too, his face inches from hers. "Honor," he breathed, and again her heart twirled like a leaf. "I want to kiss you. I'm dying to kiss you. Let me kiss you. I've wanted to kiss you for a long, long time."

It was a litany of desire. It was the kind of thing she'd longed to hear from a man, the kind of thing she'd imagined other women heard. It was deep heartfelt desire that she'd never heard from a man, not even Parker back in the early days.

Parker. The children. Alec. Templeman Energy.

"I...I don't think that would be a good idea," she managed, barely able to speak.

Joe crushed her to him and she gasped at the full intimate contact of their bodies. "Why not?" he demanded, but his voice was as soft as it had been when he'd asked to kiss her.

"I...I don't know," she whispered back. "I just think it wouldn't be such a good idea."

She felt him relax slightly and loosen his hold on

her. She felt the moment evaporating, the intensity abating...

"What *would* be a good idea?" he asked with a familiar gleam in his eye. "In your opinion."

"Dessert," she said breathlessly. "Dessert would be a good idea now. I think."

He frowned slightly. "Dessert? You mean you've got something planned for dessert? What a woman."

"Yes," she said, racking her brain for ideas. Ice cream? With maple syrup? And some of the strawberries they'd picked from Nan's garden that morning?

"And coffee, I suppose," he added, smiling now. He gently released her and she stepped back, allowing herself to breathe again.

"Yes," she said, steadying herself against the wobbly card table behind her. "Coffee would be a good idea, too."

CHAPTER ELEVEN

JEREMIAH BLAKE picked up his check and stepped into the aisle of the Chickadee Café. "Got to head out or the new cook will have my hide." Jeremiah was the manager of the Diamond 8 ranch west of Glory. The Diamond 8 was one of Joe's regular customers for a big supply of hay each year. "I promised I'd bring his grub order back with me this afternoon."

"So I'll put you down for most of that second cut?"

"Yeah." Jeremiah settled his hat on his head and glanced out the window beside their booth. A good-looking young woman was passing by. A stranger, Joe thought; at least, he'd never seen her before. He looked up at Jeremiah, noting the frank appreciation on the rancher's face.

Joe glanced back at the woman, who was well past the window now, nearly at the corner of the street. Yeah, pretty enough. Nice figure. But she didn't do a thing for him. And he used to be partial to blondes, too.

What the hell was wrong with him these days? Maybe he was just tired; Alexander had cried half the night with his teething troubles. And he hadn't been sleeping that well the past few days himself.

"Okay. See you around." Jeremiah headed for the door of the diner, pausing to hold it open for a dark-haired woman who was entering. Donna Beaton. She gave Jeremiah a smile and he smiled back and tipped his hat. Jeremiah Blake liked the ladies, no question. He'd suffered a big setback a year or two ago when one of the Galloway girls he was sweet on had dumped him. By the look of things, he'd put that behind him.

"Joe! How are you?"

"Hi, Donna. Have a seat." Joe gestured to the spot Jeremiah had vacated. She slid onto the vinyl bench.

"What are you up to these days, Joe? I haven't seen you in ages. I hear the team's been doing pretty well. I haven't been able to get to many games this summer."

"Doing okay, I guess. I figure we're out of the pennant race, though. Maybe. Nanton's got a strong team this year."

"So I hear."

"How's the store?"

"Busy. That's why I haven't been able to get away much. Whew!" She fanned her face with the napkin on the table and looked around for a waitress. "Hot enough?"

"Getting there. Jamie playing rep ball this year?"

"I wanted him to, but he's crazy about football all of a sudden." Donna sighed and nodded as the waitress held up the coffeepot. "He wants to play on the school team in September. I worry about him getting hurt. Football's rough."

"The rougher the better," Joe said, and grinned. Donna was a single parent; she worried too much.

"He'll be okay." Joe turned his attention to the slice of pie the waitress had brought him before Jeremiah left. Blueberry. Good, but not as good as Nan's.

"I met the woman who's looking after Sylvie's kids." Donna eyed him curiously and smiled. "She seems very nice. I told her I'd drive out one of these afternoons and have tea with her."

"Do that," Joe said, scooping up another piece of pie. "She'd like that. She doesn't know too many folks around here. She's from Calgary."

"I know. She mentioned she was married to Parker."

Joe met her gaze fully. He and Donna had gone to school together. He was one of the few men around Glory who hadn't dated her or tried to date her at one time or another. She'd always been just Donna to him, a good friend.

"She was." He glanced out the window to get his emotions under control. Even the thought of Parker walking out on Honor burned him up. "You know my feelings about Parker. He left her five years ago before he took up with my sister. He never got around to bothering with a divorce. Great guy, huh?" He looked sharply at Donna to see how she'd take it. She didn't even blink. It took a lot to shake up Donna Beaton. She'd been around the block a few times herself.

"Strange, isn't it, that she'd want to show up here and get involved with you and the kids?"

"She's not involved with me, Donna." Which reminded Joe of what was on his mind these days. "I've been thinking seriously about getting married, though. Now that I've got the kids and all, I figure it's time to make a move.''

Donna's sympathetic brown eyes met his. "Oh?"

"Yeah." He laughed, but it sounded self-conscious even to him. He pushed back his empty plate. "You remember Shannon Boyd? I took her out a few times this summer."

"And?" Donna's dark eyes danced with humor. "I didn't know you and she had a thing going."

"We don't." He grinned. "Not anymore. Found that out quick enough soon as she realized I intended to raise Sylvie's kids. Not every woman is real keen on an instant family."

Donna stirred her coffee thoughtfully. "I suppose not. Still, you're a fine man, Joe. I'm sure some woman would be delighted to take over those children, maybe even have a few more with you."

"Yeah." Joe reached for his hat on the vinyl bench beside him. "Well, maybe." He put the hat on. "Trouble is, I don't seem to have as much interest in finding out as I thought I'd have. Bad time of year, I guess."

Donna's eyes clouded and she placed her hand over his on the table. It was a soothing maternal gesture. "You've had a lot to deal with this summer, Joe," she said gently. "Don't overdo it. I'm sure Nan won't mind looking after Sylvie's kids for a while longer. And you can always hire someone." She patted his hand. "Don't rush into anything you'll regret."

Joe reversed their hands and squeezed hers gently, then released it. "Thanks, Donna. I'll keep that in mind." He smiled. "Okay if I leave you here? I'm trying to get over to the lumberyard before it closes. Half day on Wednesdays.''

''Sure, go ahead. I'm meeting someone in a few minutes.'' She took her coffee cup to the counter and slid gracefully onto one of the vinyl stools. She was a beautiful woman. Joe had often wondered why she'd never remarried, but maybe some women liked playing the field. The way some men did.

Joe paid his bill and went outside. It was hot all right, but every day this month had been hot. Was this the greenhouse effect you kept reading about in the papers?

The lumberyard was just closing, but Joe managed to get his order loaded, then called in at the bank for a talk with the manager. He had a mortgage there, too, a small one, and he was reluctant to get in any deeper by borrowing more money to pay out Ira. He'd just have to make do somehow. Maybe the price of oats and barley would go up this fall.

When he got back to the farm, the house was quiet. He saw that the lunch dishes were done and neatly stacked in the drainer. He'd noticed that Honor rarely used the dishwasher and had no idea why. In his opinion it was a toss-up between the dishwasher and the microwave as to the best invention going. He could do without a washing machine, if it came right down to it. There was a laundromat in town.

Joe poured himself a cup of coffee from the pot on the counter. He needed it to keep his eyes open today. Poor Alexander. He felt sorry for the little guy, but he guessed there wasn't much anyone could do about it. Getting teeth was inevitable, and besides, Honor seemed to have everything under control.

She'd probably lost as much sleep as he had last night, listening to the baby's crying. When he'd arisen about three o'clock to check on him after a silence that lasted longer than any had before, he'd discovered the child in Honor's bed across the hall, all tucked in and cuddled up on the pillow beside her. He'd stood for a moment looking at the two of them, then he'd quietly gone back to his own room, hoping she hadn't been aware of his presence.

Somehow Honor and nighttime and darkness and bed were all bound up in his mind with one thing: getting her into his. And not to sleep, either. Joe frowned. Ever since he'd been crazy enough to dance with her the other evening, he'd thought of little else.

He wandered onto the veranda and stood there, surveying the scene before him and wrenching his mind back to all he had to get done that afternoon. They were finishing up the second hay cut and just in time, too, since it was nearly time to get the equipment ready for harvesting the feed-grain crops. He glanced at the sky. Clear and blue. And the weather report called for the dry weather to continue. Barley off first, then oats. By mid-October he should be finished the harvest and could put some serious time and energy into his search for a wife, which definitely wasn't going as quickly or as well as he'd hoped. He had a few prospects, but just now, he couldn't seem to give courting the attention it required. Maybe Donna was right; maybe he shouldn't rush into anything.

Oh, well. At least he had the nanny problem pretty much solved. By the time Honor went back to Calgary, Bea Hoople's arm would have healed and she'd be ready to take on the job.

He raised his mug to his mouth, then narrowed his eyes and looked around. Ellie was playing happily in the hole he'd dug for her beside the new swing set. Where were Alexander and Honor?

Then he saw them, settled into the hammock near the windbelt at the back of the yard. Joe walked down the steps and made his way toward them. As he walked through the patio area, he picked up an aluminum lawn chair and carried it to within twenty feet of the hammock before he realized they were both asleep.

At least, Honor had her eyes closed and Alexander was sprawled across her body, facedown, arms flung to both sides, legs relaxed, the flush of sleep on his chubby cheeks.

Joe sat down and observed them. Ellie called out once, and he waved, not wanting to call back for fear he'd wake them. He finished his coffee and reached down to set the empty mug on the grass.

Mother and child. He was no artist, but what a picture that would be, the two of them sound asleep in the hammock, the shifting shadows of leaves on their faces, the tiny movements as the wind caught Honor's hair. She had one bare leg hanging out of the hammock, as though she'd been pushing gently at the ground to rock them both before she'd fallen asleep herself. Her sandals lay where she'd kicked them off in the grass.

Joe stretched out his legs, crossed his arms on his chest and studied them. It gradually dawned on him that he was staring the solution to his problem right in the face.

Honor.

She wasn't married. She liked his niece and nephew, maybe more than liked them by now. She was almost related to them. Not only that, she was used to them and they liked her, even Alexander, and he'd been a tough one to win over. She was good with them. She talked to them, took time to play with them. He'd never seen her impatient or cross.

And she was some woman. Joe allowed himself to examine the powerful deep-down feelings he'd been careful to keep hidden, even from himself, until now. He liked her, too. A lot. Maybe that was why his courtship efforts elsewhere weren't working out—his heart just wasn't in it.

Now take Honor. Seriously. She was smart, which he'd always liked in a woman, and she was incredibly sexy in her own subdued way. In his experience, she was the type of woman who was a powder keg for the right man. Was he that man? He liked to think he could be. There was definitely chemistry between them, and he had the notion sometimes that she worked just as hard as he did at keeping it out of their day-to-day relationship. She had a sense of humor; he'd seen evidence of that more than once. A sly wicked humor that he loved.

Why hadn't he thought of this before? He'd ask Honor Templeman to marry him. Maybe, just maybe he'd even let the grandfather meet the kids, if it was that important. He could hardly keep them away if he married her; she'd made it clear how she felt about the old man. It was a mystery to him why a smart cookie like Honor could be hoodwinked by an interfering old bastard like Alec Templeman, but strange things happened in the world. No way he could figure them all out.

She seemed pretty upset over this business of not being able to have kids, but did that matter? They'd have Alexander and Ellie to raise. He'd like children of his own, but if it wasn't in the cards? If she wasn't able to? Well, hell, he could live with it. And, in fact, she might be better off with him than with some guy who really did want kids, who might break her heart blaming her because she couldn't have any. And she could keep on with her career if she wanted to, drive to Calgary every day or take up with Lucas Yellowfly and old Pete Horsfall in their Glory practice.

What was missing in this situation? There had to be something. He thought it over carefully. Nope, not a damn thing. It was good for everyone all around. Him, her, Alexander and Ellie. Even the old man. The ticklish bit would be presenting it to Honor in a way that would show her just how sensible it was. He'd have to appeal to her logic; she was a logical rational person.

He made up his mind to think it over a little more before he put it to her. Then he saw her leg move ever so slightly, and he pulled his chair closer so that he could look down into her face. She still had her eyes shut.

Joe swallowed. Suddenly his throat was dry as dust. His heart rate shifted up a gear; suddenly he knew he was going to do it and he was going to do it *now*. He had to, before he lost his nerve.

He reached forward and gently took her hand. She opened her eyes slowly, her gaze clearing as she focused on him. She made no movement to take back her hand. It felt soft and small in his. Delicate but strong. The way *she* was. He swallowed again, overcome with a feeling of deep tenderness toward her, toward the kids, toward whatever kind of life they'd make together. It would be a good one. He knew it in his bones.

Their eyes met. He saw the vague query in hers, the half smile; she wasn't fully awake yet.

"Honor." He glanced down and covered her hand with both of his. "Listen to me. I've got something to say. Don't interrupt—just listen to me until I'm finished." He kept his voice very quiet so he wouldn't disturb the sleeping baby.

"Marry me." He took a deep breath as he saw her eyes widen slightly, her smile fade. She said nothing. "I want to marry you. I know it probably sounds crazy—it seemed crazy to me at first, too—but I'm dead serious. I'd like to marry you if you'll have me. It makes sense for the kids. I know you care about them. They need a mother and I've been looking for a wife. You know that. You've known that all along."

She still said nothing, which gave Joe the courage to go on. "You could continue with your job if you wanted. I could hire a nanny to take care of them if you did that." He squeezed her hand in his eagerness. "Marry me!"

"Joe," she said softly, stopping his torrent of words. Her voice sounded scratchy and thick with sleep. "What in the world are you *talking* about?"

"You and me, Honor. *You and me*. We could be good together. There's chemistry. Man-woman stuff. You feel it, too. I know I've never even kissed you, we've never even thought—" he wanted to laugh, this suddenly felt so damn right "—of something like this, getting married. But it could work," he whispered urgently. "I *know* it could." He'd never kissed her. Why not kiss her now?

On impulse he leaned forward. Her mouth was soft and sweet and trembled under his. He kept his head still, her head, too, hardly dared to breathe, fearful of waking the child who still slept sprawled across her. The very fact that they were both so restrained— had to be so restrained—was like throwing gasoline on a brush fire. Joe felt the kiss right down to his bootlaces. It was even more powerful, more exciting, than he'd dreamed it would be. He wanted it to go on and on. He went slowly, explored the softness of her mouth, gloried in her response—at first tentative, then eager—as instinctive and profound as his.

When he finally lifted his head a few inches, her eyes were closed and her face was pale. Her mouth was wet and her breathing was rapid and shallow. He noticed the flush of arousal on her throat and the peaks of her small breasts, hard and distinct under her T-shirt. She couldn't deny the effect of his kiss or her response any more than he could.

That had to be good news, didn't it?

"Joe," she said finally, and opened eyes stormy with emotion. Her voice was flat. "You shouldn't have done that."

"Why not? It felt right, Honor. It felt good. I've been wanting to do that for days, for weeks. You know that. Maybe I thought it wasn't right before, but now I do. I want to marry you. Tell me you'll think about it.''

''My turn. Listen to me now,'' she said, her voice terribly quiet. ''I can't marry you. I *won't* marry you. Ever. I'm surprised you'd have the nerve to ask me. Do you know why?''

Joe felt as if she'd dashed ice water in his face. ''No. Why?''

''Because I got married before for all the wrong reasons and I'll never do it again.''

''But, Honor, these are *good* reasons, don't you see that?'' Joe was perplexed. He'd tried to be logical; surely she could see how much sense this proposal made. ''Damn it, the kids are crazy about you. I…I'm crazy about you.'' The instant he said it he knew it was the truth. ''I'd be a good husband, a good provider. Loyal, responsible, faithful. I promise. You could do a hell of a lot worse.''

''You're *not* crazy about me, Joe,'' she whispered fiercely and her eyes flashed lightning. ''I wish you wouldn't lie about it. You just need a *wife!* Anybody will do—you've made no secret of that.''

''It's *not* a lie, it's the truth, goddamn it. I do like you, I know we'd be good together.…''

She was silent.

After a moment Joe went on, ''We could work things out with Templeman.…'' Now he was really getting down and dirty. *Shut up, Gallant.* Damn, why hadn't he taken the time to think this through properly before he presented it to her? He'd botched the whole thing.

''I never thought you'd try blackmail,'' she said

wearily. Her eyes were anguished. Joe felt like a complete heel, like he had the day she'd first come to see him and he'd sworn no way would Sylvie's kids find out about their grandfather.

"Damn it, Honor, listen to me. I'm just trying to be sensible, since it means so much to you—the kids and Templeman, I mean. I'm just trying to say that if we got married, we'd have to try and work something out, that's all."

"Well, forget it, Joe. There's no need for you to abandon your...your *principles* to marry me! Your stubborn, pigheaded, stupid grudges..."

Her eyes burned into his. What had gone wrong? Joe felt something precious and vital slipping out of his grasp. Something so precious he hadn't even known he had in his hand.

"If I ever marry again, it'll be for one reason and one reason only. It'll be because I'm in love. And the man I marry will love *me*. And maybe he won't be half the man you are. Maybe you're right that I could do a hell of a lot worse than you. I've already proved that, haven't I? But I'll love him and he'll love *me*! If it happens, great. I'll be luckier than a lot of women. If it doesn't..." She shrugged ever so slightly, but it was enough to awaken Alexander.

The boy smiled at her and she smiled back, but Joe could see the tears trembling on her eyelashes.

He stood. "Is that it? Is that your final answer, Honor?" he asked, sounding almost formal.

"Y-yes, it is," she said shakily, looking up at him and holding Alexander close to her.

"I can't change your mind? There's no chance at all?"

"No. I...I don't think so."

I don't think so. That wasn't exactly a flat refusal. There *must* be a chance for him. He'd think about that. He could accept the way she'd reacted, considering how he'd jumped right in with a double-barreled shotgun when he should have taken time to think things over. He'd work on changing her mind. Because no matter what she said, he was more convinced than ever that she was the woman for him. That kiss was proof, if he needed proof.

And he didn't think he did. He'd been more than half in love with Honor Templeman all along.

CHAPTER TWELVE

BY THE TIME Honor drove to Calgary two days later to visit Alec, leaving the children with their uncle, she'd recovered somewhat from the shock of Joe's proposal.

At first she'd worried that his out-of-the-blue announcement that he wanted to marry her would mean she'd have to cut short her time with the children and return to Calgary early. There'd be embarrassment on both sides. And maybe he'd feel resentful that she hadn't even made a pretense of taking his marriage proposal seriously.

Which she hadn't of course. No man asked a woman to marry him, bang, just like that. They'd never dated, they'd never even regarded each other in that way—Honor didn't count her occasional compelling fantasies about a quick roll in the hay with him. They'd never even kissed until then. She'd said no to a kiss on the veranda a few evenings previously, and he'd very properly accepted that.

Afterward Joe hadn't made any reference to their "date," and he'd never changed his attitude toward her in the slightest, which was a relief. It was easy to ascribe the incident to the fact that they'd had an enjoyable evening, they'd shared nearly two bottles of wine and he was feeling…well, amorous, she supposed.

After all, look at his hectic dating schedule since she'd been there. Nearly every evening he'd taken out some woman or other.

But *now*… Honor felt her breath catch just thinking about it. The kiss, and what a kiss. The passion in his voice when he'd asked her to marry him. The incredible overwhelming desire she'd had to *believe* him. It was utterly crazy. No matter how big a crush she had on him—and she was pretty sure she was getting over it—she still knew it was nothing more than that. A schoolgirl fantasy about a good-looking guy, dreamed up by a silly woman who'd spent too long without a man and who should know better. Period. She could deal with that. She *did* know better.

Joe was looking for a wife and he'd finally noticed her, that was all.

Forget what he'd said the next morning when he'd stood beside her buttering toast while she'd turned bacon in the frying pan.

"I meant it, what I said yesterday," he'd told her in a low voice with no preamble. "My offer stands. I hope you'll change your mind."

"I won't," she'd whispered back, banging the frying pan on the burner. "I think I made myself perfectly clear yesterday."

"You did, you did. But I asked you if there was any chance you'd change your mind and you didn't say no. You said you didn't think so. That means there's a chance." He brushed her shoulder accidentally-on-purpose with his. She felt the buzz of sensation and stared at him, astonished. He grinned. "I know I bungled things yesterday. Big time. But today's a new day. I'm an optimistic guy or I wouldn't be a farmer. I intend to convince you to change your mind. I haven't given up. If you absolutely mean no, Honor, say it. Say it now. Go ahead."

She'd stared at him, stunned, until he'd said she'd better watch that bacon or it'd burn. She'd been tongue-tied, unwilling and unable to give him an unequivocal final answer. It went against her nature to be so definite, and it went against all her training and experience. You never ever closed out your options. There was always that faint shred of hope....

Then he'd taken the slices of toast to the table and started entertaining the children with some story he was obviously making up as he went along about a toast monster who lived on Porridge Island in the middle of Milk Lake in a fairyland where the snow tasted like sugar.

Honor couldn't help but smile, remembering. No wonder the kids were so crazy about their uncle Joe.

When she drove up to her father-in-law's house, she saw he had another visitor. A big dark-blue Lincoln was parked in the drive. Alec's crony and personal lawyer, Conrad Atkinson. She felt a shiver at the back of her neck, then told herself not to be so suspicious. She was getting as bad as Joe. Perhaps Atkinson was only here on a social visit.

And maybe pigs could fly.

She found the two men in Alec's study. She was surprised that Spinks wasn't with them, as he'd rarely left Alec's side since the old man had come home from the hospital.

Alec greeted her with a smile and a hug with his good right arm. Honor was glad to see him looking so well. She tried to get up to Calgary to see him twice a week, and she noticed improvements with each visit. His color was much better and even his speech had improved tremendously since he'd been working with a therapist.

"Hello, Conrad. Good to see you." She shook the lawyer's hand. Conrad Atkinson was of Alec's generation, with thinning white hair thickly pomaded and combed straight back with the teethmarks showing. He favored pin-striped suits in a style always slightly out of fashion, or at least it seemed that way on Atkinson's large rangy frame. He ran a small private practice out of a downtown office, mostly longstanding clients and cronies like Alec. Honor had always thought he was a bit of a shyster, but she couldn't deny that he'd done good work for Alec in the past. And that was a lawyer's job, after all, to do the best for his client. It wasn't the sort of work Honor would care to take on, but then she'd specialized in another area of law altogether.

"How's Beryl?" she asked. Conrad had a mousy reclusive wife tucked away somewhere. Honor hadn't seen her in years.

"She's well, my dear. She's very well. I'll tell her you inquired." Atkinson was at his smarmiest; Honor contained a small shudder. He must want something. They must both want something from her.

Alec didn't beat around the bush. It wasn't his style. "What about Gallant?" he growled. "I want to see those kids. That son of a bitch can't stop me.

I'm not going to wait forever. Conrad says I don't
have to—''

"Alec!" Honor felt the hairs at the back of her
neck tingle again. "You said you'd leave it up to
me."

"Nothing's happening, Honor. You know that."
He waved one hand. "Nothing's happening. I'm an
old man. Sick." In Honor's opinion, he looked as
well as any man his age could expect to look, barring
the effects of the stroke. "I can't wait forever."

"What have *you* had to do with this?" she demanded, whirling to face Atkinson.

"Now, now, my dear. Don't go gettin' yourself all
worked up over nothing—''

"Nothing!" That was something else she'd always
disliked about Atkinson: he had very little respect for
women, including, she was sure, his wife. "Do you
call conniving to separate a couple of poor orphaned
children from the only home and family they've ever
known, from an uncle they adore, *nothing?* Because
I'm pretty sure that's what the two of you are up
to." She whirled again to glare at her father-in-law.
He had the decency to look away. She was right; she
knew she was right.

"Where's Spinks?" The dogs were missing, too.
Perhaps he'd taken them for a walk.

"Out," Alec said moodily.

"Out where?"

"He didn't say." Alec roused himself. "Damn his
hide anyway. Who pays the bills around here?
Spinks? No, Alec Templeman. Who pays his salary?
Who doesn't ask for much except a little considera-
tion now and then...."

Alec and Spinks must have had a falling-out. It was likely over this business with Conrad Atkinson. Spinks would not be in favor of Alec's trying anything sneaky in the legal department.

Honor stood. She was angrier than she'd ever been with her father-in-law. It felt strange. For so long he'd been all the family she had, he and Parker, and in some ways she'd been closer to her husband's father than she'd been to her husband.

"I won't stay, Alec," she said in as gentle a tone as she could manage. "I'm going to zip over to the apartment, see if there's any mail, and then I'll stop in at the office. I'll come by on my way out of town. When you're free." She looked pointedly at Atkinson. He grinned affably. He didn't even flinch at her words. Why would he? He'd dealt with far more difficult people than her on a client's behalf.

"I want to make my point once more. I think you should forget this," she said stiffly to her father-in-law. "Whatever you've got up your sleeve. Is it custody? Who's going to raise those children? You? Spinks? Sure, you've got money, but even a judge who was blind, deaf and drunk would see that there's more sense in two children being raised in the bosom of a family that loves them, aunts, uncles, cousins, neighbors. You'd be laughed right out of the courtroom. And what do you think the newspapers would say when they got hold of it?"

"You're just afraid everybody will find out Parker had another family somewhere while he was married to you," Conrad began silkily. "Which is indeed a most sad and unfortunate business—"

"Never!" she practically shouted at him. "Do you

think I've bothered to hide that? I haven't. Joe Gallant knows. The whole town of Glory knows. That sort of thing means nothing to me!''

"Look here. Whose side are you on, anyway?'' Alec broke in crankily. "Mine or that bastard Joe Gallant's?''

It was a very good question. Whose side *was* she on?

THE LETTER SHE DREADED came a week later. That afternoon, she was madly getting the children organized and ready to attend an engagement party for the daughter of one of Joe's neighbors. The invitation had apparently arrived earlier, but Joe hadn't told her about it. Perhaps he'd been thinking of taking one of his marriage prospects to the party and then had changed his mind. At any rate, he was insistent that the children were welcome and indeed expected to attend. Honor told herself she was only going to be able to take care of the children; she wasn't going as Joe's "date.''

She was sure his neighbors might regard her presence differently. That was Joe's problem. One he could deal with any way he wanted. In a little more than ten days she'd be heading back to Calgary and back to her regular life. She hadn't thought of it as particularly lonely before she'd spent these weeks on the farm, but now she saw everything a little differently. She knew Joe would not deny her access to the children, and she looked forward to being part of their lives, as their city "auntie,'' for a long long time.

The envelope was among a sheaf of mail that Joe

had tossed on the kitchen table when he'd come back from Glory. He said nothing, but he must have seen her blanch as she riffled idly through the envelopes, bills, flyers and magazines.

"What's wrong?" He looked at her, his hand arrested as he raised it to pour coffee into a mug.

"Nothing," she said, but her voice gave her away. She lowered herself, slowly onto one of the kitchen chairs. Ellie and Alexander had finally gone down for their nap, and she was feeling like she could use one herself.

"Something's wrong," he stated flatly, his gaze flicking to the pile of mail on the table and the envelope in her hand. "Who's that from? Some lawyer, it looks like."

Joe was of the strange—to her mind—class of people who don't open mail that doesn't interest them. She'd seen letters from automotive shops and bills from the post office for box rental stay unopened on top of the refrigerator for days. She was of the class of people who immediately open, organize and discard mail.

"Atkinson and Corbett," she read dully. There was no Corbett. Alec had told her that Corbett, a bachelor, had died shortly after Conrad became a partner and he'd never removed his deceased partner's name from the firm's letterhead.

"Never heard of them."

"Aren't you curious, Joe?" she asked, finally glancing up. What an exasperating man!

"Nope." He took a sip of coffee. "Letters from lawyers are generally not good news. If I had a rich uncle I thought might pop off anytime soon, well, maybe.'' He grinned at her. ''Open it if you're so curious.''

She took a deep breath and opened the envelope. She could be wrong. It could be nothing, perhaps some kind of conciliatory gesture from Alec.

She was not wrong. She scanned the few lines, saw past the legalese and looked up at Joe. ''He wants the kids. He's applied for custody.''

''*Who* wants the kids? Damn it, Honor, what are you talking about?''

''Alec. He's going to try to get the kids away from you.''

Joe grabbed the letter and scanned the lines himself. Then he threw it down on the table and swore. He strode back to the counter and retrieved his coffee.

''Well?'' she asked when he didn't say anything.

''Well?'' he repeated. He looked at her over his coffee cup, his face grim. ''You're the lawyer. What do you figure his chances are?''

''Not good.'' She crossed her fingers behind her back in a childish gesture and prayed she was right. ''I'm presuming your sister's will was very clear....''

''It was. I don't care what kind of legal tricks Alec Templeman plays. If it comes down to some goddamn judge awarding him custody, he's not going to get them. If I have to sell up and leave this place in the middle of the night and move to Hong Kong so he doesn't get these kids, I will.''

Honor yearned to go to him. She could feel his pain right across the kitchen. It was too much, too much for any man. To lose his sister and then to have a man he despised try to take her children from him… She wanted to put her arms around him and promise him she'd stand by him, do everything she could to make sure the children stayed with him.…

That was when Honor realized she'd answered Alec's question. When push came to shove, she was on Joe's side.

"HOW THE HELL am I going to handle this, Honor?"

She and Joe were dancing on the freshly mowed lawn at the Galloway farm, along with what looked like about thirty other couples—plus Ellie, who was dancing with both Webster twins, boys a year or two older than she was. Galloway was a prosperous grain farmer with a big farm southwest of Vulcan. He had seven daughters, and the middle one, Emma, planned to marry an insurance broker from Lethbridge in November. So Papa Galloway had thrown a big party for the whole community to celebrate. Alexander was being dandled by a group of ladies in hats who sat on the patio, where tables of refreshments had been set up. Two small boys with whisk brooms had been delegated to keep the wasps away.

Honor didn't answer immediately. She didn't know what to say. She shouldn't be giving him legal advice; he should consult his own lawyer for that. Not that she could, without doing research, but she at least knew the principles involved. Joe had been preoccupied by the news of Alec's threat ever since she'd opened the letter, although he'd denied it.

Not once had he even hinted that *she* might be tangled up in Alec's machinations. *He trusted her.* The tenderness she'd felt earlier hadn't gone away. If anything, the fact that he'd just assumed she'd be on his side regarding custody of the children—the side of right—had made her feel even closer to him. That, and being held in his arms in this delicious wonderful way in front of all these people. Why couldn't she relax, let herself go?

Like Ben and his girlfriend, whom she'd surprised one morning at the Longquists' when she'd gone over there after breakfast to feed Jill's fish. Ben, clad only in a towel, had raced into the kitchen, followed by a young woman clad only in one of his shirts, chasing him and laughing uproariously. Ben had slammed to a halt and rather sheepishly introduced Rhonda Maclean. Clearly Rhonda had spent the night. Honor hadn't known whether to be shocked— Ben was an adult, after all, and so was Rhonda—or envious of their free spirits and healthy sexuality.

"I think I'll just throw the letter in the trash and forget about it," Joe said, smiling at her.

He'd do it, too. She wrenched her thoughts back to the utter pleasure of dancing in Joe's arms. "If they're serious, they'll send you another one. It might not look good for you if you ignore it. After all, he does have some kind of claim as grandfather."

"Bullshit," Joe said cheerfully. "Now let's forget all about Alec Templeman and think about us. Hmm?"

"Joe," she began weakly, her defenses crumbling by the second. "There is no *us*."

"You're wrong—there is," he said, smiling and pulling her a little closer. Oh, yes, she liked the feeling of being in his arms. And it had to be safe enough; he could hardly try anything with sixty or seventy people looking on.

"You're the woman I want," he began in a low voice, and her heart jumped. "You're beautiful, you're sexy and you're smart. That's my idea of the woman I want to marry. You're attracted to me and you have no idea how attracted I am to you—"

"Joe!"

"In fact, I'd like nothing better right now than to dance you around that corner by the machine shed—" with a nod he indicated a big steel building nearby "—crawl up into one of Galloway's combines and make love to you—"

"*Joe!*"

"Think anybody's ever made love in a combine before? We could always be the first." He laughed as though delighted with his idea. Honor laughed, too. She couldn't help herself. When he was in this kind of crazy mood, there was no one she'd rather be with. He made her forget all her serious views about this and that, all her careful considered opinions, her naturally cautious nature. He made her laugh. No other man had ever done that. He made her laugh and he made her blood run hot. If only he wasn't such a tease and a flirt! No woman could possibly know when to take him seriously.

"Joe—"

"It's true, isn't it?" His urgent gaze bored into hers. "You're attracted to me, right?"

Honor licked her lips, which felt dry all of a sudden. "I am. I have to be honest, Joe," she began hesitantly. She had to get this straight with him! "I *am* attracted to you. You're an attractive man. Lots of women would be attracted—"

"We're not talking about lots of women. We're talking about you. And me." He grinned.

"Okay." She took a deep breath and started again. "I am attracted to you. Yes, I am. But that's neither here nor there. I could be attracted to other men, too, and—"

"But you're not," he said confidently. "It's me you want."

"Joe! If you don't take this seriously, I'm not going to say what I have to say."

"Okay. I won't interrupt. Promise." The gleam in his eye left her with a different impression.

"I am attracted to you but I'll get over it, let's put it that way." She regarded him. He didn't seem put out in the least. "I will not and cannot marry you for many reasons, most importantly because I do not love you and you do not love me."

"I know how I feel. And for you…things could change."

That surprised her. She looked at him. He was still smiling, but his eyes were very serious now. "I…I suppose it could. Anything could happen."

"You never like to say *never,* right?"

She tried to shrug but couldn't quite manage it as he whirled her around at the end of the patio. She wanted to make it clear that she was speaking generally. "Anything could change about anything. Anytime."

To her amazement he dropped a quick kiss on her forehead. "I'll remind you of that, sweetheart. I'll enjoy watching you eat your words someday."

Ellie appeared out of the jumble of children on the grass and grabbed at Joe's leg. "Dance with me, Uncle Joe! Dance with me!"

CHAPTER THIRTEEN

THE CHILDREN were both sound asleep in the back of her car by the time they returned to the farm. Honor had driven cautiously over the graveled roads, following Joe's brief directions, acutely aware of him sitting in the passenger seat beside her.

They'd excused themselves from the party about nine o'clock, saying the children needed to be taken home to bed. Ellie would have danced the night away, Honor thought, but Alexander was fussing and refused to be held by anyone but her. The molar that had been giving him trouble had popped through a week before, but Honor was sure he was getting more teeth. The fact that he'd wanted her, even over his uncle, had made her feel such foolish pride, such a strange sense of *motherliness*, that she'd nearly wept. She was beginning to dread the end of the month. They'd heard from Nan and Harry, and the Longquists were setting out on their leisurely trip back to Canada from California any day now.

Joe didn't say much on the ride home—which suited her fine—and when they arrived at the farm, he carried Ellie into the house, still sleeping, while she brought in Alexander. They got the children into their pajamas and into bed without either one of them really waking up fully.

Honor was exhausted. She was ready for bed herself. Was it too early to say good-night? Was she avoiding Joe? She couldn't help thinking about the letter they'd had from Conrad Atkinson that afternoon—then caught herself. The letter *he'd* had. Not her.

She walked into the kitchen to find all quiet. She was relieved. She was just about to head back down the hall toward her bedroom when Joe came into the kitchen from outside. It wasn't dark yet, but the sun had gone down and it was a full, rich late-summer evening. The air was cool and the scents of the ripening grain and the earth and the pungent poplars, limbs waving gently in the night breeze, wafted in through the screen door.

"Join me on the veranda for a nightcap?" he said. He looked preoccupied, almost surprised to see her standing there. Was he thinking of Alec's demands, as she was?

"That would be nice," she said. She'd be in bed soon enough. He obviously wanted some company. "What are you having?"

"Brandy."

"I'll have a brandy and hot milk," she said, moving toward the fridge.

Joe held up one hand. "You go sit down. I'll make it and bring it out to you."

Honor went outside and stood for a minute or two at the top of the steps, breathing deeply. It was so calm and quiet, such a beautiful night. She'd gained an appreciation for the small pleasures of rural life—pleasures she hadn't known about before.

"What are you smiling at?" Joe appeared at the door, a snifter in one hand, a mug in the other. He gave her the mug and she took a sip of the strong sweet brandied milk.

"Mmm."

"Not too sweet?"

"Perfect."

"So, what were you smiling at just now?" he repeated. He moved toward the old love seat at one end of the veranda, and she moved toward it with him. He sat down carefully on the creaky wobbly seat and stretched out his legs and sighed. She stood at the wooden balustrade, looking at the gently undulating fields to the southwest. She heard the cry of some strange bird, high and faraway. Not a magpie; she was beginning to know that characteristic sound.

"I was thinking how ironic it was that, when I first came here, I couldn't get to sleep because I missed the lights and the noise of the city."

"And now?"

She turned to him. "Now I think I'll miss this." She sipped her drink and made a small gesture with her other hand. "All of this. It's so lovely and peaceful."

"You like it?" His voice was gruff.

"I do."

He smiled and tilted his brandy. "I like it, too. I'm a settled-down kind of guy. Always have been." He waved his left hand toward the fields. "This is my dream. I'm living it. I've always wanted to be a farmer."

There was a comfortable silence as they both sipped their drinks. When Honor made to pull forward one of the rickety chairs drawn up against the side of the house, Joe patted the love seat. "Sit here. With me. I promise not to bite."

She sat down beside him. She believed him; she trusted him. He wasn't going to try anything. And even if he did bite, did she really mind?

"Honor…"

He paused for so long she thought he'd changed his mind about what he'd intended to say. She glanced at him and raised her mug to her mouth. He appeared agitated in profile, drawn. Even angry.

"I know you're wondering why I feel so strongly about Alec Templeman. I didn't plan to tell you, considering it happened so long ago and all. But now that I've asked you to marry me and now that I've had this letter, I want to set you straight on why I'm being so…well, what you probably consider stubborn. You think I'm crazy, don't you?"

His anguished gaze sought hers and Honor felt alarmed. What could possibly have happened between Alec and him that was such a terrible painful secret?

"I'm going to tell you." Joe took a mouthful of his brandy, then another one, as though preparing himself for the ordeal of confession. Then he looked at her again, and his eyes were lit from within. By memory, by strong emotion, by something else she couldn't quite fathom. Grief, perhaps. *Hate*.

"Alec and I go way back. You probably weren't aware of this, but Parker and my sister went way back, too."

She shook her head. This was news to her. "What do you mean? Before Parker and I got married?"

"Yes. They first met nearly fifteen years ago. Sylvie and I were twenty-two and Parker was a year or so younger. We were living in Glory then, although I'd been at college for a couple of years. My dad had left us and headed for the West Coast a few years before that. Nan was married. Nicholas had left, too. It was pretty much our mother and Sylvie living in a little rented place on Harboldt Street. I wasn't home much. School in the winter, oil rigs in the summer.''

Joe paused and didn't say anything else for quite a long time. Honor sat quietly, not wanting to interrupt his thoughts, but her mind was spinning with his news about Parker.

"Parker showed up in town one day. He was working at some farm. Driving tractor. Or maybe it was a ranch, I don't remember. Anyway, I guess his old man had sent him out for the summer to get his hands dirty, see how the other half lived. He met my sister and they fell in love. Hard. They were young and they were crazy about each other, and next thing I knew, Sylvie told me they were going to run away and get married. She told me everything in those days.''

He paused again, then ran one hand through his hair and over his face before going on, ''They had to run away, she said, because Parker's father would put a stop to it if he knew about it. By then my sister was pregnant. One day the old man showed up and there was a hell of a fight. He took Parker back to Calgary with him and she never saw him again. The old man sent her a check, which she was fool enough to tear up and mail back to him. I've always wondered if the shock of what happened interfered with her pregnancy. But I suppose it was just as well. She lost the baby.''

He looked at her and Honor stared back at him, thunderstruck. She ached for him and for Sylvie. And for Parker, weak, foolish Parker. And even for Alec. *And for the poor lost babe.*

''I tracked the old bastard down and had it out with him. He laughed. He had me thrown out of his office. He said his son was too good for trash like Sylvie Gallant. That he had other plans for him that did not include being shackled to the first woman he'd ever slept with—he put it a little more crudely than that, but you get the drift.'' Joe glanced at her. Honor was paralyzed with horror. *Was she that "other plan" Alec had had for Parker?*

''I swore I'd never forgive him and I never have. My sister never got over it. She fell into one thing after the other in the next few years, most of them not good. I pulled her out of quite a few scrapes, did what I could. She got married to some loser, then divorced, had a few years where she drank too much, worked here and there trying to support herself and my mother, waitressing. My mother finally died not too long after. She was old-fashioned. She'd never really recovered from what she'd felt was Sylvie's big disgrace.''

Joe made a hoarse sound that Honor realized was an attempt at laughter. She stared at him. She felt as if her own heart had turned to stone. No wonder Joe felt the way he did about Alec—he believed Alec had ruined his sister's life. Maybe even believed Alec's actions had killed his mother.

''Crazy, eh? Here our *maman* was, abandoned by

a husband who barely supported her and us kids, who spent his whole life chasing the horses, and she thought her unmarried daughter getting pregnant was some kind of major disgrace?'' He shook his head. ''That and Sylvie's divorce. Crazy! *Maman* was a good Acadian Catholic. She didn't believe in divorce.

''Anyway. None of it helped Sylvie. Then one day Parker showed up here in Glory again, looking for her. Nearly five years ago. It was like first love all over. This time I knew nothing would stop her. I didn't even try to do anything about it, although I had a feeling Parker was not good news. My sister was happy. She was happier than she'd ever been. So was Parker. The two kids came along and...well, I just thought that was pretty much the end of the story.

''I figured Parker had finally stood up to his father and told him what he could do with himself. I never asked him. We weren't close. The old man could have been dead, for all I knew. I never dreamed the reason Parker hadn't gotten around to marrying my sister was that he was already married.'' Joe glanced at Honor and took a big drink and coughed. ''To you.''

Honor's face burned. She hoped it was dark enough now that Joe wouldn't notice. Not that any of this was her fault, but she'd...she'd had no idea how bitter and complicated matters were between Joe's family and Alec.

''Yes,'' she murmured, and shrugged slightly, hopelessly. ''To me.'' She pushed back the pain. She felt like the pawn in this whole sordid business. Alec

had never told her about Parker's love affair with
Sylvie, probably thought it wasn't worth mentioning.
Parker had never told her, either. She felt betrayed,
as though neither had trusted her enough to tell her
the truth. Then again, how much good would it have
done? She'd known very well that when Parker married her, he'd done it mainly to please his father. And
had she refused? No, she'd gone along with everything. In a way, she was as much to blame for going
along with the too-convenient marriage as they were
for promoting it.

"Look, sweetheart," Joe said, turning to her and
taking her hand. Her hand felt ice cold in his; his
was so warm. "None of this is your problem. Parker
was a damn fool to walk out on you. Any man can
see that."

"Don't try and make me feel any better about it,
Joe. Please. The truth is, he didn't want me. He was
in love with someone else. I can accept that. Don't
make out like he was crazy to leave me. He wasn't.
I'm not that great a catch, you know." She tried for
a laugh herself, but it didn't come out very well. It
sounded more like a gulp. But when Joe leaned toward her—she knew he wanted to take her in his
arms—she stiffened. She wanted no man's sympathy.
Ever.

She stood. "Thank you for telling me this, Joe. I
wish I'd known before." She gripped her empty mug
in both hands until she felt her knuckles crack. "I
mean that. It makes everything a lot clearer. I don't
blame you for feeling the way you do."

She stared off into the shadows and blinked back
sudden tears. "I can't say I agree, though. Alec is

old and he's not well. Maybe he's had a change of heart.''

"If he's had a change of heart, why in hell is he trying to get the kids away from me?" Joe got abruptly to his feet. He was furious, but she realized it wasn't with her. "Can you answer me that?"

"I don't know, Joe. I just don't know." She shook her head and turned back to him. She reached out and put her hand on his arm. She had to touch him. The muscles beneath her fingers were iron-hard with tension. "I wish none of this had happened. But I have no answers," she whispered, searching his eyes. "None at all."

"Honor, sweetheart…" He covered her hand with his, gripped her fingers in his, pulled her toward him. "Honor—"

"No!" She snatched her hand away and ran back toward the house.

THIS WAS FAR too important to push. He knew that. If he had to take it slow and easy, he would. If he had to think more about what he should do than he ever had before, he would.

Nothing mattered but winning. And he already had so many strikes against him.

Luckily he had the short term figured out, with Nan when she got back and then Bea Hoople afterward. In the middle term, there was getting off his grain crops—he couldn't abandon his livelihood. Then there was the long-term job of convincing Honor that she was way off base in thinking his marriage offer was an impulse.

Maybe it had been an impulse at first. But as soon

as he'd spoken, he'd known it was true: he wanted
Honor to marry him. *He was in love with her.* It was
such a crazy mixed-up feeling that he almost felt like
he'd never been in love before. And maybe he hadn't
been. Not like this.

He thought of the women he'd carefully lined up
to pursue in the matrimonial campaign he'd begun.
Good decent women, all of them. But not a one held
a candle to Honor.

If Parker hadn't left her to come to Glory after
Sylvie... Joe shuddered to think of all the *what if*s.
It was so unlikely, sometimes, the way life twisted
and turned. He might so easily never have met
Honor, and now he couldn't imagine *not* knowing
her. Couldn't imagine his life going on without her.
Couldn't imagine taking another woman for a wife
eventually, if Honor really refused to marry him.

And she was leaving in less than a week, as soon
as Nan and Harry returned. He could hardly stand to
think of it.

He wouldn't crowd her. He'd give her every opportunity to see that he wasn't trying to force her
into anything. Not trying to rush her. Every opportunity to see what a gentleman he could be. So he
would quit with the marriage talk for now, hope
she'd gradually come to feel a little differently about
him. Maybe trust him more. Maybe feel a little more
the way he felt about her.

Was that hoping for too much? Joe knew he was
an optimist. He told himself that if it took time to
woo her, he'd make time. If it required particular
circumstances, he'd create those circumstances. He
intended to win by a steady process of meeting her

every objection and showing her, in the end, that she belonged with him.

He only hoped he'd be able to last. It took every scrap of self-control he had not to touch her, not to take her in his arms when he knew she was hurting, for instance, like the night after the party when he'd told her about Alec Templeman. Not to kiss her again.

He didn't dare; she didn't believe his motives for marriage. She was convinced he was just looking for a mother for his niece and nephew and that almost any decent woman would do.

There was one piece of luck and it was on his side—she loved those two kids. If he just had the patience, he had no doubt he'd get what he wanted— what they both wanted, he believed. He'd marry her.

Nan and Harry arrived on the Friday of Labor Day weekend. They'd stopped at Pincher Creek and called ahead, so Joe passed the word on to Honor, who immediately sent him to Glory to pick up several buckets of Grizzly chicken and ribs. He'd never thought he'd be so unhappy to hear from his oldest sister—damn, why couldn't they have had a breakdown in Montana and been delayed a week? Two weeks?

So that was that, he thought gloomily, driving home with the food. It was over. Honor would be on her way back to Calgary in a day or two. Maybe she'd even want to go today after they'd had a meal with the Longquists. She'd said she'd like to come to his ball tournament, which was starting tomorrow, but that was when they thought Nan and Harry might arrive home toward the end of the weekend, not the beginning.

Maybe he could hold her to it.

When he got to the farm, Honor was just putting a mammoth potato salad in the refrigerator. On the fridge shelves he caught a glimpse of other salad activities that had gone on in his absence. Her cheeks were flushed, her eyes were bright. She looked beautiful to him. And flustered. He wanted to spin her around and plant a kiss on her rosy mouth.

Maybe someday. Not now.

About five o'clock he walked out onto the veranda to see the big motor home nosing its way down the lane. He waved and grinned as Ellie went streaking across the yard, shouting, "Auntie Nan! Jill! Pheeb!" at the top of her lungs. Alexander toddled behind, slower, a little shaky on the uneven ground, but just as determined as his sister.

Joe heard a tiny sound at his shoulder and glanced around to see Honor right behind him. He moved slightly to one side and she stepped forward. Her eyes were glowing. She looked as happy to see the Longquists as, deep down, he was. Or maybe she was just anxious to be on her way.

"I think they had a good trip," he said inanely, incredibly conscious of her nearness. Jill and Trevor had leapt out the back of the RV, Phoebe following somewhat more sedately. Jill swung Alexander up into her arms and he chortled with pleasure.

"It's lovely to see them," Honor murmured, "isn't it? They look happy and healthy, all of them." She was pleating the corner of her apron between her fingers.

He gave her a sharp glance, but she didn't seem to notice. She was mesmerized by the arrival of his sister and her family. He had no idea why, except that maybe she saw their presence as the key to her own freedom.

Then there was a great deal of noise and excitement as the entire family climbed out of the motor home. Nan arranged the wheelchair for Harry, and he levered himself down into it from the passenger side, braced on his muscular arms. Dogs barked; children yelled; his sister's chatter overwhelmed him.

Honor hung back, as though she thought she didn't belong with the rest during the noisy welcome. She seemed shy. Joe hauled her forward, one arm loosely around her shoulders, and replied to all his sister's questions about the children and the garden and the events that had occurred while they'd been gone. Honor colored slightly but didn't pull away. Joe noticed his sister's interested look; no doubt she thought something was up between the two of them. Well, damn it, something *was* up. He'd asked Honor to marry him, hadn't he?

"Well," Nan said with a sigh, "I guess we should head on over to our place and see how Ben's looked after things."

"The fish are fine," Honor said. "And Joe took good care of Charlie and Mac." Charlie was the Longquists' part-collie mongrel and Mac was the terrier. Even as they spoke on the veranda, the dogs frolicked with Trevor, barking and fighting over sticks the boy threw for them.

"Please join us for supper," Honor added softly with a quick look up at Joe. He tightened his grip on her shoulders. "I confess I've raided your garden for lettuce and tomatoes all month. And your beans are pretty well finished. We've had several meals."

"I'm glad someone could use them, that's all. Well, Harry? Shall we just stay here for supper? Sounds like Honor and Joe have everything under control. Thanks, you two." She smiled at her brother. Joe allowed himself the tiniest of winks, which his sister clearly saw. Her smile broadened.

"Let me help you, Honor." The two women disappeared into the kitchen.

Joe set up a couple of tables under the trees. He filled the kids' pool with fresh water, then dumped the washtub and refilled it. He fed the dogs on the back porch where they'd been eating for the past few weeks, then went into the kitchen and pulled a couple of cold beers from the fridge to take out to his brother-in-law.

He was pleased to note that his sister was talking to Honor as though they'd known each other for years. Honor was telling her about Alexander's new tooth, and Nan was dredging up a teething story from Ben's childhood. Joe took the beers out back, where Harry was sitting under the trees, handed him one and pulled up a chair beside him. They had a lot to catch up on.

Later, during the meal, the student he'd hired for the summer, Tim Abbott, joined them. Then at about eight o'clock, a dusty pickup clattered into the yard and Ben climbed out. His mother flew down the steps to embrace him in a big motherly hug. The boy grinned and blushed, maybe a little embarrassed at all the attention. When Ben came up the steps, Joe noticed that he was careful to include Honor in his greetings. Not that there was any reason he wouldn't, but Joe could swear something passed between the two of them. Some private knowledge. He glanced from one to the other, but both looked away. What was that all about?

Honor was quiet during the meal. There'd been no mention of her returning to Calgary, so Joe was pretty sure she was staying at least one more day. He mentioned the upcoming ball tournament, casually checking for her reaction.

There wasn't much. She gazed at him, a little starry-eyed, which was how she'd been all afternoon since the Longquists arrived. More than once he'd caught her looking at him. He'd done his share of observing her, too. He thought she was even more beautiful than the day he'd first seen her, in her polished leather shoes, her matching suit, her big-city haircut. Now she looked tanned, relaxed, healthy…glowing.

At some point during dessert—ice cream and the raspberries Nan had sent her daughters to pick from the Longquist garden—Ellie engaged Honor in a serious conversation. Joe was a little too faraway to overhear, but he noticed that Honor spoke to the girl, then looked over at him. A few seconds later Ellie appeared in front of him.

"Can we sleep in the big camper, Uncle Joe? Can we? Can we? Phoebe says she'll take care of us." Joe thought back to the day Honor had first shown up at the farm. His niece had sure looked after the kids that day!

"What does Honor say, El?"

"She says it's up to you. She says it's all right with her if you think it's all right?"

Joe glanced at Honor and was stunned to see the feeling in her eyes. It was as though she was trying to tell him something. But what? He glanced at his sister. "What do you think, Nan? Ellie'd be fine out there, but what about Alexander?"

"Oh, he'll be okay. Phoebe's perfectly capable when she wants to be," she said, waving a spoon in her daughter's direction. Phoebe was curled up in the hammock, her nose in a book. "The kids have all kinds of presents for Ellie and the baby. Go ahead and let them stay. We don't have to return the motor home to the Prescotts until next week.

"All right." Joe grinned at his niece and tousled her blond head. She tore off to give Phoebe the good news. Alexander hadn't paused in his careful up-and-down negotiation of the bottommost back step. He'd been going up and down that same step for the past ten minutes.

That evening, after the children had left, the place seemed very quiet. Ben had gone back to the Double O, where he worked as a summer wrangler for Adam Garrick. Tim Abbott had gone to town. Nan had moved the motor home and parked it in front of their own house. Even the dogs had deserted him and decamped to the Longquists', definitely the more exciting of the two places at present.

Joe sat on the veranda until it got dark. Honor had disappeared after the Longquists left. He wondered if she was packing. He didn't want to find out. Finally, when he heard a coyote yip and another one answer, he got up and went into the house. Only the light over the kitchen stove was on; he snapped it off and walked to his room in the semidark. Maybe she'd gone to bed early. Joe had noticed all summer that she spent a lot of time in her room.

He sighed. Now what? He'd have to let her go. Then, after she'd had a chance to get settled back in Calgary, he'd call her. He wasn't going to quit. Maybe they'd date, the way other couples did. Maybe she'd come out to the farm from time to time to visit the kids and he'd have the chance to ask her to marry him again.

He had a quick shower and pulled on his bathrobe, then irritably picked up a magazine from his bedside table. He flicked on a reading lamp and sat down in the rocking chair by the window. It was too damn early to go to bed.

At that moment his door opened and Honor came in. She was wearing a sexy pale pink garment with a neckline that showed the tops of her small perfect breasts. Joe's magazine slid unnoticed from his lap to the floor. He felt like his jaw had dropped with it. *What the…?*

"I'm going home soon, Joe," she said. Her voice was breathless, whispery. Fear? Nerves? "I feel I've got some unfinished business with you."

"What's that?" It wasn't a croak. At least his voice was okay. Which was a lot more than he could say for the rest of him.

"I told you I was attracted to you. I've decided I want to have sex with you, if that's all right. Just once."

CHAPTER FOURTEEN

IF THAT'S ALL RIGHT? He swallowed hard. Then he carefully cleared his throat. She looked scared to death.

"Come here," he said, and held out one hand.

Honor walked slowly toward him. He called upon all his willpower and kept his eyes steady on hers when the only thing he wanted to do was feast his gaze on the rest of her.

He reached out and touched the shimmery waist of her garment and smiled and she sank into his arms. It was wonderful. Precious. A feeling he'd never had before—that she was tender and beautiful and all his. He pulled her onto his lap sideways, his arms around her, her head tucked against his shoulder. He cleared his throat again and looked at her.

"Just once?" he couldn't resist teasing. But it seemed the right thing to do, because Honor smiled back, then blinked rapidly.

"I...I didn't know how you'd take it," she said huskily.

Joe thought about that. "Take what?" He frowned slightly and reveled in the warmth and weight of her on his lap. His left arm curved around her neck and shoulders, and his right hand itched to cup the contour of her breast. He didn't dare...yet.

"You know—me coming in like this. Putting it so plainly that I wanted to have sex with you before I left." She blushed. Delightfully. Clearly she was not in the habit of asking men to sleep with her. "If you don't mind, that is."

"Honor, honey…" He tilted her chin so that she had to look at him. Had to look straight into his eyes. "I don't mind. At all. Believe me. In fact, I'm overwhelmed. I'm eager, I'm willing, I'm very very happy. It's just that, uh, this is kind of a surprise. What's it about?"

He searched her gaze. She looked embarrassed and tried to pull away. He wouldn't let her. "You say you want to have sex with me—'just once' is the way you put it, I believe." He dipped his head and kissed her lightly on the lips. She caught her breath, eyes wide, searching his. "I want to *make love* with you, Honor. Not have sex. I want to make love, and not just once, either. I want to marry you. I want to make love with you every night for the rest of our lives together and—"

"Joe," she broke in, and touched his mouth with her index finger. "Don't talk like that. I don't want that. If this is going to be complicated, I'll just go back to my room." She struggled to sit straighter on his lap and this time he let her.

He realized now that she'd given this a lot of thought. And preparation. Her hair was softly curled, she was wearing perfume. And makeup. He tasted lipstick, too. He hated kissing women who wore lipstick. He'd never seen her wearing lipstick before. What the hell was going on here?

"So what's this about?"

"It's, uh, a bit of an experiment."

"Experiment?"

"I haven't had any kind of relationship with a man for a long time." She took a deep breath. "A physical one...since my husband left. That's more than five years ago, as you know." She took another deep breath. This was hard for her. "I decided this summer that I was going to make some changes in my life. When I get back to Calgary, I...I think I'm going to start dating again. Seriously."

She met his gaze and shrugged slightly. "You seem kind of attracted to me and I'm definitely attracted to you, so I thought, why not? I want to see if, well, if it'll work. I thought if it works with you, it'll work with somebody else."

She bit her lip, as though realizing what her reasons might sound like to him.

"So, your idea is just to give sex a try again," he said. "With me."

She paused for a few seconds before replying. "Yes," she said simply. That was one of the things he loved about her: she was so damned honest.

"You're just kind of...using me? More or less?"

"I...I guess you could say that."

"So you can get up your courage to chase after some other man when you go back to Calgary?"

"That's putting it a little strongly, perhaps. But...yes," she said, then added quickly, "It must sound terrible...."

"Well, you know something?" he asked, smiling broadly. He felt good. He felt terrific. He didn't mind her reasons at all. At least she was in the marriage market, same as him. Or what she might call the *relationship* market. It was just that they saw the whole thing somewhat differently. No, a lot differently.

"What?"

"I'm not worried."

She nodded, her eyes locked on his. She looked a little bewildered.

"Know why I'm not worried?"

"Why?"

"Because after you make love with me, you're not going to want to make love with any other guy." He grinned, feeling incredibly arrogantly male, and held her tighter. It was true. This was his woman and he'd been handed this amazing chance to prove it to her.

He remained silent for a few minutes and felt her relax in his arms. He pulled her against him then and she didn't resist. Lipstick or no lipstick, he wasn't letting this chance get away from him. He kissed her, caught his breath at her response and kissed her again.

When he raised his head, her eyes were melting. His heart was melting. She was so scared he could feel it. She hadn't been with a man for a long time. He had to make this good for her. To make it *work,* as she put it.

He had an idea.

He stood with her still in his arms, then turned and deposited her in the chair. "Wait here a minute, Honor. I'll be right back."

He left her looking puzzled and walked down the hall to the main bathroom with the big cast-iron old-fashioned tub. He turned the water on full blast and shook some of Ellie's bubble-bath crystals into the water. He watched it foam up for a few seconds, then stalked back to his room.

Honor could use a couple of lessons on how to get a man's attention. A *real* man's attention.

WHAT WAS GOING ON? Honor ran her tongue over her lips and shivered. Joe's kisses were everything she'd dreamed of. It had taken every scrap of courage she'd had to walk into his bedroom and offer herself, but she'd made up her mind she was going to do it before she left. The time was now. She'd leave tomorrow. She would never have gone through with it if the children had been sleeping in the house. The fact that they weren't seemed almost like fate. She'd never have another chance like this.

It was definitely a risk. Having sex with Joe would change things between them, but the risk was worth taking, she'd decided. And she'd made it clear that she wasn't looking for anything more than one night.

She'd been thinking about it for weeks. Ever since she'd discovered Ben and Rhonda in Nan's house, laughing and tearing around in little more than towels, having a lot of fun in the aftermath of a night spent together. She'd wondered why she couldn't feel free, too. The way Ben and Rhonda obviously did. Was it because she was thirty-one and had almost no experience with a man besides her husband, and that was so long ago she'd practically forgotten it?

Maybe she'd been hiding behind her work for years now. But she was determined to change. She'd never believed she was particularly attractive to men. Spending a night with Joe might change that. She'd go back to Calgary confident, feeling more of a woman, secure in her own sexuality and ready to look for a mate and partner in life.

Was she using Joe? She supposed she was. But Joe was perfectly free to turn her down. He was a grown man. She smiled as she thought of his response, that after him, she wouldn't want anyone else—which brought on another shiver, this time of pure anticipation.

She heard his footsteps outside the bedroom door and there he was, strong, magnificent and sure of himself, with a broad grin on his face. Before she could say a word, he'd scooped her up and was striding down the hall with her.

"Joe!" She clung to his neck, afraid he'd drop her. "What are you doing?"

"Lesson one," he said, still grinning. He kicked wide the door to the bathroom and carried her in. The bath was billowing with foam and the water was running. "I don't care what you do with other guys, but I want to make love with *you*, Honor. Pure, unadulterated you."

"*What?*" She tightened her hold on his neck and gave a little scream as he stepped up to the tub.

"That means forget the makeup and perfume and all that other junk. In you go."

And he dumped her in the tub!

Honor couldn't believe what was happening. She'd spent a good hour preparing herself for her encounter with Joe, and that had included doing her hair and nails and even giving herself a very unprofessional-quality pedicure.

She screamed again. Thank goodness the children

weren't home! Joe laughed and reached across her to turn off the faucets. The water level was high and the bubbles billowed over the sides.

"Damn, I wish that tub was bigger," he said, kneeling down beside it and leaning his elbows on the rim. They were on the same level and she could look straight into his eyes. "If it was, I'd get right in there with you."

"My slip!" Honor suddenly realized she still had her silk slip on, the only garment she had with her that even remotely passed for sexy.

Joe's eyes dropped to her breasts. She didn't dare look, knowing the wet silk must be nearly invisible. She blushed. "So that's what it is," he murmured, and slowly brought one hand up to cup her breast. "A slip." His hand felt wonderful. His eyes were hot. *He wanted her.* She shivered again, then reminded herself that this…this brute had dumped her in the bath.

"Joe, this is ridiculous," she began, trying hard to put some determination in her tone. "Outrageous."

He didn't appear to have heard her. He stroked the contours of her breast lightly, then slipped his left hand under her hair and brought her close. "You are so damn beautiful, Honor," he murmured. "You take my breath away." Then he kissed her, a deep, hungry, searching kiss that went on and on until she gasped for air.

She knew her cheeks were pink, her lungs heaving. His hands were on her everywhere, under the water, dipping beneath her wet slip, seeking, finding. She was on fire.

"I love kissing you, but I sure hate kissing all that

makeup,'' he said softly, eyes gleaming. "Take a deep breath, honey.''

Idiotically she did—now, why did she *do* that? Just because he said to? He put both hands on her shoulders and pushed her under the water. She came up sputtering and swearing.

Joe was laughing. He had a sponge in one hand and began to wipe off her face. "Uh-uh. Not nice language for a lady.'' He shook his head. "Not nice at all.''

"My hair!'' Honor rubbed the water from her eyes, then glanced in horror at her fingers. Her mascara was running. "I just did my hair!''

"Yeah. It was nice, but I like it better now. Just you. And let's wipe off the rest of this stuff, too,'' he added, and gently wiped her face all over with the sponge. So much for her extra-careful makeup job.

"Whatever gave you the idea that you have to be all gussied up to make love?''

"Have sex,'' she snapped, blowing a bubble off her chin.

"Have sex,'' he said agreeably. "I want to make love to you just the way you are. Sweet, honest—''

"Plain.''

"Beautiful.'' He lifted her hair, which now hung in ropes on her shoulders.

What an irritating man she had to pick for her big experiment. "Let's be serious, Joe. I'm plain, unattractive, scrawny, ordinary—''

"You're beautiful, sexy, lovable, funny, smart and—'' he paused and his eyes met hers again "—I have a huge case of the hots for you. Cross my heart and hope to die.'' He quickly sketched an X on his chest. ''There's no other woman on earth I'd rather be with. Now or anytime.''

Could it possibly be true? That she actually was physically appealing to a man like Joe Gallant? He could have anyone. Why would he pick her?

''Look at me, Joe.''

''I'm looking.''

She lifted a dank strand of her hair. ''Look at this—boring mousy brown hair.''

''Gorgeous hair.'' He buried his hands in it and drew her close again, touching her lips softly with his. ''Silky, shiny—'' he kissed her again ''—and when it's dry, it dances around your face like something alive.''

''Yes, a mouse!''

''No, a lion. A panther. Some beautiful cat with very sharp claws that a man doesn't dare forget about.''

''My nose.''

''What about it?''

''Ordinary, straight—'' She remembered pushing up the tip of her nose as a child, thinking it would take on the interesting ski-jump profile of the most popular girls.

''Classic.'' Joe ran his finger down her nose, then kissed the tip of it. ''Beautiful. I love your nose.''

''My mouth,'' she breathed. This litany of praise was intoxicating. Crazy, nice of Joe, although completely untrue—but intoxicating all the same. ''Too wide.''

''Beautiful mouth. So generous.'' Joe kissed her lightly, softly. She could feel every nerve in her body humming, just waiting for his touch. *She wanted him so much.* "Kissable, delicious—mmm." He kissed her again. "I love your mouth. Lesson two, Honor. Trust the man you choose."

Honor felt like a volcano about to erupt right out of the foaming bath. "Oh, Joe," she whispered. "You don't have to do any of this. Say any of that stuff. I just—" her voice broke a little "—I just feel so *silly* now. I...I thought it would be a simple thing—"

"Nothing's simple, Honor." He stood, then bent over and lifted her out of the bath. Water streamed onto the floor, onto his bathrobe. He held her tight against his chest. His robe was wet. "Nothing's simple. Not the way I feel about you. Not the way I want you, which is more than I've ever wanted any woman. Not the way you came into my life."

He set her down, then toweled her hair semidry, stripped off her wet slip, which she allowed him to do as she stood there trembling, unashamed. He toweled her shivering body reverently, touched her everywhere, kissed her everywhere, set every square inch of her skin on fire. Then, with an oath—muttering that he couldn't take any more, he was just a man—he carried her back to his bedroom and set her on his bed. He tossed his bathrobe onto the chair and lay beside her and pulled her into his arms. As naked, as eager...as willing as she was.

Honor closed her eyes, but he made her open them. She tried not to touch him, fearful that she'd do something dumb or it wouldn't be what he wanted, and he made her touch him. They kissed and kissed and then, when she thought she couldn't stand it anymore, Joe entered her and they melded together, man and woman. So easy. So perfectly joined, so natural. So perfectly tuned each to the other, as though they'd done this a thousand times. As though it wasn't the first time ever.

Joe made love to her like a man possessed. He brought her to the verge of unbearable pleasure, until she cried out for completion, until at last they trembled, both at the gate of the joyous mystery they'd created between them and he whispered in her ear, "Marry me, Honor. *Marry me!*" Then he caught her up and carried her with him into that wonderful unutterable place.

There was no *just once*. They made love again, and this time Honor conceded they were making love, not having sex. Making love meant tenderness, care, satisfaction, cuddling, whispering together. Having sex...well, that was something mechanical.

Joe got up early and phoned Nan to take the kids with her to the ball tournament in the RV, told her that Honor wanted to sleep in and that she'd see everyone later. Then he scribbled a note to Honor saying he'd be back after his noon game, and he was. Sweaty, grinning, full of pride at his team's accomplishment—beating Three Hills seven to five. He took her into his bedroom, stripped off his Magpie uniform and made love to her again. In the afternoon, with the shadows of the poplars against the curtains, with the smallest of breezes coming in the open window. With no one at the farm but a few dogs dozing in the sunshine.

After he left midafternoon to go to another scheduled game, she packed up all the possessions she'd brought with her and put them in her car. As soon as Nan and Harry came back and she'd said goodbye to the children, she'd leave. She couldn't bear to spend another night here with Joe. In his arms. He'd been absolutely right—she'd made love with him and now she didn't want any other man. Ever.

Which was crazy. Which couldn't happen. Which was another reason she had to leave *now,* before she lost her focus entirely. She needed to get back to Calgary and Alec and her other life and put all of this behind her.

IT WASN'T SO EASY. As Joe had said, nothing was simple.

Moving back into her apartment was no problem. She welcomed the peace and quiet, her cool beige-and-cream sanctuary on the sixteenth floor. But within a week she desperately missed the children. She talked to Ellie on the phone twice that first week and sent them both little presents, but it wasn't enough. She wanted to hold them, to kiss them, to cuddle them.

And Joe. She missed Joe unbearably. He made no reference, in their brief telephone conversations, to what had happened that last weekend. He was pleasant, cheerful, and didn't seem to miss her at all.

Oh, well, she told herself irritably, would you want him to? He's being far more mature about this than you are, and you were the one brazen enough to invite yourself into his bed. You always knew it would go nowhere. You *wanted* it to go nowhere.

She threw herself back into her work at Templeman Energy. Summer was always a busy time for field work, and some research chores had stacked up in her absence. Nothing especially important, nothing she could really immerse herself in. She saw Alec regularly, feeling she'd neglected him a little over the summer. She stonewalled any inclination he had to discuss his bid to get custody of the children. That was one subject on which they definitely did not see eye to eye. And she'd do nothing at all to help him, even if it was in her power. Which it was not. Furthermore she'd do everything she could to make sure his bid did not succeed. She hoped it wouldn't come to that because deep down, she still loved the irascible old man. And she felt enormous pity for him because he was being denied his grandchildren. Especially now that these children were no longer just two names in a newspaper clipping.

By the end of the second week she was back, Honor realized she'd made the right decision. Joe Gallant was not for her. It had even crossed her mind once or twice that Joe's proposal could have an element of revenge behind it, against Alec. But then she dismissed the thought. There was nothing underhanded about Joe Gallant.

She went to a play with one of the men—another company lawyer—who'd asked her out a time or two. She sat in the darkened theater, waiting for the slightest frisson of energy telling her she was remotely attracted to her date. It didn't happen. She told herself it didn't matter; naturally she wouldn't be attracted to every man she went out with.

At the end of the second week Joe called, and this time he didn't put Ellie on the line. He wanted to ask her out for dinner at a fancy Calgary restaurant.

She finally said no, her fingers slippery on the receiver, her heart pounding. She wanted to say yes, oh, how she wanted to say yes. But her mind was made up. Their lives were entirely separate and had to stay that way. What was the point of getting together? There was none. She knew his reasons for pursuing her, and love was not among them.

Joe called again two days later and then he called on the weekend. She found it just as hard to turn him down the third time as it had been the first. *Was* she doing the right thing? She lay awake at night, wondering. Remembering Joe's kisses, the way her body had responded to him. The way *she* had responded to him.

But how could they start dating now? Going to movies? Going to plays? Out to dinner? They'd already lived in the same house for more than a month, they'd danced, they'd touched each other, they'd made love—how could they possibly go back to the beginning and start over? And what possible outcome could there be?

No. It was best this way. Separate lives. She didn't love him and he didn't love her. The whole business was crazy—that she'd even spent all those summer weeks with the brother of the woman her husband had…loved. It was a freak coincidence, she told herself. They'd been thrown together, and now it seemed as though they had some kind of relationship. They didn't. She prayed she'd have the strength to continue resisting him. By telephone it was a little easier. And gradually her own life got fuller and busier.

He'd forget. Joe was stubborn, but so was she. He

wanted a wife. She was not the wife for him. Soon he'd get the message and be off on another path, with another woman. One day she'd hear that he'd gotten married and she'd be happy for him and the children.

Or so she told herself.

ALEC TEMPLEMAN was another matter. More unfinished business.

"I want you to give this up, Alec. This custody nonsense. Think of the children."

She'd found the old man sitting alone on the outdoor patio, the dogs at his feet, a stack of company documents and a few bulb and seed catalogs on the table beside him. He'd been glad to see her. He'd removed his sunglasses and kissed her on the cheek when she'd bent down to greet him.

Honor had decided she'd make one final attempt to convince him to drop his legal action against Joe. If only she could offer Alec something, a chance to have a relationship of some kind with his grandchildren. If only she had something to negotiate with. If only she could make a *deal* with him. But that was hopeless, she was beginning to think. Joe would never see reason if he hadn't done so by now. As for her, she had nothing but logic and an appeal to the old man's better side.

"I *am* thinking of the children," Alec growled. "That's what this is all about, isn't it? That goddamn bastard thinks he can keep me from my own grandchildren, my own flesh and blood. Who in hell does he think he is?"

Honor restrained herself. "It's not who he thinks he is, Alec. It's who he *is*—he's the children's guardian. That's all clear and according to the law. Parker was never married to their mother. He was married to me,'' she finished quietly.

Alec stared at her for a few seconds and a grimace crossed his face. He reached out to take her hand across the patio table. "I know that, Honor. I thought the two of you would be happy together. I wanted you to be happy,'' he rasped. "Damn it, you *should* have been happy together. I don't know what went wrong. I don't know what got into that boy. You were the best thing that ever happened to him and—''

"We didn't love each other, Alec,'' she interrupted softly. "Do you see that now? I liked Parker. A lot. We were wonderful friends. I was very happy with him those first few years, and I believe he was happy with me. Maybe…'' She shrugged and smiled wryly. "Who knows? Maybe in other circumstances, we could have had a happy life together. As happy as many couples, anyway. But he didn't love me, Alec. He loved someone else.''

She squeezed the old man's hand, thinking about what she wanted to say. She was glad to have the opportunity to speak so freely to him. These were words that should have been spoken a long time ago. "I just wish he'd told me about Sylvie. I'd have been happy to give him a divorce and let him marry her. You must have known Parker and I had been pretty much separated for years. The marriage was over.''

Alec swore and looked away. Knowing what she now knew about the background of Parker and Sylvie's romance, she understood what he must be thinking. But did he regret interfering in their lives? Probably not. Yet if Parker had had the courage to face his father, accept his wrath and marry the woman he loved, the old man would have had a much stronger case for access to his grandchildren. If there were any bastards in this case—and how she hated that word as a pejorative, as Alec used it—they were his grandchildren, not Joe Gallant.

How ironic, if the old man only realized it. And Honor suspected he did. His stroke had had some physical effects, but there was nothing wrong with Alec Templeman's brain.

He let go of her hand and clasped the arm of his chair again. He glanced around irritably. "Where in hell's Spinks? He knows I want a cup of tea out here...."

Spinks materialized from within the gloom of the house, carrying a tray with three cups, a teapot with a cozy, milk and sugar and his inevitable plate of shortbread.

Honor thanked him with a smile and invited him to join them. Spinks sat down without a word. He inquired about Honor's health and asked Alec if he planned to put in any new daylilies this season. It was getting near bulb-planting time and he was thinking of digging some new beds.

When Honor got up to leave ten minutes later, Alec grabbed her hand. He looked up at her and growled hoarsely, "I wish you'd been happy with my boy, Honor. That's all I wanted—for you to be happy."

The lowering sun was full in his lined and haggard face. Honor swore she saw him blink away a tear, but perhaps it was only the sun in his eyes.

"I know you did, Alec. I know you did." She kissed his sagging cheek and left him with his paid companion, his seed catalogs and his Labradors.

CHAPTER FIFTEEN

TWO TICKETS to the Calgary-Dallas exhibition game, at center ice. It had cost him, but at the last minute his buddy at the Saddledome had come through.

Now...what about Honor? She didn't strike him as the hockey type. But how else was he going to get in her door? Tell her how much he'd missed her these last few weeks? Yeah, he could just see that—people coming and going, and him standing there in her lobby, pouring out his heart into the intercom. Come to think of it, maybe he *should* try it—she might feel sorry for him and let him in.

But he got lucky.

Just as he approached Honor's building, an impressive granite-and-brass edifice on one of Calgary's upscale residential streets, he saw the delivery hatchback. The youthful driver got out balancing a large flat box on one arm. Joe followed the kid inside and heard him talking into the intercom.

"Pizza delivery for Mrs. Templeman."

"Already? Okay. Come on up."

"Hey." Joe stepped forward and grabbed the kid by the sleeve as he reached for the brass door handle. "You like hockey?"

"Huh?"

"Two tickets—" Joe whipped them out of his

jacket pocket and waved them in the kid's face. "Center ice. Row twelve. Mrs. Templeman's a good friend of mine." He winked. "Let me take this up and surprise her."

"You kiddin' me, man? Wow! Two tickets to tonight's game? All right!" He practically threw the pizza at Joe and grabbed the tickets. "Hey—you sure she's gonna like you doin' this?"

"She's going to love it." Joe winked again, a man-to-man that had the kid beaming.

"Wow," Joe heard him say again as he walked back to his battered delivery van, shaking his head. "Wow."

"Hey, kid!"

The boy turned, still grinning.

"Let me pay you for the pizza." Joe thrust a twenty-dollar bill into his hand. "Keep the change."

"Thanks, man!"

Joe raced back to the apartment door, carefully balancing the flat box in one hand. Damn, the buzzer had quit. He pressed her number and when she answered again, sounding perplexed—or maybe annoyed—he held his hand over his nose and muttered, "Pizza-guy-sorry-missed-the-door—"

"Come in." She buzzed the door open again and this time Joe grabbed it.

An elderly lady getting her mail from the boxes at one side of the foyer gave him a suspicious look.

"Pizza," he said by way of explanation, raising the box slightly. "House special." The woman continued to frown severely as he walked to the elevator.

Inside, he breathed a sigh of relief that there was only one other person inside, a woman who'd obviously come up from an underground parking level, and pressed the sixteenth floor. Then he leaned against the wall of the elevator, racking his brain for what he was going to say to Honor when he appeared at her door.

"Mmm. Smells good." The attractive-looking woman standing across from him ran a pink tongue provocatively along her lips.

"Yeah," Joe said noncommittally.

"And I'm so-o-o hungry, too. What kind?"

"Uh—" he glanced at the box "—Reno's. Good pizza." He flashed her a quick smile.

"Maybe I should switch brands. Do all their delivery boys look like you?"

"Huh?"

The elevator stopped and the woman got off. "Bye for now." She winked and waggled her fingers at him. Joe punched the button to close the door. *Jeez, some women...*

Then he was in the carpeted corridor of the sixteenth floor. He paused to take a deep breath before knocking, and just as he raised his hand to rap on her door, it opened.

"Joe!" She was wearing a big white terry-cloth bathrobe, her hair was pulled up on her head and she was wearing glasses. He'd never seen her in glasses. She looked adorable. "What are *you* doing here?"

"Hi. Brought your pizza." He grinned, deciding to forget the deke and go for the straightforward shot on goal.

She looked quickly up and down the corridor. "Where's the pizza guy?" she demanded. But her voice sounded a little thready, a little unsure.

"*I'm* the pizza guy." Joe moved forward, box in front of him, and she moved back. He walked into her apartment and shut the door behind him. Her place was very...Honor. Expensive, elegant, modern. Conservative.

"Here you go." He proffered the box, but she didn't take it.

She frowned. "You tricked him."

He solemnly placed his left hand on his heart, the other balancing the pizza. "I cannot tell a lie. I did."

"Wh-why?" She laughed a little and stepped back. Joe followed her. One step, then two. Then they were in her living room. White carpet, big wall-to-wall city view, small television set, classy-looking furniture. Marble, steel, artsy pictures. She could use a cat, scratch things up a little, leave some hair on the carpet.

"I lucked into a couple of tickets for the hockey game tonight. I didn't think you'd let me in if I just rang the bell." He held her gaze. Would she have let him in? He'd forgotten how blue her eyes were. "I had to see you, Honor." His voice let him down; it betrayed the strain he'd been under, what the stakes in this game of theirs were costing him.

"I...I..." She took a deep breath and looked up at him. Pale brown tendrils had escaped the ribbon thing that held up most of her hair. He wanted to raise his hand and trace the curve of her cheek, brush back that loop of hair. "This isn't any good, Joe. It isn't right. You shouldn't be here. I told you I've got my life to live and you've got yours. You and the kids. Th-things have changed."

She paused, then rushed on. "What did you have

to see me about? Is something wrong with one of the kids?''

''The kids are fine. Fine.'' He smiled and stepped a little closer. ''What's changed, Honor?'' he asked softly. ''I still feel the same. Nothing's changed for me. I still want to marry you. I had to see you. I had to ask if you'd see me again.''

''I couldn't have gone to a hockey game with you, anyway. I can't go anywhere with you. I've got a date tonight. Th-that's why I ordered pizza. I didn't have time to cook.'' She was babbling. That was a good sign. ''We're going to the opera. *The Pearl Fishers*. At the Jubilee.''

''What time?'' He glanced at her watch as she did, thin and gold on her slim wrist. He already knew it was about five o'clock.

''Nigel's picking me up at eight.''

Nigel? The opera? Not that he had anything against opera. Hell, with her beside him, he'd sit through a couple of hours of overfed warblers in weird costumes screeching lyrics in strange languages any day of the week.

He tried not to smile. He knew triumph when he felt it. She looked up, but he could see the defiance had crumbled. This closeness, this physical proximity was having the same effect on her as it was on him. She was as glad to see him as he was to see her, although she was determined not to admit it. And she could be damn stubborn. He'd sure found that out in the past couple of weeks.

He set the pizza down on her coffee table, some kind of green-and-black marble affair with a bowl on it. One small thin pale-gray bowl. No peanuts in it, either.

Then he stepped forward and took hold of her shoulders. Lightly. He heard the tiny sigh, the whisper of his name.

"Joe...you shouldn't be here...."

He moved closer, pulled her toward him. Bent down, tasted the texture of her hair, reached up and tugged away the hair ribbon and tossed it to the floor. Gloried in the heavy fall of silky pale brown.

"Look, Joe..." she tried again. Her voice was wobbly. He knew she was trying to be very firm with him. But it wasn't working. She wanted him as much as he wanted her. She'd missed him as much as he'd missed her. She just didn't know it yet.

"Hmm?" He nuzzled her hair and felt a shudder run through her body. "It's just after five now," he whispered. "That means we've got about three hours before your, uh...before you have to go out. Three hours." He couldn't bring himself to say *date*. He kissed the top of her head, then her forehead, then her nose.

"*Joe!*" Her voice was hoarse. "Two and a half," she added weakly, closing her eyes to accept the light rain of his kisses. *The reverence, the offering. The promises he'd make her if only she'd allow him.*

He drew back and looked down at her, anchoring her body against him. She was so warm and slim under that bulky robe. He'd bet dollars to doughnuts she wasn't wearing a thing underneath. Just the thought made his heart pound twice as fast as it was already.

He lifted the glasses from her nose and set them

on the pizza box. Then he bent down and claimed her soft lips. Tasted the familiar sweetness, reveled in the touch and texture of her mouth. Drew her bottom lip between his teeth, bit down softly.

"Joe!"

"I've missed you, Honor." He twisted his fingers in her hair, dropping kisses on her ears, her cheek. "So much. You can't know how much...."

"Two and a half hours, that's all," she repeated, whispering. "I'll need half an hour to get ready."

She was his. Now and always. There was absolutely no doubt in his mind. He just had to figure out a way for her to discover the same truth.

"Wh-what about your hockey game? When does that start?" She opened her eyes.

"Forget the game, Miss Filofax," he growled, pressing her tightly against him. "I gave my tickets to the pizza kid. As a tip."

"Oh," she said with a small smile. "Oh, I see. Good seats?"

"The best," he murmured, kissing the delicate curve of her ear, holding back the grin. "Center ice." He kissed her temple. "It hurt like hell, but you're worth it, babe."

She arched against him and reached up to meet his smiling mouth with hers.

It was magic, just as it had been before. Somehow his left hand found the belt to her robe and he tugged and it fell open. He was right. She wasn't wearing a damn thing underneath. They had just over two hours together. It had been more than three weeks since he'd seen her, nearly four, and they had two lousy hours. He didn't intend to waste one second of it.

NIGEL HARRISON wasn't late. But then, he never was. If anything, she knew he'd be five minutes early. Nigel had emigrated from England twenty years before. He was an urbane undemanding man in his midforties, handsome in a hawkish way. Honor had dated him on and off for a year or so and had always found him to be good company. They shared a lot of interests. Since she'd had the change of heart about men and her future, she'd been considering Nigel as a potential long-term partner. *Honor and Nigel.* She'd tried hard to imagine the pair of them together. It hadn't worked before Joe's visit, and it wasn't working now.

Honor sighed and then held her breath to keep her hand steady as she applied mascara in the brightly lit bathroom. Joe was asleep, or looked like he was asleep, big, tanned, handsome, sprawled in her bed, one arm across his eyes, half-covered by a white sheet.

The pizza box rested on the floor beside the bed. At some point—Honor's memory was a little fuzzy—Joe had retrieved the pizza from the living room and they'd sat in bed feeding each other bites between kisses. The duvet and the rest of the bedclothes had ended up on the floor.

She and Joe had made love, first on the livingroom carpet with the curtains wide and late-afternoon sun pouring into the room. The intensity of her response had frightened her, the eagerness, the greed—she'd torn at his shirt, his belt, frantic to meet him skin to skin, to breathe the scent of him again, to feel the strength of his arms around her. They'd met, mated and collapsed in splendor on her cream-colored carpet, and she didn't think she'd ever be able to sit in her living room again without thinking of that.

And then he'd carried her to her bedroom and they'd made love all over again. It was hot, irrational, necessary to the sanity of both—and wonderful.

Except that she wasn't in love, nor was he, despite what he wanted her to believe. Besides, she wasn't able to have children and Joe was. He loved children. He'd want kids of his own eventually, no matter what he said now. And the doctors had told her the likelihood of her conceiving after her tubal pregnancy, the one that had required surgery, was practically zero; and even if she did, the likelihood of her carrying a pregnancy to term was almost nil. *Placenta previa.* It was a rather beautiful Latin name for the hellish situation her own body put her through. It meant losing babies at five, six months. As she'd already done twice, as she didn't think she could bear to do again.

In any event, his offer to marry her had been made on impulse, out of his own long-declared need for a wife. There was no point in even dreaming about that particular scenario. Joe was set up now with Bea Hoople; the kids seemed to like her, and Nan was there to take them on Miss Hoople's days off. The only room for her, Honor, in this picture was to continue trying to bring Alec and his grandchildren together in some sort of normal ongoing relationship. Eventually she would make it work. The old man wanted it, and she couldn't help thinking it would be good for Alexander and Ellie, too. Also their uncle. Joe needed to set aside this horrible bitterness about the whole Templeman family. If she could help him come to terms with that...

There was the doorbell. Honor gave a start, then quickly inspected herself in the mirror. Pearls, makeup perfect, no sign of the love flush she'd attempted to erase with a cool shower. Her eyes were overbright, but there was nothing she could do about that. The navy suit was perfect, too, and she'd take gloves. And her cashmere jacket. It was getting cool at night these days.

Honor tiptoed out of the bathroom and made for the door of her bedroom, carrying her shoes. She paused at the bedside, torn. Everything in her urged her to send Nigel away and come back and take off her clothes and crawl in beside Joe and spend the entire night with him. Sleeping. Perhaps making love again—but even if they didn't, just cuddling up beside him in the bed that no man had ever shared with her before. She wanted to wake up with him, shower with him, make him breakfast...

It was impossible.

The doorbell rang again—it wasn't like Nigel to be impatient—and Honor stepped back from the bed, resisting the crazy urge to reach over and kiss Joe farewell. Had he really dozed off? Or was he just pretending so he wouldn't have to say goodbye? Either way, she didn't have time to find out. She closed the bedroom door behind her.

"Coming!" she called as she entered the living room. Then, horrified, she dropped her shoes and began scrabbling around on the living-room carpet gathering up socks, his shirt, her bathrobe—all the detritus of their first, frantic coming-together. Hurriedly she stuffed the clothes into the oven in the adjoining tiny kitchen, then raced to the door.

Nigel looked a little perturbed.

"Sorry," she said. "I wasn't quite ready." He surveyed her quickly and glanced at her stockinged feet.

"No problem. Can I use your phone?" he asked. When she nodded, he strode into her apartment and headed for the phone on the counter between her kitchen and dining room. "I have a beep from the city editor. I'll just see what she wants."

"Certainly." Honor glanced at her watch. Five minutes to eight. The opera started at half-past. It would take fifteen minutes to drive there and park. Life with Nigel, she was quite sure, would be a very orderly affair. She had a sudden impulse to giggle as she thought of him methodically folding his clothing, pairing his socks, hanging up his trousers, before making love. Would he even *think* of seducing a woman on the floor of her very own living room?

Then her giggle evaporated as she heard Nigel make his connection and begin speaking into the receiver. How long was he going to be? What if Joe walked out of her bedroom now? Tousled, sleepy, clad in nothing but a towel. Stretching, maybe even scratching his chest or his belly lazily, making it absolutely clear exactly why he was in her apartment and what they'd been doing only moments before. Would he introduce himself, slap Nigel on the back in a hearty gesture, tell him to drive carefully and have her home by ten?

She wouldn't put it past him.

She spotted the ribbon that Joe had pulled out of her hair and sidled over to the coffee table, her eye on Nigel, then reached down quickly and stuffed it in her pocket.

Nigel replaced the receiver. "Ready?" He took her cashmere jacket and held it for her as she slipped it on. She checked her purse for her keys and walked to the door with him.

He paused and gave her a quizzical look. Now what?

He glanced down. Her glance followed his. "Shoes."

For heaven's sake! She hadn't put her shoes on. When they finally left the apartment Honor's face was hot, but her navy pumps were most definitely on her feet. Nigel was smiling, indulging her, enjoying her lapse. She knew very well that the incident was totally out of character. She just hoped he'd never get an inkling as to why.

Later, in the third act of *The Pearl Fishers,* in the midst of some of the most beautiful music Honor had ever heard, she fingered the crumpled ribbon in her pocket, and it struck her that she was a woman in a terrible tangle. As dreadful a tangle as had ever graced the operatic world. Here she sat, knees pressed primly together, attention visibly on the stage—yet missing whole passages of music at a time. She sat beside an attentive attractive man who must care for her, or why would he ask her out? Here she was, appearing to be one kind of woman, very proper and conventional, when she had, in fact, just risen, sated and satisfied, from her lover's arms. She still breathed the heat of their rumpled bed. She still felt the imprint of Joe's body on hers, on her very soul. What kind of woman was she? She must still smell of sex, despite her shower and her Chanel. The whole audience must know why her eyes glittered, why her cheeks were flushed and warm, why the pulse beat so heavily in her throat.

She'd fought her feelings ever since she'd met Joe Gallant way back in July. She'd used every skill she'd ever learned in law school to persuade herself that she was not involved, to deny what was happening to her—what had already happened. To convince herself of the opposite, of the rational. That black was white. The fact was, she'd fallen in love. She was in love with the brother of the woman her husband had secretly loved, the uncle of the children who should have been hers. She was in love with a man who'd asked her to marry him, but whom she could not marry. Any other man, yes—but not Joe Gallant. It would kill her father-in-law to know her true feelings for the man who had thwarted him at every turn with his grandchildren.

Alec was a sick old man. An arrogant, demanding, difficult sick old man. She owed him, yes, but how *much* did she owe him? Her happiness? And for how long? She and Joe were young. Didn't they deserve the chance, no matter how slim or how fragile or how unlikely, to have a life together? Still, now that Parker was gone—especially now—Alec needed her loyalty...and her love. He depended on it. To have her desert him, as well—Honor didn't think Alec could bear it. And to hurt the old man like that? She didn't think *she* could bear it.

As the tenors on stage poured out their final anguish in "Au fond du temple faint," Honor felt first one tear, then another slide down her cheek. She dabbed discreetly at her nose and eyes with a tissue. Nigel smiled understandingly and clasped her hand. He thought she was overcome with feeling generated by the rise and crash of the poignant duet. And she was...*she was*. Only she didn't weep for the pearl fishers. She wept for the two stubborn men she loved most. One old, one young. And she wept for herself. And for Parker and Joe's sister and her own dead mother and the dead father she'd almost forgotten.

And for all the lost babies, every one.

When Nigel brought her back to her apartment, Honor didn't invite him in for coffee. He didn't ask. When he bent to give her his usual quick good-night kiss, she twisted slightly and offered him her cheek.

Nigel was no fool. "I see," he said quietly, and gave her a small hug. He touched her cheek as he turned. "Sleep well, Honor. I'll be in touch."

But Honor knew he wouldn't.

Was Joe still asleep in her bed? Her heart beat fiercely as she entered and locked the door behind her. It was just past eleven. Perhaps he'd decided to spend the night.

But the apartment was empty. He'd thrown the pillows and duvet back on the bed and made it in a sloppy manly fashion. There was a note on the pillow, which she snatched up.

It took me over an hour to find my clothes. You are one tough, unpredictable, crazy woman, but I love you. I'm not giving up. I'm not a man who gives up easily.

Joe.

P.S.: I'll call you when I get the rest of my crops in. Still oats to come off. Another week or so, if the weather holds.

And she knew he *would* call. Honor stripped off her clothes and crawled into bed, burrowing into the rumpled side where Joe had slept. She swore she could still smell his skin on the sheets. She stared at the ceiling, resisting the childish impulse to pinch herself, to see if any of this was real. Was true.

The question was, when he called—as she knew he would—what would she say?

CHAPTER SIXTEEN

BUT SHE WAS WRONG about Nigel. He did call back, and she agreed to go to dinner and a poetry reading with him the following Saturday evening.

Early Friday morning—she was still in bed—she got a call from Joe. He didn't refer to their encounter the previous weekend and, typically, came straight to the point.

"I'm going to an equipment auction up in Red Deer on Saturday and wondered if you'd like to have the kids for the day."

"Oh, Joe, that would be wonderful!" she said immediately. Was it a good idea, though, to renew her relationship with the children before she and Joe had settled things between them? Well, *she'd* settled them, but she didn't think Joe had.

She didn't care; she wanted to see the children.

"I'll be back about five, if that's okay." He sounded diffident, even uncaring as to whether he took the children or not. That puzzled her a little.

"What about Bea? Is she all right?"

"She's fine. I try and give her weekends off. She's around, but I just thought you might like to see Ellie and Alexander."

"I do. I can hardly wait." Already her mind was churning with things to do with the children. She'd take them to the Bow Island Valley Zoo, she'd take them for lunch at McDonald's, they'd get some books from the library and she'd read them a story before their naps.... Then she remembered Nigel. It was a shock to realize how annoyed she felt the moment she remembered her commitment to Nigel.

"I...I have something planned for that evening, Joe," she said stiffly. But it was probably a good thing. He might as well realize right away that there was nothing in this for *them,* that she was agreeing only to look after the children. Maybe she'd had a lapse last weekend, maybe she'd found Joe Gallant hard to resist, but she was well warned now, and it wouldn't happen again.

"A date?" He didn't sound surprised. Or even that interested.

"Mmm. Yes." She restrained herself from confiding the details. She'd have to get ready, though, before Joe picked up the children, as the poetry reading was for seven and Nigel had suggested they eat earlier. "I'll need you to pick up the kids by five at the latest."

"Sure." Joe paused. She thought for a moment that he'd finished the conversation, but unexpectedly he went on. His voice was rough. "The old man still wants the kids, Honor. I got a notice that there's going to be a hearing on the twenty-second."

"Oh, Joe!" She couldn't say anything else. She ached for him. Damn her father-in-law, anyway! "I...I just hope it goes your way," she whispered.

"It will." He sounded determined. "No matter what happens, Sylvie's kids are staying with me. The old man can go straight to hell."

And if Alec thought this sort of threat would improve his chances with the children's legal guardian, perhaps his stroke *had* affected his mental powers. He was dead wrong on this issue. Honor knew that Joe wasn't a man to back down from a bully. If it came to a fight, it would be ugly for everyone involved, including the children. And her. Would she have to choose, in the end, between her relationship with her old friend and father-in-law and her relationship with Joe and with Parker's children?

Joe arrived at the condominium bright and early Saturday morning. Honor was ready, dressed in corduroy slacks and a fine-knit Nordic sweater. The weather was warm for early October.

"Auntie!" Ellie flew straight into her arms, and Honor lifted her and spun her around, blinking back the tears. She laughed to cover her emotion.

"Oh, sweetie! I've missed you so much." She hugged the little girl and kissed her all over her smiling face. She didn't miss Joe's grin or speculative glance. She didn't care; of course he knew how much she loved the children. She had nothing to hide.

"And Alexander!" She reached for him and Joe handed him over. "You've grown, my little man." She kissed his nose and he tucked his head bashfully against her shoulder. He clutched a rubber car in one hand and was wearing a long-sleeved red T-shirt and striped train engineer's overalls, with a flannel-lined zipper jacket. She couldn't believe it had been less than a month since she'd seen them.

She appealed to Joe. "Hasn't he grown?"

"Maybe." Joe shrugged. "Look, I've got Tim with me in the truck. I'll go down and bring up the kids' stuff.'' He didn't touch her or greet her in any way that might indicate their relationship was—or had been—closer than that of simply two friends, but his eyes were warm, and she felt a responding heat right through her bones.

"I never thought of that,'' Honor admitted. "I guess there's a lot of paraphernalia that comes along with this sort of thing, even for a day.''

"Stroller, diapers, favorite toys, extra clothes…'' Joe ticked the items off on the fingers of one hand, then grinned. "I'll be right back.''

Honor watched him walk toward the elevators. He wore black jeans, a dark-hued plaid shirt and a sports jacket. Boots and a cowboy hat of course. He looked terrific.

A child on either side, she stepped into the apartment and closed the door, leaving it ajar for Joe's return.

He brought the children's gear in one load, most of it piled onto Alexander's stroller, and then, with a quick, "See you at five,'' he was gone.

Honor thought a trip to the library might be best to start with. They could choose some books, perhaps a children's video or two, and after that, they could have lunch at McDonald's and go to the zoo. Then, if Alexander looked like he needed his nap, they'd come back to the apartment and Ellie could watch a video while the little boy napped and…and then… Oh, Honor couldn't wait!

It didn't work out quite that way. The children were bored in the library and Alexander kept shouting to hear his own echo among the stacks. Honor hurriedly picked out three children's books with lots of pictures and grabbed two videos from the children's section. *Pippi Longstocking* and one other.

Then Ellie insisted on pushing Alexander's stroller along the city sidewalks, but she wasn't as strong or as careful as she thought she was, and was constantly running Alexander dangerously close to the curb. It took all of Honor's vigilance and good humor to finally get them to the McDonald's with the big children's entertainment center. She discovered that Ellie was allowed in the play area, but Alexander was too small to go there unattended. So she let him play for a short time while she watched, then removed him, kicking and yelling, while she went to order their lunch.

All in all, the day was far more exhausting than Honor had expected. However, they spent a lazy couple of hours at the zoo, and luckily both children were delighted with the animals, especially the hijinks of the monkeys in their cages. The Siberian tiger, Honor thought, looked very sad, padding endlessly around his enclosure. He'd worn the grass next to the fence right down to the clay in his relentless patrol of his artificial steppes.

Finally, about half-past four, Honor struggled into the elevator with the stroller and all their packages and up to the sixteenth floor. She was perspiring, her hair was a mess, and both Joe and Nigel would be arriving in less than half an hour.

Honor put one of the videos she'd borrowed from the library into her VCR and left Ellie sitting on the cream-colored sofa, legs sticking straight out, happily watching *Pippi Longstocking* and chewing on a fruit-and-nut bar. Alexander followed her into the bedroom where she was about to effect possibly the quickest change of clothing in history. She zipped into the bathroom for a three-minute shower, leaving the boy sprawled on the floor making *vroom, vroom* noises while running some of her leather pumps over the carpet. She peeked out into the bedroom as she toweled her hair: all was well. Alexander was parking her shoes now in neat rows in the middle of the floor.

Kids. What a ball, she thought, wiping the fogged-up mirror, then squinting to quickly apply a little makeup. She blow-dried her hair in record time, and came out into the bedroom wearing just her bra and panties. Alexander paid her no attention, happily drooling as he zoomed her shoes here and there along roadways only he could see.

Honor picked out a simply-cut skirt and jacket, in a matching coral shade, and pulled on a pink-and-white striped top. Alexander was still playing cars with the Italian sandals she usually wore with that outfit, so she dug in her closet and found a pair of patent-leather pumps which she traded him for the sandals. Alexander got to his feet and, carrying a shoe in each hand, followed her to the living room, where Ellie was still absorbed in the adventures of little Pippi.

Honor poured a glass of cold water from the refrigerator and drank it standing at the counter. Whew. She glanced at the kitchen clock. Ten minutes past five. What a day. Joe was late and Nigel was due any moment. As she set the glass back in the sink, the doorbell rang. Thank goodness.

But it wasn't Joe. Nigel raised one eyebrow as he

spotted Ellie sitting rapt on the sofa before the television set. Alexander was busily parking her shoes under the coffee table, making regular trips back to the bedroom for more.

Honor raised her shoulders in a shrug and laughed.

"Baby-sitting?" Nigel smiled and came in, shutting the door behind him.

"Yes. This is Ellie—" the little girl smiled shyly, then promptly returned her attention to the television set "—and this is Alexander." The little boy didn't even look up.

"Oh?" Nigel's expression asked volumes.

Honor took a deep breath. "Yes. They're Parker's children. My husband's. He'd, um, he'd been living with another woman, their mother, since we were separated about five years ago and...well, these are his children!" She smiled at Ellie and Alexander, who appeared not to have overheard her comments to Nigel.

But Ellie must have been listening. "My mommy and daddy are in heaven," she announced seriously. "They're angels." She nodded several times, then looked back at what was happening on the screen.

"I see," Nigel said, but Honor wasn't sure he did. "Are we dropping them somewhere—?"

"No. No, their uncle's picking them up here." Honor checked her watch. "He's running a little late, I guess. Is that okay? I'm sure we won't be late for the reading. I'm expecting him any moment."

She was flustered and afraid that it showed. Nigel, always the perfect gentleman, agreed, and sat down in her armchair. He picked up a magazine from the rack beside him and began to leaf through the pages. He appeared to be relaxed; she hoped he was.

Not, she thought quickly, that it mattered all that much. They were in plenty of time for their date. If they were five minutes late for a dinner reservation at some neighborhood bistro, big deal. Then she was appalled at her disloyal thoughts. Was she making excuses to herself for Joe? She'd *told* him how important it was that he pick the children up by five.

Just then the doorbell pealed again.

This time it was Joe.

"Sorry I'm late, Honor. Hope I didn't interfere with your plans," he said as he stepped into her apartment. She didn't miss his long look over her shoulder at Nigel, who must have been wondering what on earth was going on. She couldn't see Nigel, positioned as he was behind her in the living room.

"Not at all," she replied breathlessly. Why, oh why did Joe have this effect on her? "I've gathered all the children's stuff here...." She indicated a neat stack of the folded stroller, the toy bag, the diaper bag and the rest of the possessions Joe had brought in that morning.

Joe continued to smile, a cat-that-swallowed-the-canary smile, in Honor's opinion. Honor remembered her manners. "Joe? I'd like you to meet Nigel Harrison. Nigel, this is a friend of mine, Joe Gallant. He's the children's uncle I was telling you about."

Nigel came forward and the two men shook hands. It looked like a too-firm shake to her, a knuckle-buster. Both men smiled and spoke pleasantly enough, but the smiles didn't quite make it to their eyes.

"Well, I won't hold you up any longer," Joe said easily. He bent to scoop up the children's gear. "I bought a grain truck at the auction and Tim's driving it home for me." He opened the door. "Be back in a minute."

Honor quickly retrieved Alexander from under the coffee table and wriggled him into his flannel jacket. Ellie popped her thumb in her mouth and climbed slowly down from the sofa. She yawned, apparently not all that sorry to leave Pippi and her adventures behind. She had the stuffed apatosaurus Honor had bought her at the zoo firmly under one arm. Honor was sure she'd be asleep in her car seat before Joe had left the city limits.

Just as she'd finished dressing the children, a light rap announced Joe's return.

"Ready, kids?" He took Alexander from her. The boy seemed reluctant to go, which warmed Honor's heart. She had really enjoyed the day. It was a precious unexpected gift that Joe had given her.

Joe nodded to Nigel and thanked Honor for taking care of his niece and nephew. Then he was gone, and Honor leaned against the closed door for a few seconds, wondering at her sudden feeling of abandonment. The children were such life and joy. Their company today had been a total change from her quiet daily life in Calgary, such a reminder of how full and happy her summer had been.

"Tired?"

"No, not at all," she said, turning to Nigel. He was standing and had put down his magazine. "It was a lot of fun looking after those two today. I enjoyed it."

Nigel's raised eyebrow and smile told her that he wasn't convinced she was being entirely truthful. A man who had no experience of children, like Nigel, could not possibly imagine the joys they might bring, along with the chaos and, yes, sometimes frustration and confusion and weariness.

There was a loud rap at her door.

"Yes?"

It was Joe. She poked her head out. The children were halfway down the corridor, looking back at them. "Did you forget something?"

"Yes, as a matter of fact, I did." She didn't trust his grin. She saw him peer at Nigel behind her. "Could I, uh, see you privately for a moment?"

Heavens! What did he want? "Sure." She glanced quickly over her shoulder at Nigel, who was frowning slightly, and stepped outside into the corridor with Joe. She shut the door quietly. "What do you want?"

"This." He moved forward and put his arms around her and pulled her roughly against him. He lowered his head, covering her mouth in a glorious, demanding, possessive kiss that went on and on and on. She could hear Ellie giggling somewhere in the distance, and the startling sound of the elevator bell as someone got off on her floor.

"Joe!" she gasped, pushing against his chest. "What are you doing?"

"Kissing you," he said, completely unrepentant. "I consider it very bad form to kiss a man's date in front of him, don't you?"

"But—"

"I figured you could stand a reminder about who

loves you and who wants to marry you." He grinned. "Me. Just in case it slipped your mind."

And with that, another big grin and a tip of his hat, he disappeared down the hall, shepherding the children ahead of him.

Honor waited a few seconds to catch her breath before returning to the apartment. How in the world did Joe *do* this to her? Every single time. She fanned her heated cheeks with the flat of her hand.

Nigel didn't seem to notice anything amiss. "Well, did you manage to shake off that farmer?"

"Yes," she said tightly. "Shall we go?"

Honor decided that, despite what she'd thought, she really had very little in common with Nigel Harrison, after all.

THE JUDICIAL HEARING was on a Thursday. Honor dressed carefully that morning. She intended to drive out to Glory after lunch and show up in the courtroom. She couldn't do anything about what Alec Templeman and his lawyer had hatched, but she could show Joe and Nan and Harry that they had her full support. Alec would be furious, but she was past caring. He'd just have to accept the facts, and the facts were that she cared about Parker's children— and Joe—too much to pretend otherwise.

The Glory courthouse took up one side of the town's new provincial building, which housed several regional government offices, including the motor-vehicles branch and the public-health clinic. The district wasn't large enough for a full-time judiciary presence, but circuit judges presided every Tuesday and Thursday.

This Thursday afternoon the docket was full, and when Honor slipped into the courtroom just after two o'clock, the judge was hearing a driving-under-the-influence case. He dealt with it in about ten minutes, suspended the driver's license for six months and then conferred with the court secretary before calling up the next case, a jaywalking charge. Ten past charges, all guilty. The defendant was fined twenty-five dollars, and he left the court muttering about the injustice of it all.

Next up was Alec Templeman's petition to acquire custody of Eloise Marie Gallant and Alexander Samuel Gallant. Honor was shocked to hear the children's legal names; she'd always assumed they'd taken the Templeman name.

Well, that was another mark in Joe's favor. It had to be clear to everyone in the courtroom that the children belonged with the Gallant family, many of whom were present today.

Honor craned her neck. She could see Nan and Harry in his wheelchair at the end of the second row. Ellie and Alexander weren't there. They must be home on the farm with Bea Hoople. Jill was there and so was Ben. Honor recognized several of Joe's neighbors, some of whom she'd met at the Galloway party. A gloomy-looking man in an ill-fitting suit sat next to Nan. From Joe's description of his friend and neighbor, she figured that was Ira Chesley.

Joe hadn't turned around, but she saw him clearly, sitting in front of Nan, shoulders straight, hair freshly cut and in a dark suit. He looked good—what she could see of him.

Honor sat back and took a deep breath. For Joe's sake, she hoped this would be over soon.

"Will Alexander Royston Templeman please come forward," announced the sergeant-at-arms. There was a murmur as Alec's name was linked to Joe's in description of the matter before the court. Honor glanced around. She hadn't seen Alec. Or Conrad Atkinson.

"Will counsel for Alexander Royston Templeman please step forward," demanded the judge. He took off his reading glasses and looked swiftly over his courtroom. Then he peered at the big clock on the south wall.

"Mr. Templeman is not present? His counsel is not present?" He glanced once more over the courtroom, then picked up his gavel. "Case dismissed. Next!"

Honor was stunned. Over already? Even she hadn't hoped for such a summary result. Where was Alec and why hadn't he shown up after going to these lengths to stir up trouble between himself and Joe Gallant? Had her arguments finally had some effect on him? It was out of character for the old man—unless he had other tricks up his sleeve and this was only the first volley, designed to put Joe off his guard. If it wasn't custody Alec wanted, though, what *did* he want? Was he planning a campaign of delay? To drag out the legal process?

Several people had risen and were leaving the courtroom, among them Joe and Nan. A tall, nattily dressed man with the dark good looks and high cheekbones that denoted First Nations ancestry had shaken Joe's hand as they stood. Presumably he was

Lucas Yellowfly, Joe's lawyer. Honor moved to the end of the row, past two empty chairs. There was a babble of excited voices over the shouts of the sergeant-at-arms for quiet in the courtroom.

Honor's gaze met Joe's. She was reminded almost viscerally of that first time she'd gone out to the farm to take care of the children, the day Nan and Harry had left for California. The connection between them now was as strong, as vivid, as compelling.

Joe pushed through the crush of people that surrounded him and came straight to her.

"Honor!" He reached for her. His arms were tight and strong. She shut her eyes, prayed desperately that she wouldn't weep.

She didn't, but blinked hard. "I'm so glad, Joe," she whispered hoarsely. "So very glad."

"Can you stay?" he asked quietly, releasing her and looking deep into her eyes.

"No, I've got to get back to the city," she said, shaking her head. "I just…wanted to be here today." *With you.*

He held her again, tight against his chest, and she heard him whisper into her hair, "You don't know what this means to me, Honor. Thank you."

CHAPTER SEVENTEEN

BY THE TIME of the court date, Honor had begun to wonder about her own body. Normally she was regular as clockwork, but when she drove out to Glory that Thursday, she was already a week late. She was too young to start missing periods.

She tried hard not to think about the possibility that she might be pregnant. She and Joe had used no protection; she'd told him she couldn't have a child, which was largely true. But the slimmest possibility did exist. She hadn't dared to hope.

The specialists had told her that with only one functioning ovary and with complications from the emergency surgery that had saved her life after her tubal pregnancy, her third, it was extremely unlikely that she'd ever conceive normally again. Even if she did, she'd already had two disastrous *placenta previa* pregnancies. There was a higher-than-average probability that the condition would occur again. All this had been burned into her brain long ago. She had not become pregnant again during her marriage and, going with the best advice, she hadn't thought it at all likely that she'd ever become pregnant in the future.

Now she had to consider the possibility all over again. Her first reaction, to her dismay, was absolute and unequivocal hope. And joy. To have Joe's baby—to have *any* baby—was such a cherished dream, so long put aside, that she could scarcely bear to think about it. The other prospect—the likelihood of losing that baby, if in fact a baby existed—was too terrifying to contemplate. Because that was the other side of the coin. To conceive was extremely unlikely; to carry a pregnancy to term was even more so. She was damned both ways.

But she could still hope.

Thinking about that, and making an appointment with her doctor for the end of the month, brought Joe's proposal to her mind again.

If she could have his baby... *If* he really did care for her the way he said... *If* he wasn't just looking for a wife to take care of Ellie and Alexander, as she'd begun to believe... *If* she could live with Joe out on the farm and make a life with him...

Oh, she knew she could. That last moment in the courtroom had brought it all home to her: she cared for Joe more than she'd ever cared for any man. More than she'd ever dreamed she could care. She loved him. And she loved Ellie and Alexander. It was perfect—or it could be perfect.

The doctor was skeptical, but even he had to smile when he came back with a positive reading and witnessed Honor's jubilant reaction. She threw her arms around him and kissed him, then stepped back, both hands to her hot cheeks, shocked and amazed and absolutely ecstatic. It wasn't like her to kiss her doctor—or to throw her arms around *anyone* like that. She was so happy she could hardly stop herself from throwing her arms around Liz, too, back at the office and blurting out her news.

She couldn't wait to tell Joe. But she forced herself not to be impulsive, to think it all through carefully and come, point by point, to the conclusion she realized she wanted to come to—that she'd marry him, after all.

And there was Alec to consider. But right now she didn't want to think about that.

For seven days she lived with the quiet intense joy of knowing that her baby—hers and Joe's—was growing inside her, cells dividing and multiplying, implanting firmly to the wall of her womb. *Hang on, little miracle baby, hang on and I promise I'll do everything possible to keep you safe until you're ready to be born.*

Then, after the full week—a period of reflection, she told herself—she decided to drive to Glory to tell Joe. It wasn't the sort of thing she wanted to do over the phone. Besides, she had more news for him if he wanted to hear it. Christmas could come early, for both of them.

She drove down after a long day at the office, and by the time she arrived in Glory, it was dark and cold and the wind was blowing out of the north. November was turning out to be a miserable bone-chilling month, although there hadn't been much snow yet. She hoped a major snowstorm blew in before Christmas. Christmas wasn't Christmas without snow, in her view.

There were lights on at the farmhouse, but when she knocked at the door, Bea Hoople answered and told her Joe was playing hockey in Glory and wouldn't be back until late.

"Come in, dear. Do come in and get warm," Bea

said, waving her inside the cozy kitchen. "The children will be so excited to see you. Well, Ellie will. Alexander's in bed already."

"Thank you, but no." Honor felt shy suddenly. She wanted to see the children, yes. She wanted to scoop them into her arms and kiss them until they giggled—but she wanted to see Joe more. She didn't dare stop and visit now.

"Is he at that rink on the edge of town toward Longview?" she asked, pulling her collar closer around her throat.

"I think so. You want me to call and find out?" Bea offered.

"Never mind—I'll just drop in. If he's there, he's there." She smiled and shrugged as though it didn't matter all that much. "If not, I'll see him another time."

"Well, suit yourself, dear. Drive careful, won't you? The roads are awful icy." Bea Hoople shut the storm door and the inner door firmly.

Honor hurried back to her car and headed for the rink. He had to be there; she couldn't wait a minute more to tell him. Not a minute.

She recognized Joe's pickup when she drove into the lot, parked among an assortment of other pickups and utility vehicles. A thrill went through her. Now, in just a few minutes, she'd know what direction her life was going to take. Everything that happened from now on she'd mentally date from this cold November evening.

The slam of hockey pucks and sticks and bodies against the boards and the blunted echo of male voices in the steel rafters greeted her as soon as she opened the big double doors. She entered a small lobby area, with a hot-drinks dispensing machine, a snack machine, a skate-rental booth with a Closed sign propped on the counter and a bulletin board fringed with community announcements, upcoming events and items for sale. There was no one there.

When Honor pulled open the heavy wooden door that led to the rink itself and the few risers of seats on either side of the ice, the noise heightened. She shuddered slightly at the thuds and shouts—why did men enjoy this form of organized violence so much? Women, too—Liz's eldest daughter played women's hockey. Baseball was okay in the summertime, Joe had told her, but hockey was...well, hockey *mattered,* in his words.

The Glory Old Guys were playing the equivalent team from a town a few miles south, Pincher Creek. Mostly, she knew, the teams just played pickup hockey in their own towns, from among their own ranks. Occasionally they played exhibition games with other towns.

There were some wives and girlfriends sitting on the wooden risers, perhaps twenty, bunched together under an overhead radiant heater. Honor joined them. As far as she could determine, the heater wasn't making much difference. She decided to watch for a while, rehearse exactly how she was going to tell Joe about the baby.

She picked him out immediately, dressed in a tattered old Montreal Canadiens home jersey. He was playing right wing. She winced as he slammed into an opponent, yelled and managed to dig the puck out of the corner and pass it to a teammate. The teammate took a shot and missed the net. She glanced up at the scoreboard: Home team 3, visitors 2. Five minutes left in the second period. She'd wait and catch his attention between periods. Or when the game was over, if he didn't see her first.

She watched as the puck moved rapidly from one end to the other and back again. The game was too fast for her to grasp what was going on. Baseball, she had to admit, was more her speed.

"Honor!"

She turned, bewildered.

"Honor!"

She smiled and waved one gloved hand. Joe was standing at the boards, visor lifted, yelling at her. "What are you doing here?"

She waved again and gestured toward the clock. The game was going on without Joe, and some of his teammates were yelling at him to get back in the game.

"Honor!"

Embarrassed, Honor made her way down from the wooden bench toward Joe, fielding curious looks.

"Time!" Joe hollered at the Old Guys' bench, making a high T-sign with raised hands. He'd thrown his gloves down on the ice. "Time-out!" She saw the coach repeat Joe's sign. The referee's whistle blew.

"Honor, what are you doing here?" He was drenched with sweat and his eyes were worried. He surveyed her quickly, head to toe, as though looking for evidence of a broken leg or something.

"Can't we talk after the game?" she whispered

urgently, glancing around at the interested spectators. This was embarrassing.

"No. Talk to me now. Tell me why you're here."

He was on the ice, on one side of the boards; she was on the wooden floor on the other side. She thrust her hands firmly into the pockets of her fleecy jacket and took a deep breath. "I'm pregnant, Joe."

He paused for only a second, long enough for his eyes to light up and a big grin to split his face. *"We're* pregnant," he corrected, reaching forward and clutching her shoulders. *"We're going to have a baby."* His eyes were fastened on hers. His voice was hoarse. She couldn't have looked away if the Zamboni was about to run them both down.

"Yes," she said, knowing her cheeks were pink and her smile just about as wide as his.

He tossed off his helmet, then leaned forward over the boards and planted his mouth on hers. Vaguely, as though in a fog, she heard a ragged cheer go up behind her and on the ice. The players on the bench stamped their skates and thumped the boards with their sticks. She could hear the referees' frantic whistles. She sensed a camera's flash going off near them and heard another cheer.

Then to her shock and amazement, he lifted her right over the boards and began to skate around the ice with her in his arms.

"Joe! Put me down. For heaven's sake..." She glanced at the ice whooshing beneath her and grabbed him tightly around the neck.

"So—" Joe's eyes were lit with triumph and pride and joy and every emotion she'd dreamed of seeing on his face "—*now* you're going to marry me, right?"

But it wasn't a question. Somehow she'd known it wouldn't be.

"Yes," she said simply, and Joe let out a whoop that echoed off the rafters. The crowd was on its feet now and both teams were milling about the center of the ice, alternately cheering and banging their sticks.

"When?" he said, eyes gleaming.

"Tomorrow, if you want. Or the next day. Or next week. Or next month."

"Tomorrow."

"I can't believe I'm having this conversation."

"Me, neither." He grinned. "This isn't exactly how I'd pictured it, but it'll do." He kissed her once, briefly, for which she was grateful, as she had no desire to pitch onto the ice if Joe stumbled.

"The news about the baby is fantastic, wonderful, absolutely terrific, but you know what, Honor? It's second-best." He looked into her eyes. "You know what's first-best?"

"What?" She had an idea of what he was about to say.

"That you're finally going to marry me."

She wanted to believe that—oh, how she wanted to believe that.

"I love you, Honor," he said softly. "I've loved you all along. I've told you that often enough. *Now* do you believe me?"

She blinked rapidly to clear the tears and nodded.

"This is about us. You and me. It isn't about the kids or the old man or any of that. Or the new baby.

It's about me loving you and you loving me. That's all that matters. Right?''

"Right," she agreed shakily.

"I love you and I want to tell the whole world about it," he said, grinning. "I never was good enough to make it to the NHL, but this—'' he gave her an extra squeeze and took a powerful stride "—is *my* kind of victory lap.''

Joe turned to the crowd when they reached the spot where she'd been standing and yelled, "Hey, everybody! I want you to know this is Honor Templeman. We're getting married tomorrow." He kissed her. Another ragged cheer went up, another flash went off, and Joe deposited her neatly on the spectator side of the boards and released her. He bent to pick up his gloves and helmet.

Then he turned to her again and enveloped her in a last hug, a hug that was lumpy with chest pads and shoulder pads and elbow pads. "Don't go away," he warned her, still grinning. "You're coming with me after the game."

"All right," she said weakly, and turned away to stumble back to her seat on the bleachers. The spectators, mostly women, flashed friendly smiles and thumbs-up signs. The reporter who'd taken their picture came and sat beside her and asked her a few questions, which she answered in a daze.

She couldn't believe it—she was marrying Joe Gallant, after all.

And he loved her.

HONOR DIDN'T NEED to worry about telling Alec her plans. He already knew. The whole city knew as soon as they picked up their morning papers. It wasn't every day, Honor guessed, that the newspapers got a picture of a marriage proposal in a hockey rink for the front page.

Spinks opened the door to 33 Elbow Lane with a wide grin on his face. "Congratulations, Honor. I'm so pleased for you." He clasped her hand in both of his. "It's about time you saw some happiness. No one deserves it more. And I'm sure any man you'd choose to marry is a fine man."

"What about…?" Honor nodded toward the dark interior of the house.

"Oh, he'll get over it," Spinks said, shrugging. "It's none of his business, anyway, is it? Coffee, my dear?"

"Coffee would be very nice, Spinks. Thank you."

Honor entered Alec's den. He was sitting in a leather club chair to one side of the hearth, where a wood fire burned brightly. The two Labradors lay sprawled on the hearth rug. Alec turned to face her as she came in but said nothing. She could see the front page of the *Calgary Herald* in front of him on the coffee table, the huge above-the-fold photo of Joe in his tattered hockey uniform with her in his arms. They were both smiling, with eyes only for each other. The local reporter had put his photo on the wire, and newspapers right across the country had picked it up. Honor felt terribly embarrassed, yet at the same time, the sentiments expressed in the photo were exactly what she felt. She was as happy now, after a night spent with Joe at Glory's Tropicana Motel, as she'd been the evening before. They'd spent most of the night cuddling and talking in the big oval bed in the honeymoon suite, with the baseboard heater cranked up high. Somehow, she didn't think too many couples really honeymooned at the Tropicana.

"Good morning, Alec," she said heartily, pulling off her gloves and throwing her jacket down on the sofa. She'd left Glory after an early breakfast and driven straight back to Calgary. Joe planned to return to the farm after picking up a marriage license as soon as the provincial offices opened.

She rubbed her hands briskly and stepped close to the fire. "Cold, isn't it?"

Alec gazed balefully at her. "You could have told me."

"I planned to. You know that, Alec." She moved closer to him and bent to kiss his cheek. "It's all brand-new to me, too."

"What about that?" He waved one hand at the newspaper. "It's a hell of a note when a fellow has to find out something like this in the local fish wrap."

"I understand how you feel." Honor paused. Alec's reaction so far had been more subdued than she'd expected. She'd prepared herself for outrage, anger at least. "I had no idea this would show up anywhere—this photograph. There was a reporter at the game last night, sure, but I just thought it was somebody covering it locally."

"So it's true?"

"Alec!" She sat down on the hearth rug and ran her hand over Major's shiny black back. "Of course it's true."

"You're really going to marry that bastard?"

"I'm going to marry Joe Gallant, yes. And I don't want to have to ask you again not to speak of him in that way."

"Ha!"

She met his eyes levelly. "I love those children, Alec, and I want to bring you and them together one day—"

His eyes lit up. "So *that's* why you're marrying him?"

Honor felt disgust that the wily old man would even *think* she'd marry Joe for such a reason. "Absolutely not. I'm marrying Joe Gallant because I love him and for no other reason."

Alec stared into the fire. "He's taken my grandchildren. And now he's taken you away."

"It's not like that, Alec." She reached out and put her hand on his arm. "It's not like that at all. Believe me. I want you and Parker's children to have a relationship. I'll continue to work toward that. Joe's not taking me away, if that's how you want to put it. I'm marrying him because I want to and because I love him. I...I think I deserve a chance at happiness, Alec," she finished softly.

He covered her hand briefly with his. When he spoke his voice was gruff. "No need to remind me, Honor. Of course I want your happiness. I just don't see why you have to find it with that son of a—"

Luckily he bit back the words before he uttered them. Honor did not want to have to chastise him again. Just then Spinks came in, beaming.

"Coffee for three! And coffee cake." He set a large tray on the butler's table. "To celebrate Honor's happy news."

Honor hesitated, wanting to tell the two old men her other news. At the last second she decided against it. Somehow she felt superstitious, that the fewer people who knew, the better.

"Coffee cake?" Alec growled. "What happened to your shortbread?"

"New day," Spinks said, grinning and rubbing his gnarled hands together. "New recipe."

THEY WERE MARRIED on Friday. Nan and Harry and their children came to the courthouse—the same courthouse they'd sat in a few weeks before—to witness the brief civil marriage ceremony. Ellie and Alexander were there with Bea Hoople. Ira Chesley was there, and so was half of Joe's Old Guys' hockey team, including Jeremiah Blake and Jeremiah's brother, Cal, and his wife and baby girl. Ben was there, with a new girlfriend Honor hadn't seen before. Adam Garrick, Ben's boss, was there, with his wife and children, little Rosie and baby son. Honor recognized other neighbors and friends she'd met at the Galloways' and that summer in Glory. Donna Beaton and Myrna Schultz, the postmistress. It seemed the whole town of Glory was there, to Honor's dazed happy eyes, and on such short notice, too.

As she walked out of the courtroom on Joe's arm, carrying Alexander, she spotted a broadly grinning Cecil Spinks, who had taken a seat in the last row. He took off his old-fashioned bowler hat and bowed.

There was no sign of Alec Templeman.

CHAPTER EIGHTEEN

WITHIN A WEEK Honor had cleared out her personal things from the apartment—with the help of Joe and Ben—and moved into Joe's bedroom at the farm. She'd taken some furniture with her and put the rest in storage until she made up her mind what to do with it. Joe was being hopelessly overprotective, in her opinion, not letting her lift anything heavier than her handbag and refusing to make love with her until they had the doctor's okay. He didn't say he was terrified she'd lose this baby, but she knew he was. As terrified as she was herself.

That first night they'd spent at the Tropicana, Joe had turned to her after they'd talked for a while and asked, "What's the risk, Honor?"

He'd never been more serious, and she knew immediately what he meant. "It's so hard to say," she whispered back, heartsick. "What happened to me only happens once in a couple of hundred pregnancies. But then it happened again, which the doctors said was rare. I'll have to see what my doctor says now. What if…" She couldn't bear to say, *What if I lose our baby?*

Joe had sighed and gathered her close and stroked her hair. "Look, sweetheart," he said, "it'd be terrible if you lost that baby, but I care more about it for your sake than I do for the baby's sake. Do you know what I mean? I know that sounds bad, but…''

He'd paused and gently kissed her. When he went on, his voice was hoarse. ''I'm marrying you for *you*, Honor, not for any baby we might have. If this goes wrong and we never have a baby together, I can live with that. We've got two kids already—Ellie and Alexander. That's good enough for me.''

Then she'd wept for a little while, both because she was so scared and because she was so happy.

In some ways she couldn't believe she was a married woman again. When she opened a checking account in Glory and signed Honor Gallant, the name seemed so strange. Who was Honor Gallant? She filled out forms for a new driver's license, for new credit cards in her married name, for a library card. It gave her an odd feeling, as though the woman she had been for eight years, Honor Templeman, was slowly and thoroughly being wiped out. In her mind Alec Templeman would always be her father-in-law, although Parker was dead and she had a new father-in-law now. Sam Gallant. A mysterious elderly horse-crazy stranger who lived on the West Coast and whom none of the family had seen in more than a year.

Nan was delighted about her brother's marriage, and Honor was thrilled to have her as a sister-in-law. The entire Longquist brood welcomed her with open arms, and the fiction of being Parker's sister was laughed away in an instant. The feeling of being part of a large generous family was so welcome to Honor. It felt as though she'd spent most of her life alone— an only child, so often the new kid in school with no special friends, the student trying desperately for scholarships that would open up the future for her. Her own father was just a distant memory and her mother had been dead for fourteen years. It seemed forever since she'd had any family besides the remote Parker and the crusty demanding old Alec.

Joe wanted to take her on a honeymoon somewhere, even for a few days, but Honor refused. Somehow, being pregnant and with a husband who was reluctant to make love were not the ingredients for a successful honeymoon. She agreed that when the baby was born—they never, not for moment, really considered otherwise—she and Joe would try to get away for a few days. With the baby, of course. For now, just being at Swallowbank Farm was better than any honeymoon. And she was beginning to make plans for Christmas with Joe and the children. This would be the best Christmas ever.

Ellie was thrilled to have her back at the farm, and Alexander seemed happy, too. He didn't say much yet, beyond a few single words that translated to those in the know as "milk" or "juice," but his exuberant smile was enough for Honor. This was her new family; this was where she wanted to be.

For the first two weeks, she drove to her office at Templeman Energy in Calgary every morning and drove home every night. Bea Hoople continued looking after the children on a daily basis. Finally, though, Honor made her mind up to take a leave from her legal work. She found the commute tiring, and her doctor had warned her that if her pregnancy ended up being at all high risk, he'd want her to quit work. If she showed signs of another *placenta previa* pregnancy, she might even be faced with bed rest for much of the nine months and a caesarean in the end. Anything, Honor vowed, to save her baby.

After discussing it with Joe, she decided to tell Alec she'd be leaving for at least the duration of her pregnancy. Joe wanted to go with her, but Honor refused. There were things she had to do on her own, and she didn't want all the Templeman and Gallant personal baggage mixed up with what she had to say to her employer and old friend.

Luckily she found Alec in a good mood. He'd just had a session with one of her colleagues in the legal department at Templeman Energy, Don Wetherall, and the old man was buoyed up by the prospect of outscoring one of his oil-patch enemies on some northern-Alberta mineral rights. He was practically rubbing his hands together in glee when she showed up.

"Congratulations, Alec," she said, not entirely meaning it. Sometimes she found the push and shove of the oil and gas business distasteful. She knew Alec reveled in it. "I'm glad to hear you're finally getting somewhere with those Murphy leases."

"You bet." Alec gestured for her to sit down. They were in his study again, the part of the house where he spent most of his time. "If we find what we think we'll find, why, Bill Dexter's gonna be wishing he'd gotten up a little earlier in the morning to get the jump on me!" he said with satisfaction. "Now, Honor. What's on your mind?"

"I'm pregnant, Alec."

The old man stared at her. "Didn't take too long, did it? You been married, what—two, three weeks?

I guess you musta been a lot friendlier with Gallant this summer than I'd thought.''

"Alec!" Honor poured herself a cup of coffee from the vacuum flask that stood on a side table. "I'm sure you know what this means to me," she finished softly, looking up at him.

Alec said nothing for several minutes. Several emotions crossed his lined face: anger, fear, pity. Honor sipped her coffee, prepared to wait.

"I…I know what it means to you, Honor. Nobody felt worse than I did when you lost those babies, you and Parker," he said gruffly. "I hope this time works out for you." He took a deep breath. He seemed to be making an effort. "What does the doc say?"

"He says I should take it easy. That's partly what I came to see you about, Alec. I'm going to leave Templeman Energy, at least until after the baby's born. Maybe longer."

"I see." He was silent a few more minutes. The sadness on his face tore at Honor's heart.

"I'll still come and see you, Alec. Every week. I promise. Maybe even twice a week." How she wanted to say he could come out to Glory and visit her. So far, Joe hadn't said anything about Alec and the children.

"Hell, no. You go ahead and forget about me," he muttered. "You've got your own life now. New husband, Parker's kids—" he waved one hand in an angry gesture "—new baby coming."

"I won't. I'll never forget you. You mean a great deal to me. I'll never let you down," Honor said.

"You mean that, don't you?" Alec stared at her

curiously, an odd look on his face. Affection mixed with disbelief.

"I do."

"Come here." Honor put down her mug and went to him. The old man awkwardly put one arm around her and patted her back. "You're a good person, Honor. A real good person. An angel. You're more than an old bastard like me deserves. Your ma and pa would have been proud of you."

Honor felt her eyes fill with tears as she kissed him goodbye. Was it true she'd forget him as her life became busier with her new family, her new concerns? Old Alec had seen a great deal more of this world than she had; he'd seen a great many who mattered to him come and go.

HER FORMER FATHER-IN-LAW might have a heart buried beneath that crusty exterior, Honor thought a week later, but who could say it was in the right place? Joe had come storming home from Glory, fit to be tied and ready to tear Alec Templeman limb from limb if he could just get his hands on him.

The custody threat had not amounted to anything in the end, but Alec had obviously not been deflected from his single-minded battle with Joe over his grandchildren.

Joe's news was that Alec or his agent—Honor was pretty sure it was the smooth-talking Conrad Atkinson who had handled it—had taken over Ira Chesley's mortgage and was threatening foreclosure.

"Can you beat that?" Joe threw a handful of papers on the kitchen table. Honor had never seen him so furious. "Goddamn lawyer's papers telling me I pay out the mortgage or I agree to a new contract on his conditions.''

"New terms?" Honor ventured. She'd had chills when she heard Joe's news. Her premonition had been right all along—Alec was never going to give up trying to get his grandchildren.

"The works." Joe flung himself down into the chair opposite her and ran both his hands over his face.

"Tea?" She pushed the pot toward him.

He glanced at it. "No, thanks." He scrubbed his face with his palms again, then sat straighter. "I just don't see how the bastard managed to find out about Ira's mortgage, that's all. And Ira!" Joe snorted. "He's pleased as punch. Figures he's done me a big favor finding someone to buy out the mortgage so I don't have to come up with it early. He knows it's tight for me right now.''

Honor stirred her tea warily. "There's no way you can pay out the mortgage?"

"Nope." Joe looked at her. "I haven't got the money. I was hoping for a higher price on barley this fall and maybe it'll be better in the winter and I know it'll be better in the spring, but I can't wait that long. *Bastard!*'' Joe stood and began pacing back and forth in front of the stove. Suddenly he turned to her. "And don't you say one goddamn word in his defense!''

Honor flinched. She hated it when Joe swore like that. He rarely cursed in her presence. But then she'd never seen him this riled before, either. "What are you going to do, Joe? Go to the bank?"

"I could do that," he muttered. "I damn well hate

to. But I'd rather be on the hook to the bank than to Alec Templeman.'' Then he shrugged. ''I could sell the place. Why not? That'd be just what he'd like, run me out of business. Ha. If he thinks I'd give up the kids, he's crazy. I don't care what he pulls. I'd just start up someplace else, smaller place, move there with you and the kids. Maybe leave the province.''

Honor sipped her tea, willing herself to be calm. He didn't mean it. He'd never leave Harry and Nan in the lurch. Where would Harry work then? If he didn't work for Joe? Where would they live?

''I'm selling the condo,'' she said quietly. ''That should bring in enough money to pay off that mortgage. Maybe even put some savings away. I've got money from selling Parker's condo last July, too. I was investing it for the kids, but it can go toward the mortgage.''

''No damn way.'' Joe stared at her. ''I'm not taking money from a woman to settle my affairs. I've always stood on my own two feet and I intend to keep on doing that—''

''Joe—'' Honor interrupted, putting her teacup down and standing. His words had hurt her to the quick. ''I'm not a *woman,* Joe. I'm your wife.''

''Oh, babe.'' Joe's voice was rough with emotion as he came toward her. He put his arms around her. *Her haven. Her safety. Her man.* ''I didn't mean it that way, sweetheart.''

He kissed the top of her head. She could hear his heart thumping wildly beneath her cheek. She pulled his head down to hers and looked him straight in the eye. ''The condo will sell soon. I'm paying off that mortgage with the money and we're staying here. Right here, with Nan and Harry and all your neighbors. Christmas is coming in a few weeks. We've got a lot to do. We're not going anywhere. We're partners. We're not moving. This is your place. And now it's my place, too. It's where we belong." She met him in a hungry kiss that went on and on.

Finally Joe threw back his head and laughed, a ragged sound. "I guess we're in this together, babe. No matter what."

"I guess we are," she said, and kissed him again.

CHRISTMAS WAS ONLY a few weeks away. This year would be a real contrast to the Christmases Honor had known since her first marriage. Those had begun with breakfast with Alec and Parker—a custom she and Parker had kept up long after they'd ceased living together. After that, she usually went home alone. And Parker? Well, the last few years he'd obviously gone to Sylvie and his children in Glory.

The two of them, she and Parker, hadn't even bothered with gifts for each other. She'd exchanged gifts with Alec and Spinks at the breakfast and had given her associates at the company small mementos the last day of work before Christmas Eve. Then, Christmas Day itself, Honor usually made herself a small Cornish hen with all the trimmings and ate it in front of the television set. There was always some Christmas special to watch.

This year would be different. Nan had suggested the Gallants spend Christmas Eve with the Longquists, going to midnight Mass together and then coming home for a late-night supper of the traditional *tourtière* and rhubarb chutney. Honor had tentatively volunteered to have Christmas dinner at the Gallant house and been a little dismayed when Nan had agreed so enthusiastically. From a Cornish hen to a twenty-plus-pound turkey?

Still, Honor looked forward to every detail leading up to the event and busied herself in mid-December baking and doing crafts with the children. Ellie helped with the thumbprint shortbread cookies by pushing her little thumb repeatedly into the soft dough to make the depressions that would later be filled with jam or lemon butter. They made ginger-bread—joyfully decorated by both children—and cinnamon squares and sugar cookies in the shapes of Christmas trees and bells and sleds. The house was warm and filled with spicy scents, and the cookie tins stacked up slowly but surely in the cool back porch, on shelves that reached to the ceiling, and in the freezer.

Late though it was in the season, Honor borrowed from Nan's extensive recipe collection and picked out a fairly uncomplicated recipe for Christmas fruit-cake. With Ellie's help—and little Alexander set to the useless but absorbing task of counting raisins—she managed to turn out three very presentable cakes. She was proud of her accomplishment, which brought back tender memories of the times she'd spent in the kitchen with her mother, baking and sew-ing and planning for their simple Christmases.

Joe helped, too, and carried out her specific orders for running Christmas lights along the veranda and outside trees and bushes. The entire front of the farm-house was lit up at night in a varicolored glow that entranced the children and dogs. Honor wondered if Joe had even bothered to decorate in years past.

Then there were all the community events to attend. There were bake sales, craft sales, Christmas bazaars—all the busy preparations of a small town for an important annual event. And a week before Christmas the entire town came together for the Glory Christmas Concert.

CHAPTER NINETEEN

"HERE," JOE WHISPERED. "Let me take him for a while."

Alexander was squirming on Honor's lap, trying to peer over her shoulder at the people sitting behind them. His angel costume, which Honor had ironed so carefully before they left the farm, was already twisted and crumpled. Ellie, he noticed, sat quietly on her chair beside Honor, next to the aisle, awaiting her turn to go up to the front. Her curls were still neatly brushed, golden and glossy, and she was the model of decorum, sitting carefully forward so as not to disturb her wire-and-gauze angel wings or her glittery halo. Joe had suggested fastening on Alexander's wings at the last minute. No halo. Every time they put it on him, he snatched it off, seemingly affronted.

Joe figured he knew why: at nearly nineteen months, the boy was no angel.

"I'm fine," Honor whispered back with her special smile. The one she saved for him. Joe felt it right through his body—heat, pride, pleasure. He'd looked forward to tonight, welcoming the chance to show off Alexander and Ellie and his new wife to the whole town. There'd been talk, he knew, when Honor's identity had become widely known after the now-famous photograph of the two of them at the hockey arena appeared in the newspapers. A lot of people were stunned that Joe would up and marry the widow of the man who'd fathered his sister's children. Sylvie Gallant had shocked the townsfolk plenty in her life, but her children being fathered by a bigamist passing as a respectable Glory citizen, albeit a man who spent a lot of time away from home, was the final blow to the town's sense of propriety.

Most people in town, Joe was convinced, didn't give a damn. But the ones who did, and there were a few, could make life difficult for his new wife if they decided to. Small towns could be funny that way. Myrna Schultz, for one. The busybody postmistress. She always seemed to know everything that went on. And Hattie McCormack, head of the ladies' hospital auxiliary, and very much a role model for many Glory matrons of a certain generation.

A lot of them thought his marriage had been somewhat speedy. Not speedy enough, in his view. He was just damn glad Parker had walked out on Honor and she'd come into his life at all. Let Glory folk talk. Let them see how happy he was with his new family. The baby was still a secret. There'd no doubt be more talk when the stork arrived, as more than one town biddy could count up to nine on her fingers.

Honor was almost superstitious in wanting to keep news of the baby quiet until she was farther along in her pregnancy, but he was willing to accommodate her. He'd go along with anything she said if it'd put her mind at ease. Too many nights since their marriage he'd soothed her tears as she relived the past. It was almost as though her grief over those losses had been brought back, fresh and strong, with the changes going on in her body now.

If it was in his power—and he knew not much was—nothing would go wrong this time. She'd have the best possible medical care and she'd have the best possible pregnancy. If the doctor told her after her next checkup that bed rest was required, he'd personally sit beside her bed to make sure she stayed there.

The annual concert was held at the high school, but several town groups joined with the students, including the seniors' choral group that had ''borrowed'' Alexander and Ellie as tiny angels for their presentation. The children had approximately ten minutes onstage; he hoped Ellie would be able to handle her little brother up there for the duration.

The low hum of voices from the audience rose, then fell, as the lights went down on the paper stars, the twisted red and green crepe-paper streamers and the greenery pinned to the basketball hoops. Several people coughed.

Finally, Joe thought with a sigh, crossing his arms and stretching out his legs, preparing himself for a long evening. First up, after the principal's remarks, would be the grade-three class presenting a medley of songs and then a short skit. Alexander and Ellie were slated for fourth on the program, just before a brief intermission.

Just as the principal began to speak, Joe became aware of a small disturbance. A late arrival in a wheelchair came down the aisle and parked at the end of their row. No doubt one of the seniors wanting to get a good look at the stage, Joe thought. There were several other elderly spectators in wheelchairs in the front row and along the aisles. Joe didn't even glance at the recent arrival. He frowned, focusing on the spotlighted principal, who was giving every indication that she'd prepared a lengthy speech. At present she was going through individual thank-yous to various town businesses that had supported the concert and various school functions over the past months.

Suddenly he became aware of Honor's agitation. Her face was flushed and she seemed distressed. Was she all right? He'd better take the kid.

"Give him to me," Joe said firmly, and lifted Alexander onto his lap. The boy began to inspect the earrings of the woman to Joe's right.

Joe realized Honor was still distressed. She was staring at the man in the wheelchair. Joe glanced his way—damn, that looked like Alec Templeman! He hadn't seen the man in nearly fifteen years, but he'd recognize that bold eye, that arrogant expression anywhere. The man was gray and haggard; Honor had said he was sick and he definitely looked it.

The old man was staring at Ellie as though he wanted to eat her alive. Ellie seemed oblivious, humming to herself, alternately smoothing her gold-and-white costume over her knees and folding her hands angelically in her lap.

The old man looked up and Joe knew for sure. It was definitely Templeman. He had a lot of nerve coming to the concert like this after what he'd put them through in the past couple of months.

Joe had made it clear through his lawyer that Templeman was to stay the hell out of their lives. Honor had never mentioned he was in a wheelchair. He wouldn't put it past Templeman to have thought that one up just to make sure he could get positioned at the front where the children were. This visit to Glory was designed just to defy him. Templeman knew Joe couldn't do a damn thing about it if he showed up at a public event. The old man had outwitted him; he was determined to see his grandchildren, and now he had.

Joe felt his blood boil. He took a deep breath and tried to concentrate on the stage. What could he do? He could hardly throw a sick old man in a wheelchair out of the town Christmas concert, the way he'd like to.

He glanced at Honor again. She caught his eye, a stricken expression on her face. He hoped she was all right. Damn Templeman, anyway, showing up here. He tried a quick comforting smile, but he knew it wouldn't work. It was hard to smile with your jaw clenched. He looked at Templeman again; to his horror, Ellie was speaking to him. Joe couldn't hear what she was saying and was relieved to see her put her fingers to her lips in a hushing motion and gesture toward the stage. At least the kid had the manners to keep quiet. He peered at his watch. Two hours minimum for the whole show. Maybe they'd be able to leave at the intermission.

There was never any kind of confrontation with Templeman. As soon as Alexander and Ellie had completed their roles on stage with the seniors' choir, as two little angels around the nativity scene, he disappeared. A gloomy-looking man materialized from the back of the auditorium, grabbed the handlebars of the wheelchair and wheeled him out. Must be that man Friday Honor had mentioned. Spinks. The guy gave him the creeps.

Joe and Honor left after the intermission. Joe had trouble greeting friends and neighbors casually and manufacturing small talk when he was burning up inside. Somehow he managed it, for Honor's sake. He wanted to show off his wife to the community and he was damn well going to do it. Templeman wasn't going to rob him of that, too.

That bastard. It looked like he'd try anything, do anything, to get close to his grandchildren. The custody ploy hadn't worked, the threat to foreclose on Joe's mortgage hadn't worked—so now what? Was he going to start stalking them? Showing up at every public function they attended?

Honor was silent on the way home. She might be tired. Or maybe she just didn't want to talk about Alec Templeman's coming to the concert. Joe tried to keep quiet, too, but he couldn't. There weren't many things he and Honor didn't talk about, but Templeman had been a closed subject for weeks now, ever since the foreclosure attempt. Still, no one was closer to the old man than she was.

"Did you know he'd be there?" he asked bluntly when they were five miles out of town.

"I didn't, Joe. I swear to God I didn't." Honor put both her hands to her cheeks. She glanced into the backseat. Joe had already checked in his rearview mirror; both kids were asleep.

"You must have told him about it. I mean, how would he find out the kids were going to be in that damn concert?"

"I told him—sure I told him! I don't feel the way you do about him, Joe, no matter what he's done. You know that. If you hadn't been so stubborn about not letting the kids get to know him, none of this would have happened."

"So now it's my fault."

"Yes!"

He could see the fire in her eyes even in the dim light from the dashboard. He couldn't believe it. They were having their first fight—and over that old carpetbagger! There was no justice in the world.

"Your fault *and* his fault," she went on fiercely. "You're both a couple of stubborn...fools, that's what you are!"

Joe couldn't comprehend what he was hearing. "After everything he's tried, you still stick up for him?"

"Yes, I do. He was wrong to act the way he's acted toward us, but to tell you the truth, Joe, you've driven him to it. Oh, never mind!" She made a weary gesture and pressed her fingers over her eyes. "I don't want to discuss it. I'm sick of thinking about it. There's nothing more to say, is there?"

"Maybe not," Joe said grudgingly. "Except, how long is he going to hound us like this?"

"Until it kills him!" she snapped. "Until he's dead. Don't you see? He has absolutely nothing to lose and everything to gain. His son is dead, everybody he loves is dead, all he's got left are these kids—"

"He's got you."

"What's that supposed to mean?"

"He obviously cares a lot about what happens to you. And you about him."

"We've always been close, you know that. That's no crime. He needs me. I'm his connection to his grandchildren. I bring him news of the kids when I visit—"

"Well, he's got a great way of showing his appreciation, doesn't he?" Joe burst out. He couldn't help it. The way Honor always took the old man's side was frustrating. "Coming all the way to Glory, interfering like this."

"He didn't interfere," she said wearily. "He just wanted to see Alexander and Ellie. I guess he figured there was no other way...."

Her voice drifted off and Joe suddenly felt guilty that he'd dragged her over the coals. She was tired. She was pregnant. It wasn't as though any of this was her fault. She'd tried her best to keep them all happy—him, the kids, Templeman.

"He's done a lot for me in my life, Joe," she said quietly, resignation in her tone. "I owe him. But even if I didn't, it would make no difference. I still believe he's got a right to know those kids. What's past is past. They're his only son's children—"

"Maybe you feel you've made a mistake hooking up with me, Honor. Maybe you're regretting it now."

"I don't regret it, Joe. I love you. And I love him. But when push came to shove, I picked you, didn't I? Not him."

That night, after they'd put the children to bed, Honor gathered up her nightgown and slippers and a down quilt and said she was sleeping in the spare room. She had a headache, she said, and just wanted to be alone for a while.

Joe had to accept that. It was the first night since they'd been married that they hadn't slept together in the same bed. He had plenty of time to think things over while he stared up at the ceiling, and he didn't like the conclusions he came to. He didn't like them at all.

JOE HAD NEVER BEEN to Templeman's residence, but he had no trouble finding the address. And there were plenty of places to park on the tree-lined street. He walked through the big cast-iron gates, which were open, and stood for a moment looking at the house.

It wasn't as impressive as he'd expected. Kind of low-slung and stretched out. He saw smoke coming from a chimney somewhere and bare flower beds lining the walks, dusted over now with last night's flinty snowfall. They'd had a little more snow in Glory, nearly an inch, which had excited the children tremendously this morning. He hoped there'd be a big snowfall before Christmas, for their sake.

Honor's clear eyes and smile at breakfast told him she wasn't holding last night's argument against him. He'd held her close and kissed her and told her how much he'd missed her in bed. But he didn't tell her what he had in mind.

He'd barely admitted the notion to himself, until the moment he actually saw the address on the gatepost and parked his truck. He took a deep breath and shrugged his shoulders to settle the tension he felt. *No time like the present.* He stepped forward and rang the doorbell.

The spectral creature he'd seen pushing Alec Templeman's wheelchair opened the door. His face broke into a big smile. "Mr. Gallant, I believe?" He extended a knotty paw. "Cecil Spinks. I recognize you from your picture in the paper. And, of course, I was at your wedding. Maybe Honor mentioned it. Please accept my congratulations on your marriage. Honor is a wonderful woman and I'm sure you deserve her." The majordomo's little speech surprised Joe, but he accepted it in the spirit it was offered.

"Thank you." He nodded and walked into the foyer. "I intend to do my best to deserve her, you can be sure of that." The other man grinned, an expression that gave his gaunt face a skeletal look.

"You're here to see Mr. Templeman, I presume?"

"I am." Joe took another deep breath as he followed Spinks down the polished floor of the hallway. At an open door, Spinks preceded him and announced, "Mr. Joe Gallant to see you, sir!" then stepped back and bowed low as Joe entered the room.

Odd.

Joe found himself in an old-fashioned gentleman's study. The fire burned merrily on the hearth, the walls were lined with bookshelves and hunting prints and photographs, and the air was faintly laced with the scent of fine tobacco mixed with wood smoke. Two huge Labradors got to their haunches on the hearth rug and yawned loudly.

Alec Templeman sat in a club chair, a tartan rug covering his knees. He glared at Joe, his eye as fierce as an eagle's.

"What the hell do you want?"

"I want to talk to you."

"What about?" the old man snapped. The male Labrador growled low in his throat, then flopped back down on the rug and closed his eyes with a sigh.

Joe felt his temper rise. He'd told himself that no matter what happened, he wasn't going to get angry. He was going to say what he had to say and leave. He choked back the retort that had sprung to his lips at Templeman's rude reply and reminded himself that he held all the cards.

"May I sit down?"

The old man glared at him again, then averted his eyes and made a grudging gesture with one hand. "Suit yourself."

Joe sat on the leather club chair on the other side of the hearth. He immediately regretted it. Maybe what he'd come to say would be better delivered standing, kept short and sweet. Then he could leave.

"I'll get right to the point—"

"Fine," the old man said with a snarl. "I haven't got all day."

That was good, Joe thought, looking quickly around the room. As if Templeman had things to do, places to go. It was a comfortable room, lived-in, filled with books and newspapers. Joe spotted a framed photo that might have been a young Parker on the wall behind the old man's chair.

"It's about Honor and the children."

Templeman stared at Joe. "What about 'em?"

Joe wasn't going to be rushed. "As you know, Honor is my wife now..." He pinned the old man with his gaze.

Templeman nodded and frowned. "Go on."

"I love her and she loves me. We married for that reason and that reason only. Anything that's going to hurt her or bother her is my business. I *make* it my business. Do you understand?"

The old man said nothing.

"And you've hurt her."

"Like hell I have!" The old man's eyes flashed and he held out one shaking hand to point at Joe. "*You've* hurt her, you bastard. You're the one who won't let me see my own grandchildren. You're the one standing between me and a young woman I care about. She's like a daughter to me, a daughter I never had. She means more to me than...than my god-damned company! Now—do you understand *me?*"

"Is that why you've interfered? Why you've tried to get custody of my sister's children?"

"My son's children!"

"Is that why you tried to run me off my farm? Threatened to foreclose?" Joe realized he was furious—and showing it—despite his best intentions. "Is that why you sneaked out to Glory the other night to get a look at Ellie and Alexander?"

"Just trying to make you see reason, that's all. I thought it'd get your attention if I tried to shut you down. Ha!" To Joe's shock, the old man actually cackled, a dry unpleasant attempt at laughter that quickly degenerated into a harsh gasping sound. Joe wondered if he was having an attack of some kind. How sick was he? Joe started to stand, thinking he should call for Spinks, but Alec gestured for him to remain seated.

Joe didn't say anything, waiting for the old man to regain control of himself. The harsh sounds stopped and Alec Templeman raised his head. His eyes were bright. His voice, when he spoke, was hoarse and rasping. "All I ever wanted was her happiness. All I ever wanted was for my girl to be happy. And my boy."

He looked away into the fire, and Joe remained silent. Somehow he knew the old man was trying to tell him something. Something important.

For a long time Alec stared into the fire, and Joe thought he wasn't going to speak again. Spinks knocked lightly, deposited a coffeepot, cream, sugar and two mugs on the table and left as quietly as he'd entered. Alec appeared not to even notice the interruption.

"I met Honor one day when I was having lunch at the Prince of Wales. I used to go there regularly. We talked a few times. I recognized something in her, y'see?" He looked up, eyes distant. "She had backbone. Spark. I liked that. She knew what she wanted and was doing her damnedest to get it. She didn't have much going for her. Her ma was dead. Her dad had been some kind of loser and he was dead, too. I liked her.

"I made up my mind I was going to do what I could for her. And I did." The old man glared fiercely at Joe. "I gave her a job. I treated her like my own daughter. I only had the one son, you see. My wife didn't want any more after he was born. I pushed my son into marrying Honor. I thought they'd be happy together."

"Parker was in love with my sister. He'd always been in love with my sister. You knew that."

Alec stared at him again. Joe wasn't sure if he was

really seeing him sitting there in the club chair, or if he was seeing his dead son, who had likely often sat in that exact place. "Your sister was no good for him. She'd drag him down, I knew that right away. I couldn't let him marry her. He was too young. He didn't know his own mind."

"He never knew his own mind," Joe suggested softly, then added silently, not until he decided to take up with Sylvie again years later, despite everything.

"No. He was his mother's son," Alec said, shaking his head. "No balls. I waited for him to fight back, but he never did. He wasn't a fighter."

"He was a wonderful father to those two children," Joe said.

"Was he? Was he?" The old man looked up eagerly. "He beat me there." In an odd way he seemed almost pleased. "I was a washout as a father. Never had time for the boy. Thought that was women's business. I was more interested in making a dollar. That's the way I saw it—a man's job was to provide. To make money." He shook his head sadly. "I'm still making money, more than I'll ever need. But I don't have a son anymore."

Joe felt emotion clutch his throat. It had to be tough for the old buzzard to sit here and tell him, someone he'd always regarded as an enemy, what was in his heart. Joe had no doubt that the old man had never told anyone what he'd told him today. Not even Honor. Maybe especially not Honor. Alec Templeman wasn't the sort to reveal his personal secrets and shames.

But he had revealed them to him. Why? Maybe

Alec felt he owed Joe the truth, now that he was the man providing for the woman he'd regarded as a daughter and for his grandchildren. Maybe he'd realized he'd met his match when Joe hadn't backed down from any of his threats. Maybe this was just one more strategy designed to get the old man what he wanted. Somehow Joe didn't think so.

Joe stood. "I'd better go."

Alec glowered, as though just now remembering that he had a visitor. He waved him away. "Yes, you'd better go." Then he peered up at Joe. "Does she know you came here?"

"No." Joe stepped forward and stuck out his hand. After a few seconds of hesitation, Alec stuck out his own. The old man had a surprisingly strong grip.

"Goodbye, sir. I'm going to put this all behind me." Joe took a deep breath. It felt good. "Parker and Sylvie are both dead. What's past is past. I'm going to make sure things are different now. My wife loves you. She's never stopped loving you, no matter what I said about you, and believe me, I've said plenty. She misses you. She's pregnant with my baby and I want her to be happy. She wants you and the children to get acquainted. She wants everyone to be one big happy family. I'm going to do my best to make that happen, sir. You have my word on that."

"All right." Alec blinked rapidly, then cleared his throat. "Now get out of here, Gallant," he growled. He grabbed his cane and used it to point to the door. "Speak to my man on your way out. He makes all my arrangements."

CHAPTER TWENTY

HONOR AWOKE SLOWLY, conscious first of Joe's large warm body beside her, then of the fact that the room was light and bright. It was Christmas morning, late Christmas morning, and it must have snowed again.

She rolled over and nestled against Joe's back, her right hand on her still-flat belly. The last checkup, three days ago, had given her hope beyond hope. It was a little too early to tell, the doctor cautioned, but the ultrasound had indicated that this time the placenta had become fastened to the wall of the uterus in a higher position than any of her previous pregnancies. That meant the baby would be delivered before the placenta, not the other way around, as had happened before. The doctor had warned her that this early, just over twelve weeks, it was impossible to say exactly how the placenta would position itself, and that it could move throughout the pregnancy, but to Honor, there couldn't have been better news. She *would* have this baby; she and Joe *would* have a child, a third child, a little cousin for Ellie and Alexander. And maybe even, God willing, a fourth.

He hadn't allowed her to help get the tree, which they'd cut on a nearby forested part of the farm, nor to help drag it in, but he'd let her decorate it. She could hardly wait to see it again this morning. Last night she'd gone to candlelit midnight Mass with Nan and Harry and their family. She hadn't been brought up as a churchgoer of any kind, certainly not as an Acadian Catholic, but she wanted to share in the Gallant family's traditions. The babe in the manger had special meaning for her, and she'd prayed fervently that she'd one day hold her own babe in her arms. They'd come home from the country church in the softly falling snow.

Honor slipped out of bed. The floor was cold and she put on her slippers. She shrugged on her fuzzy housecoat and belted it snugly, then went to the window and pulled back the curtains. Yes, it had snowed all night, and every fence post and every wire and tree branch was dimpled with white glistening powder. She glanced at the radio alarm. Even Ellie and Alexander were sleeping in. Ten o'clock! She'd better get the turkey in the oven.

Honor quietly left the bedroom and went down the hall to put on a pot of coffee, detouring into the living room to turn on the tree lights. Ah! She stepped back and clasped her hands. It was beautiful. A tall rather scraggly spruce tree, special because it had been chosen by Joe and the children and had grown on Swallowbank Farm, it glittered and glowed with lights and baubles and bells and tinsel. A ruby velvet-clad angel smiled down from the top. Ellie had remarked that they should have two angels, one for her mommy and one for her daddy. Honor had resolved that next year they *would* have two angels on the tree.

She tiptoed into the kitchen to start the coffee, but Joe had beat her to it.

"Merry Christmas, darling," he said, and pulled her into his arms. He had on his old plaid robe, no slippers. His hair was tousled and his eyes were warm. He bent and kissed her gently, and Honor felt overwhelmed by all her blessings.

"Merry Christmas, my love," she whispered back, and returned his kiss.

The coffeepot sputtered to its noisy conclusion, and Joe poured them each a cup. He handed her mug to her and suggested they sit in the living room and admire the tree until the children got up.

Honor cuddled up beside him on the sofa, happy just to be with the man she loved. They sipped their coffee in companionable silence. *What a year this had been.*

"When are Nan and the gang coming over?" Joe asked, putting his arm around her shoulders and pulling her close.

"About two, I think. Dinner at four, Nan suggested." She was terrified. They'd spent Christmas Eve at the Longquists' house, and today the entire Longquist family, plus Tim and Ben, who were home from college for the holidays, would be over for Christmas dinner. "I'd better get that bird in the oven," she said, trying to sit straight. She had a monster of a turkey, twenty-six pounds, already prepared and on a shelf in the spare refrigerator in the laundry room.

"Sit still," Joe said, smiling, drawing her back. "There's no rush. If we eat late, what's the problem?"

"Easy for you to say," she said, trying to look severe. "Nobody's going to blame you if the turkey's dry or the gravy's gluey or the brussels sprouts are overdone."

"Brussels sprouts?"

"Yes, brussels sprouts. It's tradition, at least it was in my family. So there!" She grinned and got an answering grimace. "Better get used to it, Joe Gallant."

"Hey," he said, glancing over her shoulder, "look who's here."

Ellie was peeking around the corner of the doorway, dragging one of her dolls behind her. She appeared to be half-asleep, still in her creased flannel nightie. Honor held out her arms and the little girl scrambled forward with a giggle.

"Can we open our presents now? Did Santa come last night? Shall I go wake up Ale'sander? Is that big one for *me?* When are Jill and Pheeb coming over?"

"Hold on, sweetie. One question at a time." Just then they heard Alexander's loud demand from the children's bedroom. "Up! Up!"

"Guess who else is awake?"

Joe got up and in a minute was back with Alexander, tousled and smiling in his blue Dr. Denton's pajamas. The little boy's eyes were wide as saucers when he saw the tree with all the gifts heaped beneath. He immediately popped a thumb in his mouth and reached for Honor. She took him onto her lap, cuddling the firm little body and inhaling the sweet sleepy little-boy scent.

Joe stood at the window, his coffee mug in his hand. "I'd better get out there and get the driveway plowed. Looks like we had quite a snowfall last night.''

''Sit down and relax,'' she said, mimicking him. ''What's the rush? Nobody's coming to visit until this afternoon.''

''No?'' Joe turned to her and smiled. ''I guess you're right. Well? What do you say, kids—is it time to look under the tree?''

''Yes!'' Ellie ran toward the tree and pulled out the large present she'd had her eye on. ''Is this for me, Uncle Joe?''

''Let's see...'' Joe made a great show of examining the parcel, then pronounced that, yes, it was for Ellie Gallant.

Ellie squealed with delight. It was a doll-size bunk bed, with tiny mattresses, pillows and duvets, just right for the doll she'd carried into the room. Ellie immediately got busy putting her doll to bed.

Alexander unwrapped a big dump truck, with a dumping mechanism easily operated by little fingers. He immediately began driving the truck along the floor, *vroom-vroom*ing as he went, loading the truck with discarded ribbons and paper and repeatedly dumping it.

''Couldn't have been better,'' Honor murmured to Joe.

He laughed. ''I seem to recall getting something like that when I was a kid, too. Should keep him busy for a while.''

''I've got something for you, but you can't open it now,'' Joe said mysteriously, glancing at his watch.

''Oh?'' Honor went to the tree, bent down and

picked up a small package. She handed it to Joe. "This is for you. I know how you like to keep your eye on things."

Joe unwrapped the gift she'd given him—a small powerful pair of binoculars. Waterproof, the works. He leaned forward and kissed her, then looked out the window with them. "Hey, these are pretty good. I could be a bird-watcher." He grinned.

"Or a wife-watcher," she said, grinning, too. "Just to see if she's lifting anything she shouldn't be."

"Or opera," he said, eyes wide. He waved the binoculars at her. "I could take these to the opera."

"You could," she agreed, knowing very well what he was referring to. She'd had a note of congratulations from Nigel Harrison on her marriage, and he'd even sent them a silver cream-and-sugar set, which she was quite sure they'd never use. He'd been very decent about losing her to "that farmer," she thought.

The phone rang and Joe jumped up to answer it. Honor was happy to remain on the sofa, enjoying the children with their new toys and mentally running through the list of things she had to do that morning to make sure Christmas dinner got on the table in time. Joe was back a moment later.

"Who was that?"

"Uh, just Christmas wishes from someone." Joe peered out the window again. "I see Ben's got the plow out. I guess he'll clear the lane."

"Oh." Honour rose and began gathering paper and ribbons to put in a box to be discarded later. She wasn't very interested in whether or not the lane was plowed today. "Time for me to start getting things organized."

"Let me help."

"You can put on another pot of coffee. And I guess we'd better have some breakfast."

"Sure." Joe went down the hallway and returned in a few moments, dressed. He whistled as he took down the coffee and filters and rinsed the pot.

"You seem awfully happy," Honor remarked, opening the refrigerator.

"Christmas, sweetheart. I'm always happy at Christmas. You just never know what that old Santa guy will bring. Pancakes?"

"That's true," she admitted, laughing. "Does that mean I can open my gift from you now?"

"Soon. I'll let you know."

"Okay." She was enjoying the mystery. "Pancakes will be great, if you feel like making them."

Ten minutes later they were sitting around the table, the children delighted with the reindeer pancakes Joe had created for them. Joe was telling them one of his crazy stories, this time about a pancake hill with pancake kids and pancake reindeer. And the little pancake boy and girl had a pancake grandma and grandpa—

"Know what?" Ellie asked suddenly. "I wish we had a real grandpa and grandma. I wish Grandpa Sam would come and see us."

"How about if we drive out to visit Grandpa Sam in British Columbia sometime?" Joe asked. He glanced at Honor. She nodded. She'd like to meet Nan and Joe's father, not to mention their brother who lived out there. Perhaps in the summer...

She popped her last pancake "letter" in her mouth; she'd discovered that Joe had loaded up her plate with pancake letters that spelled I LOVE YOU. She'd grinned at him, remembering his vow to watch her eat her words. Life with this man was never going to be boring, she could see that.

The kitchen doorbell rang.

"I wonder if that's Santa now?" Joe said, winking at her. He got up and went to the door.

"Yay! Santa!" Ellie stood on her chair, eyes wide. Alexander yelled and beat his spoon on his highchair tray.

Honor set down her fork and knife. What was *this* all about?

"Ho! Ho! Ho!" A thin man dressed in a red Santa suit came through the door, stomping snow off his knee-high black boots. "Ho! Ho! Ho!"

"Santa!" screamed the children.

He actually carried a sack on his back, which he set down and rooted around in. Who could it be? Honor wondered, amused. Ben? Tim? The fake beard and Santa hat covered most of his face, but Honor had a sudden suspicion that he was very familiar to her. Who was it, though?

Ellie was handed a nearly lifesize doll with golden curls like hers and a pretty green gingham dress. "Oh, Santa!" she breathed and clasped the doll to her chest. "Thank you!"

"T'uck, t'uck." Alexander was on the floor—Joe had lifted him down—viewing his newest acquisition with awe. Another truck, this one a tractor-trailer rig with "Templeman Energy" emblazoned on the door.

The light dawned. It couldn't be…?

Honor stared at Joe. He was grinning broadly.

"What else have you got for us, Santa?" he said, clapping the red-suited man jovially on the shoulder. "Anything else out there on the porch? Let's see…" He opened the door again and "Santa" went out, then Alec Templeman, clad to the jowls in a huge fur overcoat and scarf, limped in, leaning heavily on his cane.

"*Alec!*" Honor gasped. She couldn't believe it. She couldn't get up. Her eyes blurred and tears caught at her throat. She'd never dreamed she'd ever see Alec Templeman here at Swallowbank Farm.

"Well, look what else Santa's brought you, Ellie."

"Me?" Ellie looked up, eyes full of stars.

"You and Alexander. A grandfather," Joe said. "A real live grandfather. This is your Grandpa Alec, Ellie. Your daddy's daddy."

"Alec." Joe straightened and shook the old man's hand heartily. "Meet your grandchildren, Ellie and Alexander. Parker and Sylvie named the boy for you. I know they'd have wanted you to meet one day," he finished gruffly.

Honor found her tongue at last. She stood and threw her arms around Alec. "Oh, Alec. This is so wonderful, so fantastic."

"Thank your husband, girl," the old man growled. "I want to see my grandchildren. I've waited damn long enough."

Honor felt the release of tears as her husband's warm strong arms enfolded her. He patted her back and held her close, allowing her to weep all over his shirt. Finally she drew back.

"Can I open my present now?" she asked, laughing and crying at the same time.

"You go right ahead, babe," Joe said, still smiling broadly. He looked like a very happy man.

"Coffee, Spinks? Alec?" Joe poured out two more cups. Honor hadn't noticed that "Santa" had taken off his red suit, stowed it somewhere, possibly in the Cadillac which Honor had glimpsed out the window, and reemerged in the kitchen, the dour and accommodating Cecil Spinks again. She appreciated that he hadn't ruined the children's perception of Santa Claus by pulling off his beard right there in the kitchen.

Honor carefully tugged at the wrapping on her gift. When she pulled it off, she discovered a large silver photograph frame that opened like a book, with several photos already in it: one of Joe and her, Ellie and Alexander, still others of Alec, Spinks, Parker and Sylvie, and several people she didn't recognize. It was a family album. And there were a number of spaces left—for her mother and father, and for their baby when he or she was born.

Honor looked at her husband across the crowded noisy room—Alexander played with both his trucks under Spinks's careful eye and Ellie chattered away on Alec's knee—and mouthed, "Thank you, my darling."

Joe just winked and blew her a kiss.

Looking For More Romance?

Visit Romance.net

Look us up on-line at: http://www.romance.net

Check in daily for these and other exciting features:

Hot off the press

View all current titles, and purchase them on-line.

What do the stars have in store for you?

Horoscope

Hot deals

Exclusive offers available only at Romance.net

Plus, don't miss our interactive quizzes, contests and bonus gifts.

PWEB

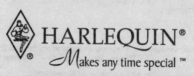

MEN at WORK

All work and no play?
Not these men!

October 1998
SOUND OF SUMMER by Annette Broadrick

Secret agent Adam Conroy's seductive gaze could hypnotize a woman's heart. But it was Selena Stanford's body that needed saving—when she stumbled into the middle of an espionage ring and forced Adam out of hiding....

November 1998
GLASS HOUSES by Anne Stuart

Billionaire Michael Dubrovnik never lost a negotiation—until Laura de Kelsey Winston changed the boardroom rules. He might acquire her business...but a kiss would cost him his heart....

December 1998
FIT TO BE TIED by Joan Johnston

Matthew Benson had a way with words and women—but he refused to be tied down. Could Jennifer Smith get him to retract his scathing review of her art by trying another tactic: tying him *up?*

Available at your favorite retail outlet!

MEN AT WORK™

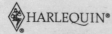 

IN UNIFORM

There's something special about a man in uniform. Maybe because he's a man who takes charge, a man you can count on, and yes, maybe even love....

Superromance presents *In Uniform*, an occasional series that features men who live up to your every fantasy—and then some!

Look for:
Mad About the Major
by Roz Denny Fox
Superromance #821
Coming in January 1999

An Officer and a Gentleman
by Elizabeth Ashtree
Superromance #828
Coming in March 1999

SEAL It with a Kiss
by Rogenna Brewer
Superromance #833
Coming in April 1999

Available wherever Harlequin books are sold.

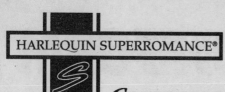

HARLEQUIN SUPERROMANCE®

Come west with us!

Start in January 1999 with *Twilight, Texas,* the next installment in our popular "West Texans" series by Ginger Chambers. West Texas—home of the Parker Ranch. And there's nobody Karen Latham loathes more than a Parker.... Then Lee Parker, her ex-fiancé's brother, shows up in the small town of Twilight—*Karen's town.*

Then in February 1999, come to Wyoming and find out *What a Man's Got To Do.* In this dramatic and emotional book by Lynnette Kent, you'll meet rancher Dex Hightower. He has to get custody of his young daughter—and get Claire Cavanaugh to help him win his case. Then he discovers he wants more from Claire.... He wants her love.

Available wherever Harlequin books are sold.

Look us up on-line at: http://www.romance.net

HSRWT